# BARBARA FAITH
# Mr. Macho Meets His Match

*Silhouette Special Edition*

Published by Silhouette Books New York

**America's Publisher of Contemporary Romance**

For Bettina Jones—
who will always be ''Betsy'' to me.

**SILHOUETTE BOOKS**
300 East 42nd St., New York, N.Y. 10017

MR. MACHO MEETS HIS MATCH

ISBN: 0-373-09715-8

First Silhouette Books printing January 1992

## BARBARA FAITH

is a true romantic who believes that love is a rare and precious gift. She has an endless fascination with the attraction a man and a woman from different cultures and backgrounds have for each other. She considers herself a good example of such an attraction, because she has been happily married for twenty years to an ex-matador she met when she lived in Mexico.

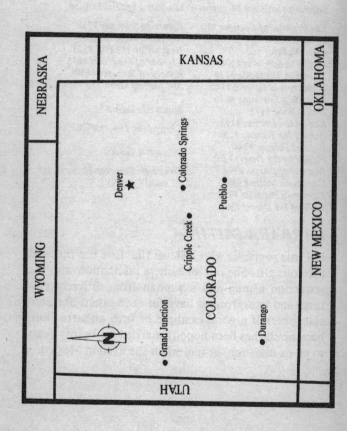

## *Prologue*

The telegram brought back a flood of memories, memories of that long-ago summer, of the accident and of the uncle she had known so briefly and had loved so dearly.

The minister of the First Baptist Church and his wife took care of Abigail for the first few days in July after the accident that had hospitalized both her mother and father.

"Your Uncle Jonah is coming to Toledo tomorrow," Mrs. Pedigrew said after that first week. "He's going to be taking care of you till your folks are well again. Won't that be nice?"

Ten-year-old Abigail really didn't care much for either Reverend Pedigrew or his wife, but the thought of spending the rest of the summer with an uncle she had never seen before wasn't all that pleasant, either.

When she saw him get off the plane, she thought, *Oh, my goodness!* and Mrs. Pedigrew said, "Well, I never!"

Neither had Abigail.

He was wearing patched blue jeans, scuffed boots and a red flannel shirt under a faded jean jacket. His long hair had been pulled back into a ponytail, and there was a gold-nugget earring in his ear.

From stories her father had told, Abigail knew that Uncle Jonah was the black sheep of the family, that instead of going into the family hardware business as her father had done, he had left Toledo to prospect for gold in Colorado.

"Irresponsible," her father had often said. "No sense of family duty. Broke our poor mother's heart when he left."

But black sheep or not, Abigail found, after the first few days, that she rather liked her uncle.

A quiet, mousy child brought up by parents who had been in their midforties when she was born, Abigail rarely spoke unless she was spoken to because, as her mother often said, "God meant for children to be seen, not heard."

Abigail had never been asked her opinion on what she liked or disliked, so she was surprised that first morning when her uncle asked her what she wanted for breakfast. For as long as she could remember, her mother had alternated between soft-boiled eggs—which, although she had never said so, were always too gooey for Abigail's taste—and bran cereal.

"I usually eat bran flakes," she answered, hoping Uncle Jonah didn't know about the soft-boiled eggs.

"Bran's fer mules," he said with a snort. "You'n me're goin' to have flapjacks."

She was delighted when she learned that flapjacks were really pancakes smothered with thick maple syrup, and that they were accompanied by small, brown sausages.

For lunch, almost every day, they had hot dogs or bologna sandwiches. For dinner Uncle Jonah either fixed hamburgers with canned baked beans and what he called his hardtack biscuits, or they sent out for pizza.

For dessert, they had heaping dishes of rocky-road ice cream, something her mother never let her have, "Because sugar isn't good for you, dear."

At night, Abigail and Uncle Jonah watched television—shoot-'em-up Westerns mostly—and once or twice a week they went to a movie, where they shared the large-size tub of popcorn and drank orange soda pop.

When Uncle Jonah discovered that Abigail didn't have any play clothes and that she always dressed in what he called her Sunday-go-to-meeting duds, he took her to the local department store and bought her some overalls and T-shirts.

Abigail wore them the rest of the time he was there, except when they went to visit her mother and father in the hospital.

Her mother's injury was worse than her father's and it scared Abigail every time she went into the room and saw the bandages wrapped around her mother's head and the tubes in her arms.

"Your mother very likely will never be strong again," her father told her when she and Uncle Jonah saw him toward the end of Uncle Jonah's stay.

He looked at Abigail over the top of the two broken legs that were raised above the bed. "You're going to have to take care of the house now," he said. "I can't afford to hire a woman, so I'll expect you to do the cooking and the cleaning and the taking care of Mama."

Uncle Jonah started to say something, but Abigail's father stopped him with a frown.

"That doesn't mean you'll do any less well in school," her father went on. "You've always gotten good marks, and I'll expect you to continue to get good marks. Is that clear?"

Abigail looked down at her shoes and whispered, "Yes, Papa."

"How in the hell do you expect her to do it all?" Uncle Jonah's jaw thrust forward and there was fire in his eyes. "When in the blue-damn blazes is she supposed to have any fun?"

His lips pursed into a thin, hard line, her father glared at Uncle Jonah. "Abigail is a dutiful daughter," he said. "But duty isn't something you'd understand, is it?" And then he said, "I'll be out of here in another two weeks. I appreciate your taking care of my daughter, but it won't be necessary for you to stay after I'm home."

Abigail held tightly to Uncle Jonah's hand when they left the hospital, but she didn't say a word. They went to a movie and afterward, they each had a double-chocolate soda. That night when he tucked her into bed, Uncle Jonah gave her a big bear hug and said, "You're a mighty fine little girl, Abby. I reckon these next few years are going to be hard, but they'll pass and pretty soon, you'll be a young lady." He kissed her forehead. "I want you to remember you've got an uncle who loves you, and soon's you're old enough, maybe you'll come on out to Colorado to visit me."

The night before her father came home from the hospital, Uncle Jonah took Abigail to a visiting carnival. They rode the Ferris wheel, the carousel and the whip, and drove the dodgem cars. Hand in hand, they wandered the midway while she gazed in amazement at the tattooed man and the bearded lady, and gasped when the strong man flexed his muscles and lifted a three-hundred-pound weight.

They had hot dogs with mustard and onions and relish, and when they passed the cotton-candy machine, Uncle Jonah said, "Let's get us one of those."

Abigail watched the young man in the candy-striped jacket whirl the pink fluff into a big, sugar cloud. And she laughed aloud when, at the first bite, the sweet fluff disappeared on her tongue.

That had been the happiest night of her life, and it was what she remembered when she read the telegram telling her that her Uncle Jonah had died.

She had never forgotten him.

Or the taste of pink cotton candy.

## Chapter One

The alarm rang, as it did every morning at precisely ten minutes before seven. Abigail got out of bed and without bothering to put a robe on over her tailored, navy blue pajamas, padded to the kitchen and switched on the radio.

"Good morning," a too-cheery voice said. "It's a bright sunny Toledo morning. The temperature today will be in the high eighties—"

Abigail frowned and switched the radio off. For the past two days at work, she had been cataloguing stacks of old law books in the downstairs storeroom. It was something that didn't need to be done, certainly not in the summer heat, but Eloise Zircle, the new office manager and Alan Greenway's niece, had assigned the job to Abigail. "I want this finished by Monday," she'd said, "even if it means working through the weekend."

Still frowning, Abigail put water into the old, blue tea-kettle that had belonged to her mother, then went into the bathroom to shower. By the time she came out, the morning paper had thudded against the screen door. She put it on the breakfast-nook table, put herbal tea into the teapot and spooned prune yogurt over a dish of bran flakes.

Just as she opened the paper, the phone rang. When she picked it up, a voice said, "Miss Sedgewick?"

"Yes."

"This is Henry Crimms, Miss Sedgewick. I'm handling your late uncle's estate."

"Oh?" Abigail took a sip of tea. "You're calling from Colorado, Mr. Crimms?"

"No, Miss Sedgewick, I'm here in Toledo. I prefer discussing the terms of your uncle's will in person rather than over the phone. I need to return to Colorado as soon as possible, however, and I'd like to meet with you some time today."

"I have got to go to work at nine, Mr. Crimms."

"Ah, yes. I'd forgotten. Your uncle said you were a legal secretary. Could we meet for lunch?"

"Lunch would be fine. I only have forty-five minutes, though."

"Then that will have to do. Is there a restaurant nearby?"

"The Country Kitchen. It's at Fifth and Main."

"Very well, I'll meet you there at twelve, if that's convenient."

"Twelve is fine," Abigail said, and following a polite "Goodbye, Mr. Crimms," she replaced the receiver and went back to her yogurt-covered bran.

She couldn't imagine why the attorney had come all the way from Colorado to talk about her uncle's will, for surely her uncle had died as poor as he'd lived.

Uncle Jonah had written to her regularly after he'd returned to Colorado. His letters had been funny and warm, and they had showed his concern. She had faithfully answered, at least at first, but little by little, the burden of taking care of her mother as well as doing all of the household chores and trying to keep up with her schoolwork had eaten into what spare time she had had. Her letters had dwindled, and after a while, so had his.

But he had always remembered her at Christmas and on her birthday, and when she'd graduated from high school, he'd sent her an inexpensive wristwatch.

She had been saddened by his death and sorry that she hadn't kept in closer touch. She hadn't forgotten him, but she'd been too preoccupied with her duty to her ailing mother, and then to her widower father, to spend time reflecting on the pleasant memories of that long-ago summer or of the uncle who had been so kind.

But all of the memories had come flooding back with the news of his death. She still remembered how they had hugged each other goodbye and that he had said, "I'm here for you if you ever need me, Abby girl."

Now he was gone, and though she had only known him for that one brief summer, she felt a terrible sense of loss and of guilt because she hadn't gone to Colorado when he'd invited her or written when she should have.

She wondered what Mr. Crimms meant by what he had called Uncle Jonah's "estate," because it had been obvious that her uncle had not been a prosperous man. But perhaps because he, too, remembered that long-ago summer, he had left her a keepsake, a pocket watch or a trinket that he valued. And very likely, because Mr. Crimms had other business in Toledo, he'd thought to bring whatever memento Uncle Jonah had wanted her to have with him.

At eight-thirty, dressed in a plain gray-and-white summer suit and sensible shoes, with her brown hair pulled back off her face and skewered into a tight French twist, Abigail got into her father's ten-year-old Chevrolet and drove to the downtown offices of Wintz, Greenway and Strasburg.

It was cool inside the old building, but the storeroom was hot and dusty. As she set about her task, she turned on the radio that she'd brought with her to a classical-music station. At ten-thirty, Eloise, looking cool and poised as always, appeared to check on Abigail.

"A radio?" she said. "You've brought a radio?" Delicately arched eyebrows rose half an inch. "Really, Miss Sedgewick."

Abigail turned it off.

Eloise frowned at the stacks of law books still to be cataloged. "I certainly hope you'll have all of these finished by Monday," she said.

"So do I," a tight-lipped Abigail answered.

She stopped work at fifteen minutes before twelve and went to the ladies' room to wash her hands and splash cold water on her face. She wished that she could have had her lunch in the park across from the library, as she usually did, and that she didn't have to meet Henry Crimms.

It was cool inside the Country Kitchen. Because she had no idea what the lawyer looked like, Abigail approached the hostess and said, "I'm meeting a gentleman. A Mr. Crimms."

The hostess nodded. "He's expecting you," she replied, and led Abigail to a corner table where two men were seated.

A middle-aged man in a conservative business suit and steel-rimmed half glasses rose as soon as he saw her headed his way. Holding out his hand, he said, "I'm Henry Crimms, Miss Sedgewick. It's a pleasure to meet you."

Abigail murmured a reply and looked at the other man, who pushed his chair back and stood. He was tall, broad shouldered and green-eyed, black-Irish handsome. Instead of a business suit, he wore unreasonably tight blue jeans, an obviously expensive tweed jacket and boots. There was a Stetson hat on the chair beside him.

"I'd like you to meet Nicholas Fitzgerald," Mr. Crimms said. "Nick, this is Abigail Sedgewick."

Three women at the next table turned and stared at him.

"How do you do?" His hand, when he took hers, was large, roughened with calluses and tan.

Abigail straightened her shoulders and smoothed back her hair.

"Nick is a mining engineer," Mr. Crimms said when he'd seated her. "He has an interest in what I have to tell you, so I asked him to join us."

Abigail nodded uncertainly and stole a quick glance at the tall man sitting across the table from her.

He smiled the kind of a smile good-looking men reserve for their maiden aunts.

"I thought I would tell you about the will now," the lawyer continued. "Tomorrow, we can meet and sign the necessary papers. But let's order first, shall we?"

Abby ordered iced tea and a spinach salad. The two men asked for steak, potatoes and a bottle of red wine.

"I really don't understand why you couldn't have mailed the papers instead of coming all this way," Abigail said when the waitress left.

Mr. Crimms tapped long, skinny fingers against the tabletop. "Actually, Miss Sedgewick, there's rather a large sum of money involved. I thought it best to speak to you in person."

"I see," Abigail said. But she didn't. A large sum of money? How large? She said a silent prayer for enough to fix the roof.

She glanced across the table at Nick Fitzgerald. He met her gaze with cool green eyes and a wry smile that curled up the corners of his mouth.

Abigail looked away and turned back to Mr. Crimms.

"Your uncle was a very wealthy man," he said.

"Uncle Jonah?" She shook her head because her rag-tag uncle had looked like anything but rich to her. The thought that he might have left her his gold-nugget earring flitted through her mind and made her smile.

Mr. Crimms steepled his fingers. In a solemn voice, he said, "Your uncle left you an estate of eight and a half million dollars, Miss Sedgewick. There are other—"

Abigail, who had just taken a sip of her tea, gasped and choked. "Eight and a half..." Her hands started to shake.

"As well as the Lucky Lady Mine, of course."

The floor tilted. She clenched her hands together in her lap. This couldn't be happening. Any minute now she was going to wake up. She—

"The only stipulation," the lawyer went on, "is that you get the mine running again, which is why Nick has come with me, and that you stay in Cripple Creek for a year. At the end of the year the money will be turned over to you."

Abigail shook her head. "I—I have a job. I—"

"You won't have to worry about ever working again," Nick Fitzgerald said, before he turned his attention to the approaching waitress, a tall blonde with a short skirt that hugged her hips and showed off her long legs.

The young woman smiled at him and when she left, his gaze followed her. He looked back to Abigail and knew she'd been watching him watch the waitress.

A blush rose to her cheeks and she turned away from him to nod at something Henry had said.

It's a damn shame, Nick thought. Here was a woman who had suddenly come into eight and a half million dollars, and she probably hadn't the slightest idea in the world what to do with it. She looked as plain as a country church mouse with her hair pulled tightly back off her face and skewered into a kind of knot, and face scrubbed clean of makeup. The gray-and-white suit didn't do anything for her figure, if indeed, she had one. The skirt was too long, and her shoes were too flat.

He wondered how she was going to get along in Cripple Creek and how a wonderful, go-to-hell guy like Jonah, who'd loved wine, women and song, and who'd lived every one of his seventy-five years, could have a niece like her.

Over the years, Jonah had told Nick all about Abigail Sedgewick. "She's my brother's girl," Jonah had said. "Never married. Took care of both her mother and father till they died. My brother was a crotchety old son of a bitch, and I don't guess poor Abby had much fun growing up. But she was a nice little girl, real quiet and ladylike, and she had this sort of wide-eyed look about her, as though she was just waitin' and expectin' something wonderful to happen."

And Nick remembered that, later, after Jonah had come back from Toledo after his brother's funeral, he'd shaken his head sadly. "She's lost the look," he'd said. "She was nice enough, of course, polite and all, but whatever spark she'd had as a child is gone. I sure would like to get her out here to Colorado. Might loosen her britches some."

Nick looked at Abby, who was looking at Henry and shaking her head as though she didn't believe what was happening. It'll take more than Cripple Creek to loosen

her britches, he thought, and he tried to pay attention to
what the lawyer was saying.

"Jonah kinda adopted Nick some years back. Before he
died, he gave Nick a fifty percent interest in the Lucky
Lady. That makes you partners."

Thoughts skittered in Abigail's brain....

She had a partner who was the best-looking man she'd
ever seen.

She had just inherited eight and a half million dollars.

She owned half a gold mine.

Ridiculous.

"I don't know anything about mining for gold or anything else," she managed to say. "I've never been in a
mine. I—I don't even like caves."

"Nick's an expert," Mr. Crimms said. "Got his degree
at the Colorado School of Mines, and he's worked mines
all over the world. You couldn't be in better hands."

Abigail looked at the large, tan hands that encircled
Nick's wineglass, and a shiver that was akin to both fear
and excitement ran down her spine.

His powerful maleness showed in every movement he
made, in every line of his body. When he shrugged, she
could almost see the play of muscle under the tweed jacket.
When he'd appraised the waitress, Abigail had sensed the
raw sensuality of his gaze, the slight contemplative smile
that played across his full mouth.

In all of her thirty-three years, she had never met anyone like Nicholas Fitzgerald.

When they rose from the table after their meal, he closed
his hand around hers and a wave of dizziness made her
cling to his hand a moment longer than she should have.
"Goodbye," he said politely, then he turned and smiled at
the blonde who had waited on them.

It was almost one-thirty before Abigail returned to the law offices of Wintz, Greenway and Strasburg where Eloise was waiting for her with fire in her eyes.

"Do you have any idea what time it is?" Eloise said.

"Yes, I do."

Eloise bristled. "I want those books cataloged by Monday. That means you work this weekend."

Abigail's hands tightened around her purse. "I'm afraid I can't do that," she said politely.

"Can't...?" Eloise's voice rose an octave. *"Can't?"* She took a step closer. "You will if you plan on keeping your job."

"But I don't plan on keeping my job." Abigail's voice, though more firm than usual, was still polite.

"You don't..." Eloise's eyes widened. "What in the world are you talking about?" she sputtered. "You've been here for almost ten years. You need the job. You—"

"Not really. Not anymore. You see, I've just come into some money—"

"Money!" Eloise's smile wasn't pleasant to see. "Oh, I see. Someone has left you a few thousand dollars, and so now you're going to retire?"

"Actually, it was a few million," Abigail said kindly. "Eight and a half million, to be exact. And a gold mine." She opened her desk drawer and took out the pen-and-pencil set her father had given her and a pair of sunglasses. Then she looked at Eloise and said, "You really are a dreadful person."

And turning on the heel of her sensible shoe, she left.

That night, unable to sleep, Abigail paced the worn living room carpet. This was the home she had grown up in. All of her memories were here. She'd done her homework on the table in front of the bay window, where she could watch Tim Griffin going in and out of his house across the street. She had dusted all of this furniture, had vacuumed this carpet at least a million times.

She touched the back of the black leather chair in which her father had sat reading his paper when he came home from the store. She thought of how the last ten years of his life had been a struggle for him because the big warehouse-type chains had all but pushed the small hardware stores out of business. When he had told Abby he couldn't afford to send her to Ohio State and that, instead, she'd have to go to a city college, she'd held back her tears and told him that she understood.

But though she'd understood, she'd been bitterly disappointed. For years, she had looked forward to going away to college, to being free at last from all of the restraints that had been set upon her as a child. She wanted to live in a dorm, go to frat parties and date all of the boys she hadn't been allowed to date in high school.

When, a week before her high school prom, her mother had said, "I suppose you're disappointed about not going," Abby had shrugged. "It doesn't matter," she'd murmured.

But it had mattered, and she'd wanted to say, "Why would anyone ask me? You didn't allow me to date while I was in school, and when I went to a movie with Tim Griffin, Papa didn't speak to me for a week.

Over the years, she had told herself that parents did the best they could. If her parents had made mistakes, they had been made out of love and because her parents had wanted to protect her.

She had loved them and she hadn't minded putting her life on hold for them. But they were gone now and she was alone to face a new set of circumstances, to meet new challenges.

It would be difficult to leave—even for a year—and while there was a sadness in leaving, as well as a fear of the unknown, there was also a sense of excitement, a feeling that she was setting out on a new adventure.

She took a *Rand McNally Road Atlas and Travel Guide* down from the bookcase shelf and turned to the map of Colorado. She had to look in the index to find Cripple Creek because it was little more than a dot on the map an inch from Colorado Springs.

She had never been to Colorado or anywhere else in the West. The farthest she'd gone from home had been a week's trip to Chicago with her parents when she was nine.

Colorado. She wouldn't know anyone there except Mr. Crimms and Nick Fitzgerald.

Nick Fitzgerald.

A smile played across her lips.

At last, tired from all the excitement of the day, Abigail went upstairs to bed.

But it was a long time before she went to sleep that night. And when she did, it was to dream not of the eight and a half million dollars she would inherit if she agreed to spend a year in Colorado, but of a man with black-Irish looks and sea green eyes.

The next morning, she had breakfast with Henry Crimms, and when she had signed all of the papers he had placed in front of her, he handed her a cashier's check for one hundred thousand dollars.

''To tide you over,'' he said.

The next day, Abigail began preparing for the move to Colorado.

## Chapter Two

There were things she couldn't leave behind: photographs, the patchwork quilt her grandmother had made,
her own goose-down pillow, the stuffed animal with sad
brown eyes and long floppy ears Uncle Jonah had sent her
for her eleventh birthday.

And books. Hard as it was, she limited herself to books
that she had read and wanted to read again, and books that
she had bought but had never had time to read.

Finally, on the last day of August, Abigail packed everything into the small, conservatively priced station
wagon she had bought with part of the hundred thousand
dollars Henry Crimms had given her.

She stood in the driveway and looked back at the slate
gray, two-story house that had been her home for the past
thirty-three years. Susie Braesek, her next-door neighbor,
had taken her African violets, and Susie's husband, Fred,
had agreed to keep the furnace going during the winter.

For the past three weeks, Abigail had felt a sense of exhilaration, but now that it was time to leave, she was overcome by a feeling of uncertainty. Wintz, Greenway and Strasburg hadn't been the best company to work for, but she'd had the security of a steady job. She thought of what her father had told her a year before he died. "You likely won't get married, Abby," he'd said. "Just be sure to hang on to your job so you'll have that pension when you're sixty-five."

Even now, with the promise of eight and a half million dollars dangling before her eyes, she felt a niggle of fear.

What if? she asked herself a dozen times a day. What if there really isn't all that money? What if I can't get the mine running again? What if I can't stick it out in Cripple Creek for a whole year?

She had dreamed about Eloise Zircle the previous night. Eloise, dressed in a long, gray robe, waggled a red-lacquered fingernail under Abigail's nose. "There isn't any money," she whispered. "There isn't any gold. You'll end up with nothing... nothing... nothing...."

Abby had awakened sitting straight up in bed, her body bathed in perspiration.

But this morning, she squared her shoulders, got into the station wagon and fastened her seat belt.

By the time she reached the rolling plains of Iowa, she had started to relax. When it came time to stop for gas, she began looking at the prices in the gas stations of the small towns she passed through. When she found one that was two pennies cheaper than the others, she stopped—at the self-serve pump—and filled up the tank.

It was only when she was once again on the road that she thought, I don't have to do that anymore! I have almost a hundred thousand dollars, and pretty soon, I'm going to have eight and a half million! She smiled, then the smile became a laugh. Finally, laughing so hard she couldn't see to drive, she pulled off to the side of the road and stopped. When the laughter died, she leaned her head back against the seat.

It was really true. She didn't have to pinch pennies anymore. She could buy high-octane gas or anything else she wanted—a pair of shoes that weren't on sale, a winter suit, a chateaubriand for one. She could even pay a dentist's bill in one fell swoop instead of a little bit at a time.

And yet, with the money would come new challenges, new decisions to make. That frightened her and she wished she was more worldly, that she had traveled, dated more, knew more about life. She wished, as she had not wished since she had been sixteen, that she was not so plain.

By noon of the fourth day, Abigail made Denver. She spent the night there and drove to Colorado Springs very early the next morning. There was still mist in the air. As Abigail rounded a curve, she saw a doe grazing on the side of the road ahead of her. Other than in a zoo, the only deer Abby had ever seen had been the head of the buck that hung in the living room over the fireplace, and so she stopped and rolled down her window.

"Well, hello," she said softly.

The doe lifted its head and looked directly at her. It stayed like that for a few moments, watching her with wide and lovely eyes, then turned and went into the brush.

And Abigail, feeling inordinately happy, drove on.

When, an hour later, she came up over the rise of a mountain, she saw two cars pulled off the road. She stopped and walked to the bluff, where several other people were standing.

Below her lay a town, a very small town, nestled in a volcanic bowl and rimmed by the snow-tipped Sangre de Cristo Mountains.

"What is that place?" she asked a woman standing nearby.

"That's Cripple Creek."

And Abigail got back into her car and drove down the mountain, toward the town that would be her home for the next twelve months.

The Majestic Hotel, built in the days when Cripple Creek had been a booming gold mining town, was a half block north of Bennett Avenue, the town's main street.

"You'd best stay there until you find a house," Henry Crimms had told Abby when he'd seen her in Toledo. "Your Uncle Jonah's place belongs to you, of course, but it's way on out at the mine, and I don't reckon you'd want to stay there. I'll line up a few places right in Cripple Creek that might do, and you can take a look at them once you get there."

As soon as Abigail registered at the hotel, she was shown to a vintage 1900s room on the second floor. All of the furnishings and decorations reflected Victorian charm and elegance. An antique, embossed copper bed stood against one wall. On the other side of the room was a bird's-eye-maple chest of drawers, a dressing table and a lady's chair with a needlepoint-covered seat.

There was a wardrobe instead of a closet, and the plumbing in the partitioned off bathroom, though obviously old, looked efficient.

Abigail gazed out of the open window at the mountains. She knew she should call Mr. Crimms to let him know that she had arrived, but she didn't. She needed time to adjust to her new surroundings, to get used to the old-

world strangeness of this Western town. When her heart
beat faster, she told herself the cause was the altitude, that
it wasn't the endless miles of rolling land or the fearsome
rise of the mountains. Or the fact that for the first time in
her life, she was really on her own.

On her own. Abigail breathed in the clear mountain air
and knew she was glad that she had come.

That evening, wearing a simple, blue cotton dress with
white collar and cuffs and neat white shoes, Abigail went
down to the dining room for dinner. She had washed her
hair, and because it hadn't completely dried, she had
brushed it out and let it curl naturally around her shoulders instead of pulling it back in its usual twist.

The dining room was crowded and pleasantly noisy. Like
her room, the dining room was furnished in Victorian
style. There were heavy, red velvet drapes at the windows,
and the pristine white tablecloths were edged in lace. The
last rays of the sun seeped in through stained glass windows, patterning the polished plank floor with splashes of
gold.

Abigail was led to a candlelit table against the wall. She
declined a drink when asked, and because she felt uncomfortable being alone, she buried her face in the menu and
didn't look up until the waiter came to take her order.

Feeling more comfortable, she looked up and smiled at
the waiter when he placed a deep bowl of chicken soup in
front of her, and she saw Nick Fitzgerald being led to a table in the middle of the room.

He seemed bigger than other men, taller and broader of
shoulder. He wore a black knit shirt and black trousers
that fit tight over his flat stomach and narrow hips. The
same tweed jacket that he'd worn in Toledo was hooked on
a finger and hung over his shoulder.

Men called out to him and grasped his hand when he passed. The women with them sat straighter in their chairs, smoothed their hair and touched the linen napkins to their lips.

The woman with Nick clung to his arm. A gamin-faced redhead, she was dressed in jeans and a bright pink T-shirt that stretched somewhat alarmingly over her bust.

Abigail quickly lowered her gaze because she didn't want Nicholas Fitzgerald to see her, but try as she might, she couldn't help an occasional peek in his direction.

The redhead entwined her fingers in his. She moved her chair closer and, once, she put her arm around his shoulder and nibbled on his ear.

Abigail tried to concentrate on her rice pudding.

She looked up when the waiter approached with her check, and she saw Nick Fitzgerald watching her. Before she could look away, he said something to his companion, stood and threaded his way through the tables toward Abigail.

"Good evening, Miss Sedgewick," he said. "I didn't know you'd arrived."

"I got in this afternoon." She caught the scent of musk and old leather and breathed it in.

"Had a chance to look around yet?"

Abigail shook her head.

"Henry's got a few houses for you to look at."

"I'll phone him tomorrow."

He hesitated. "If you've finished your dinner, perhaps you'd like to join my friend and me for a drink."

"No, I...no, thank you, Mr. Fitzgerald. I'm rather tired. I think I'll just go up to my room."

"I'll call you in a few days, then. There are some things we need to talk about—about the mine, I mean."

He tapped his fingers on the table and because she knew he was anxious to get back to the redhead, she said, "Thank you for stopping to say hello, Mr. Fitzgerald."

"We're partners. Why don't you call me Nick?"

She nodded. "Please call me Abigail."

"How about Abby?"

"If you prefer."

"Well then..." He cleared his throat. "I'm glad you made the trip safely. It's nice to see you again."

And oddly enough, it *was* nice to see her. In a way that Nick could not explain, he rather liked her primness and her well-bred manner. The blue dress with the white collar and cuffs gave her an old-fashioned, ladylike look that he found strangely appealing. She looked younger with her hair free about her shoulders, and when she'd inclined her head, he'd caught the scent of springtime apples.

"Who was that?" Merilee demanded when he reached her.

"Jonah's niece. She's just arrived in town."

Merilee looked at Abigail. As she rose and made her way out of the dining room, Merilee said, "Plain as an old-maid schoolteacher, isn't she?"

Nick's lips tightened. "Tell me about the new quarter horse you bought last week," he said.

Although he smiled and said all of the right things when Merilee spoke to him, Nick kept thinking about Abigail Sedgewick in her neat little blue dress with the white collar and cuffs. And of how, in the flickering light of the table candle, her brown eyes had been the color of very fine Spanish sherry.

The following day, Henry Crimms showed Abigail the houses in town that were either for rent or for sale, and while there really wasn't anything wrong with them, they simply didn't appeal to her.

"Maybe I'll have a look at Uncle Jonah's house," she said that afternoon when Mr. Crimms returned her to the hotel.

"You wouldn't want to live way out there, Miss Sedgewick. It wouldn't be right, a woman like you all alone."

"There's electricity, isn't there?" Abigail asked. "And water?"

"Yes, of course. But it's a good way from town, and there aren't any neighbors."

"But I have the car. I can drive in for anything I need."

And though he argued that she shouldn't live that far from town, he gave her directions on how to get there, and the next morning she drove on out to the mine.

Two miles out of town, Abby turned onto a rutted dirt road. There were no other cars here, and the only sounds came from the wind whispering through the quaking silver aspen. The farther she went, the more beautiful the country became. She was surrounded by fields of Indian paintbrush, columbine and mountain laurel. Ponderosa pine and blue spruce rimmed the landscape and the distant hills.

Now and then, a rail fence marked the land, and at one point, she passed an old mill that had been built high up on a rock. The slanting roof showed gaping holes, the walls sagged inward, and the wooden stairs leading to the structure were broken and rotted.

Abby smiled wryly. *I hope Uncle Jonah's house is sturdier than that,* she thought.

Ten minutes later, she came to a split-rail fence and a wooden gate with a sign that read, Lucky Lady Mine.

She opened the gate, drove through, then got out of the car and stood looking out at the distant mountains and the clear, blue sky. It was beautiful here, but more than the beauty, it was the quiet that touched her.

Though it was only the first part of September, there was already a hint of autumn in the air and she wondered what it would be like in the winter when the fields were no longer green. She was used to snow, but she had a feeling that Colorado winters, especially way out here, would be far different than the winters in Ohio.

She turned when she heard a scratch of sound, and she saw a small rabbit creep cautiously out from the shade of a pine tree and toward the wild grass. She stayed very still, watching with a smile, when suddenly, out of nowhere, a red-tailed hawk swooped down. The rabbit froze, scooted forward, stopped and ran in a circle.

"Oh, no!" Abby cried.

The hawk snatched the small animal in its talons and flew upward. She heard the rabbit squeal as it died, then hawk and rabbit disappeared behind a stand of silver birch.

Suddenly, the air seemed colder than it had been, and the clouds that only a few moments before had looked so powder-puff white now looked gray and threatening.

Sobered, Abigail went back to the car and drove until she came to a curve in the road and saw the house.

Almost surrounded by a stand of piñon pines, it stood low and rambling, built of logs with a base of heavy, gray stone. A wide front porch ran along the front. Yellow wood sorrel and lupine grew along the path that led up to it.

She parked and got out of her car, but before she had taken more than two steps, a dog bounded down off the front porch and raced toward her, barking as it came.

The back of Abigail's neck prickled, but she stood her ground. "Easy," she said softly. "Easy, fella."

He stopped six feet away and growled. Abby didn't move.

He was a big, blackish brown dog, probably a mix of German shepherd and black Labrador.

"It's okay, boy. Okay." Her heart beating in double time, she put her hand to her side, fingers curled inward, the back of her hand slightly extended.

The dog came toward her. She didn't move, but continued talking softly, reassuringly.

The dog's tail started to wag. The animal came closer and sniffed her hand.

"Good boy," she said, and slowly, so she wouldn't startle him, she patted his head. When Abigail turned and started up the front steps, the dog followed her.

He didn't look like a stray, nor did he look underfed. But there were no other houses around, and she wondered who he belonged to.

"Wait out here," she told him. He cocked his head, then settled down on an old rug just to the right of the front door.

Abby took the key out of her purse and unlocked the door. A hand-hooked rug covered part of the polished wood floor. Nubby, earth-tone curtains hung at the windows. The furniture, except for a comfortable-looking, worn leather chair and an overstuffed Victorian sofa, was rough-hewn and serviceable. A beautiful old desk stood beneath the windows that overlooked the porch and the fields beyond.

There were papers on the desk, an open accounting book, a magnifying glass, pens and pencils.

Everything in the room looked neat and clean. It was as though her uncle had only stepped out for a moment and the house, like the dog on the front porch, was waiting for him to return.

Had the dog belonged to Uncle Jonah? And if so, who had been feeding him?

Thoughtfully, Abby began to look at the books in the bookcases on either side of the fireplace. When she found a volume of Robert Service poems, she began to leaf through it, smiling as she read aloud, "'A bunch of the boys were whooping it up in the Malamute saloon...'"

Abby put the book down and picked up a pipe from the pipe rack on the table next to the chair. She ran her fingers around the bowl. Lifting the pipe to her nose, she caught the scent of the tobacco her uncle had used.

She could almost picture him sitting here before the big, stone fireplace on a cold winter's evening. Had he hunted with the rifle that hung above the mantel? she wondered.

There was a basket filled with wood to the left of the fireplace, along with a set of andirons and a bellows. An old moonshine jug had been placed at one end of the mantel, several photographs on the other. There was one of a group of workmen in front of what looked to Abby like a big, black hole with open wooden doors in the side of the mountain. A sign read, The Lucky Lady.

Next to that was a picture of Uncle Jonah with Nick Fitzgerald. The two of them were standing by a rail fence. Nick, hands in the pockets of his jeans, had one foot up on a rail. Her uncle was grinning up at Nick and they looked so outdoorsy male that Abby smiled. Her uncle had been right to leave Toledo. This was where he had belonged.

Still at the fireplace, she surveyed the room. And suddenly she knew how it would be on a winter's evening. She would be warm and cosy here, and though it was far from town, this was where she wanted to spend the year.

Exploring farther, she discovered that the household had a big, old-fashioned bathroom with a claw-foot tub.

In the smaller bedroom, a copy of *The Old Man and the Sea* lay on the nightstand beside the bed, and next to it was a picture of a woman. Her eyes were crinkled with laughter, and she had an old, felt hat pulled down over her curly, gray hair. The photograph was signed, "Love always, Evie." The room had surely been Uncle Jonah's.

The other bedroom had white lace curtains covering windows that looked out over the mountains. There was a bishop's bed, an old-fashioned dresser with a beveled glass mirror, a wooden rocking chair and a fireplace.

This was the room Abigail decided she would take for her own.

She went into the kitchen next. Red-checkered curtains had been hung over the old granite sink. There was a round oak table and six ladder-back chairs in the middle of the room, and a modern stove and refrigerator stood side by side against one wall.

She looked through the cupboards, hoping to find something for the dog to eat and was surprised to find them stocked with food. She found a can of dog food and opened it, then put the contents into a dog's dish she found next to the back door.

A few moments ago, it had seemed to her as though Uncle Jonah was still living in the house. Now, Abigail knew she'd had that feeling because someone else, a very live someone else, had a key to the house. Someone had been here, someone had been feeding the dog.

Frowning, Abby took the dish out to the front porch. "Here you go," she told the dog. She leaned against the porch railing while he ate, wishing the animal could tell her what had been going on.

When she went back into the house, she decided to take a look at the mine, so she hunted through neatly arranged drawers until she found a flashlight. Remembering the wooden doors in the photograph of the mine, she searched until she found a large ring of keys.

As soon as she opened the back door, the dog came racing around the side of the house. She scratched him behind his ears, said, "Coming with me, fella?" and began to look for a path. When she found it, she followed it through a stand of pines for less than a quarter of a mile before she came to the side of the mountain that held the large wooden doors she'd seen in the photo on the mantel.

By trial and error, she found the right key and managed to unlock the doors. The entrance looked to be about ten feet wide and perhaps six and a half feet high.

"Come on," she said to the dog, who had followed, but he stood right where he was. She started in and he began to whimper.

"There's nothing to be afraid of," she said, more to herself than to the dog, and taking the flashlight out of the pocket of her skirt, she tightened her hand around it and started in.

The floor of the mine seemed to be level, but after she had gone a few steps, it began to slant downward.

Abby didn't like caves, even the tourist caves with electric lights and guides that said, "Right this way, folks," but she made herself go on.

"It's half mine," she said aloud. "I should see it." And she kept telling herself that because her uncle left her a half interest, she had a responsibility to get used to being in here. There would be workers, of course, and Nick Fitzgerald would run things, but she wanted to know what was going on. She couldn't if she was too frightened to set foot inside.

The passageway narrowed and the ceiling lowered. Abby went a little farther, and when she flashed the light on the ground, she saw narrow railroad tracks and, empty, open carts that probably were used to transport the ore.

The ground slanted even farther down, and ahead of her she saw the mine shaft and what looked like a wire cage that she thought was what the miners used to lower themselves into the mine.

She decided then that she wouldn't go any farther and turned around, expecting to see light from the entrance ahead. But there wasn't any light. There was only blackness.

Her throat closed with fear. She hadn't branched off to the side, but the tunnel must have curved and she hadn't noticed. All she had to do, she told herself, was to go straight ahead, step by step, one foot ahead of the other.

And not panic.

"Just keep going," she whispered. "You're not too far from the entrance...."

A rock clattered to the ground somewhere behind her.

Abby smothered a yelp and tightened her hand around the flashlight. A little farther, she told herself. Just a little...

She saw the light at exactly the moment a slide of rocks clattered to the ground. As though the devil himself, pitchfork poised to strike, were right behind her, she sprinted toward the entrance. Another few yards, another few feet...

Gulping for air, her chest heaving with fear, Abby streaked out of the mine...right into Nick Fitzgerald's arms.

## Chapter Three

"Hey!" Nick said. "What...? Take it easy. You're okay."

But Abby was too frightened to take it easy. She burrowed her head against Nick's chest and tightened her hands on his soft, leather vest. The total blackness of the mine had scared her out of her wits and she welcomed the arms that tightened around her, liked the feel of his hand against the back of her head, the arm around her waist.

But little by little as her breathing evened, she became more aware of him, the masculine him, and stepped away.

"I'm—I'm sorry," she managed to say, embarrassed because she'd clung to him like a frightened child. "Some rocks fell and I got frightened. I—"

"What in the hell were you doing in the mine?"

The dog had been barking and prancing around them. Now, he jumped up against Abby's legs and began to whine. Instead of answering Nick, she reached down to pat the animal's head. She was ashamed of the fear she'd shown in front of Nick, and yes, a little shaken because she'd liked the feel of his arms around her.

"I—I just wanted to have a look around," she said finally.

"By yourself?" His lips tightened to a hard, firm line. "Dammit, Abby, the mine's been closed for over a year. There's work that needs to be done before we start operating. If it hadn't been for Jasper, I wouldn't have known where you were."

"Jasper?" She looked down at the dog. "Is that his name?"

Nick nodded. "He was Jonah's dog. I took him home with me after Jonah died, but he kept coming back here." Nick pushed the Stetson back on his head and absently scratched the dog behind the ears. "I tried keeping him in the house, hoping he'd get used to it. He'd been with me a week this time, but a couple of days ago, I let him out and he took off."

He ruffled the dog's ears. "It's a long run, isn't it, boy?" he asked, then knelt to inspect Jasper's paws. When he saw that a thorn had wedged its way between two pads, he took a penknife out of the back pocket of his jeans.

"I'll get it out," Abby said.

"The dog doesn't know you."

"That's the idea, Nick. I want him to." She sat on the ground and took Jasper's paw in her hand. "Easy now, boy," she said soothingly. "Easy does it."

Jasper whined, but he let her minister to him, and when she had pried the thorn out, she hugged the animal and said, "Good dog, Jasper. Good dog."

"Looks like you've had some experience with animals," Nick said.

"Actually, I don't have any experience." Abby stood and brushed her skirt off. "My parents wouldn't let me have a pet when I was a child. I suppose I could have gotten a cat or a dog after they died, but it didn't seem fair to an animal, leaving it alone all day while I worked." She patted Jasper's head. "It'll be fun having Jasper around."

"He won't stay in the city with you any more than he would with me."

"I'm not going to be in the city. I've decided to move out here."

"Here?" Nick frowned. "You can't do that."

Abby glared up at him. "I like the house," she said testily. "It's cosy and comfortable and—"

"Too far from town."

"I have a car."

"It's not a good idea for a woman like you—"

"What's that supposed to mean?"

"That you're a city girl and the first time you hear a coyote howl, you'll be on your way back to town."

"No, I won't!" She turned away from him and started toward the house.

Jasper looked up at him, then went loping after Abigail.

Nick stared after her, hands clenched at his sides, trying to resist the temptation to tell her to take his share of the mine and welcome to it. He hadn't wanted Jonah to give him half, and he'd done his damnedest to talk the old man out of it. But Jonah, who'd known for months that he hadn't long to live, had been adamant.

"I'm giving you half and that's damn final," he'd said. "But I'm giving it to you with strings attached. My brother Elbert's girl is going to be coming out here and she doesn't know spit about operating a mine. I've got a hunch she doesn't know spit about anything else, either, and I want you to keep an eye on her. That's partly why I'm makin' you'n her partners. I want you to have half of the money that'll be there when you find the gold.''

"You've given me enough as it is," Nick had argued. "You took me in and gave me the home I'd never had. You set up a trust fund for me and put me through college. You've been more of a father to me than my own father ever was."

"And you've been the son I never had," Jonah had answered. "That's why I want you to have half the Lucky Lady. It's goin' to pay off again one of these days, you just see if it don't.''

Jonah had been so sure there was gold even though the vein they'd been mining had been worked out almost five years before. He'd kept a skeleton crew on, and he'd worked night and day trying to find another vein. He hadn't closed down until he'd been too sick to get out of bed, and only then because Nick had promised to open the mine again.

"I'll do it, Jonah," Nick muttered to himself. "I'll find the gold if it's there, but I sure wish to hell you hadn't saddled me with your old-maid niece."

Still mumbling to himself, Nick padlocked the big wooden doors and started back toward the house.

Abby was in the kitchen making coffee when he went in. Jasper was stretched out in front of the refrigerator.

"I don't think you should live out here alone," Nick said without preamble, "but if you're determined to, then by all means keep Jasper here with you. I'll be hiring men this week, and I'll arrange to have a watchman keep an eye on things."

"I don't need a bodyguard," she snapped, swinging away from the stove.

Nick crossed the kitchen in two strides and glared down at her, just as angry as she was now. "And you are never, repeat, *never*, to go into the mine by yourself. Is that clear?"

Abby lifted her chin. "We're partners," she said. "You're not the boss, and I'm not your employee."

His eyes blazing, Nick said, "No one's been in the mine for over six months. Every inch of it has to be inspected to make sure it's safe before we can start work. Beams need to be shored up, tracks have to be replaced and the cage— the elevator—and shaft have to be checked."

A muscle jumped in his cheek. "Cave-ins have been known to happen, Abby, and men have been trapped a thousand feet below the surface. If something happened . . . a slide, a fallen beam . . ." He shook his head. "I want you to promise me you'll never go in alone again."

Abby looked up into his angry green eyes, and though it cost her to say the words, she managed them. "I promise." Then, dropping her gaze from his, she stepped away and poured coffee into the two mugs she'd set out.

He took the Stetson off and sat at the big, round table. "I think maybe you'd better know that before Jonah died, he was approached by some men, a group from Denver that, as far as I'm concerned, are a bunch of ruthless bastards. They wanted to buy the Lucky Lady, and they offered three million dollars. Jonah wouldn't have anything to do with them. They've approached me with an offer of four million, and I told them to get lost. But you're my partner, you have the right to know about it."

"Four million dollars is a lot of money."

"Yes, it is." He waited.

"Uncle Jonah left us the Lucky Lady," she said. "All he asked was that we give him a year." She sat down across from him. "Whether we find gold or not, we owe him that year, Nick. If they approach you again, tell them no deal."

He let out the breath he didn't know he'd been holding and studied her across the rim of his coffee cup, surprised that she had surprised him, that maybe there was a little something more to her than he'd first thought.

"There's something else," he said. "The last couple of times I've been here, it looked to me as though somebody had been prowling around."

"Nothing seems to have been disturbed in the house. Actually..." There was a puzzled look on her face. "Actually, everything is in perfect condition. Inside, I mean. Uncle Jonah's been gone for over two months, and the furniture isn't even dusty. The stove and refrigerator are clean, and there's canned food in the cupboards."

"That'd be Evie," Nick said with a smile.

"Evie?"

"Evie Montgomery. She used to spend a lot of time out here with Jonah."

"Is that her picture in his room?"

Nick nodded.

"Were she and Uncle Jonah...?" Abigail blushed. "You know."

"Yes," Nick said. "They were."

"Oh." She looked down at the coffee cup. "But they weren't married?"

Here comes the moral indignation, Nick thought. "No, they weren't married," he said in an even tone.

"How long were they...together?"

"For almost thirty years."

"Thirty years! That's terrible."

He'd been right. Her face was red and her lips were tight. Here came the indignation.

"All those years, and he didn't mention her in the will?" Abby said hotly. "She's the one who should have the house and the money."

Surprised, Nick took another drink of his coffee before he answered, "Jonah built her a house and, a few years ago, he set up a trust fund for her. Evie's well taken care of."

"And she's the one who's been coming out here?"

"Yep." He pushed his chair back from the table. "I'll give her a call tonight and tell her you're moving in. She won't want to come out and bother you if she knows you're here."

"I'd like to meet her."

"I'll arrange it." He stood up. "Guess I'd better be getting back to town."

A heavy date with the ear-nibbling redhead? Abby tried not to look at his ears. She took the cups and went to the sink to rinse them.

"I'll follow you back if you're ready," he said.

"I think I'll stay a bit longer. I want to check the closets and take a look around to see what I'll need to buy."

"You're determined to move in?"

"Absolutely. I'm paid up at the hotel until the end of the week. I'll move in here on Monday."

In spite of himself, Nick grinned. Eight and a half million or not, she'd paid for something and she was going to make sure she got her money's worth. That answered his question about what kind of a partner she was going to make. She'd keep a tight rein on their purse strings and account for every penny they spent.

He fished his car keys out of the pocket of his jeans and reached for his hat. "I'll help you move in," he said.

"Thank you, but—"

"I'll be at the hotel at seven on Monday."

"I really don't need any—"

"Seven o'clock." He started out the door. Turning back, he said, "And stay out of the mine unless I'm with you. Is that understood?"

Abby resisted the impulse to salute. "Understood." She closed the door behind him with a little more force than was necessary and watched him from behind the curtains. Other men walked, sauntered or trudged. Nick's long legs covered the ground in easy, purposeful strides.

She wondered if he did everything that purposefully, and with a smothered sigh, she let the curtain fall back into place.

Nick found himself thinking about Abby at odd moments during the next few days. He told himself that was because she didn't belong in Cripple Creek and that she certainly didn't belong hell gone living out at the mine all by herself. It surprised him that she wanted to because he'd have bet anything that she would have chosen to stay at the hotel or in an apartment in the center of town. She was, as he'd told her, a city girl. And he knew damn well that no matter what she'd said, the first time a coyote started howling, she'd hightail it right back to town.

Saturday night, telling himself that the only reason he wanted to see her was to try once again to talk her out of moving out to the mine, Nick stopped by the hotel. He asked the desk clerk to ring Abby's room and when there was no answer, he looked into the dining room.

She was there, having dinner with Henry and Blanche Crimms, looking prim and proper in a blue, summery dress.

Henry stood up and pulled a chair out when he saw Nick. "We've just ordered," he said. "Come on and eat with us."

"Yes," Blanche said. "We don't see enough of you, Nick. Please join us."

He looked at Abby. She gave him a tentative smile and lowered her gaze.

Nick sat down opposite her.

"Has Abby told you she's planning to move out to Jonah's?" he asked after he'd ordered.

Henry nodded. "I think she ought to stay here in town. It'll be winter in another couple of months and the roads'll be bad."

"Convince her if you can," Nick said. "I tried, but she wouldn't listen to me."

Blanche, a comfortably plump woman in her middle sixties with warm brown eyes and a generous mouth, smiled at Abby. "I can understand why you want to live there. Henry and I drove out a few times when Jonah was ailing. It's a good sturdy house, and I bet you're going to love living there. A woman listens to a man and she'd never do anything. Half the time, they don't think we've got the sense to cross the street by ourselves."

"Now, Blanche, Miss Sedgewick's not used to being out in the country all by herself. A young woman like her—"

"I'm thirty-three years old, Mr. Crimms," Abby said. "For the last five years, I've lived alone in a ten-room house. I've shoveled snow in the winter and mowed grass in the summer. I appreciate your concern, but I'm quite capable of taking care of myself. Uncle Jonah's house is in good condition. There's electricity and a phone, and I've got a car whenever I need to get into town." She raised her chin. "I'm moving in on Monday."

"I told you she wouldn't change her mind," Nick said. "Anyway, the mine'll open in another week or ten days. I've hired some of the old crew back, and I've arranged for a night watchman to keep an eye on things." He looked across the table. "And on you," he added firmly. "He starts Monday."

After that exchange, Henry and Blanche carried most of the dinner conversation. It was when they were finishing their coffee that Blanche suggested they go to Zeke's and listen to some music.

"Good idea." Nick turned to Abby. "You'll enjoy it," he said, and he wanted to chuckle because he knew damn well she'd probably hate it.

"I'd planned on making it an early night," Abby said.

"Oh, come on, it'll be fun." Blanche smiled at her.

Henry called for the check, paid it over Nick's protests, and when they'd pushed back their chairs, Blanche, without giving Abby another chance to refuse, linked her arm through Abby's and led her toward the door.

It was a little after eleven and except for a few cars, the streets were empty. They walked the few blocks to Zeke's and even before they reached it, Abby could hear the music.

She didn't know what she'd expected, but certainly not this old-time type of saloon. And that's exactly what it was, a saloon. A banged-up thirty-foot bar ran the length of the big, crowded room with a beamed ceiling. A four-piece band was playing foot-stomping Western music, and jean-clad couples were dancing. Everybody seemed to be in a Saturday-night, go-to-hell, party mood.

Abby took one look at the place and tried to think of a reason to leave. But before she could, Henry Crimms said, "There's a place," and with an arm around his wife's waist, he led her toward the only empty table in the room.

Abby looked uncertainly at Nick. He raised one dark eyebrow, gave her a look that was both amused and challenging, and with his hand in the middle of her back, guided her after the Crimmses.

When they reached the table, he seated her and was just pulling out a chair for himself when the redhead Abby had seen with him the first night launched herself at him.

"Nicky!" she cried, and throwing her arms around his neck, she kissed him full on the mouth. Then she turned to yell back over her shoulder, "Hey, Jake, over here."

A tall, lanky man ambled toward them. "Hi, Nick. H'lo, Miz Crimms." He shook hands with her husband and looked at Abby.

"Abigail Sedgewick," Nick said. "Jonah's niece. Abby, this is Jake McClinton, Sheriff McClinton." He turned and grinned at the redhead. "And this is Merilee Beals."

"How do you do?" Abby said.

Merilee nodded and dismissed Abby. "Party time," she said with a laugh.

Jake McClinton borrowed two chairs from the table next to them and sat down. An inch or two over six feet, he had a boyishly rugged look. His hair was a sandy brown, and his eyes were a nice, honest blue.

"I'd heard you were in town," he said. "Is everything all right? Have you found a place to stay?"

"I'm moving into my uncle's house on Monday."

"It's a little far from town, isn't it?"

"That's what I tried to tell her," Nick put in. "But she's determined that's where she's going to live." He looked up as the waitress approached. "What'll it be?" he asked.

"Beer's fine for Blanche and me," Henry said.

"Abby?"

She hesitated. "I don't . . ." She hesitated when she saw the look on Merilee's face.

"I don't reckon they have any milk," the redhead said.

"Then I reckon I'll have whatever you're having, Miss Beals."

Merilee looked up at the waitress. "Two boilermakers," she said.

"Well, now." Henry looked nervously across the table at his wife.

Nick leaned back in his chair. He wanted to tell Merilee to cool it and to tell Abby she didn't have to keep up with Merilee. But there was something in the thrust of Abby's chin that stopped him.

The waitress brought the drinks. "Whiskey with a beer chaser," she said.

Abby stared at the whiskey. She'd never had anything stronger than a glass of white wine at Christmas. She didn't know what whiskey tasted like, and she hated the smell of beer.

Merilee raised the whiskey glass and, looking at Abby, said, "Here's to you and here's to me. Should we ever disagree, then to hell with you and here's to me." In one gulp, she downed the drink.

Abby picked up her glass. She drank it down, wiped the corners of her mouth and smiled.

She had to smile because she knew that if she opened her mouth, flames would spurt out. The fiery liquid scorched her mouth and burned its way slowly down to her stomach. She lifted the mug of beer and took a big drink. She didn't like the taste, but the beer helped bank the fire.

Jake McClinton stood up. "Would you like to dance?" he asked.

Abby, still afraid to speak, nodded.

"You all right?" he said when they were away from the others.

She took a deep breath. "I think so."

"You shouldn't mind Merilee. She never did like competition. Anybody younger and prettier than Blanche Crimms and she starts acting up." Jake grinned down at

Abby. "You're a whole lot prettier than Blanche or anybody else this town's seen in a long time."

"Sheriff, I—"

"Jake. Okay? I hope you're going to like it here, Miss Abby. I know it's hard getting used to a new place, but everybody's friendly, and we sure did think a lot of your uncle. He was everybody's friend, and now, we're your friends. You need anything, you can call on me or anybody else here in Cripple Creek." He grinned as Merilee and Nick danced by. "She'll be in a better mood now that she's got Nick dancing with her," he whispered. "She's been after him since they were in junior high school together. One of these days, I figure she's bound to catch him."

The music ended, and before it could start up again, Abby said, "I'm not a very good dancer, Jake. Do you mind if we sit down?"

"Of course not." He took her arm and led her back to the table.

Where another whiskey-filled shot glass awaited, along with another beer.

"Can't walk on one leg." Merilee, thumbs hooked into the waistband of her cutoffs, grinned a challenge at Abby.

Abby took a deep breath, then a tentative sip. Before she could take another one, Nick said, "Let's dance," and he all but lifted her right out of the chair.

"What're you trying to do?" he asked when he put his arms around her. "If you think you can keep up with Merilee, you've got another think coming."

"I'm not trying to keep up with her. I'm just..." Abby hiccuped.

"Ever drink straight whiskey before?"

"I've never even tasted whiskey before."

"Then what..." Nick shook his head. "You let Merilee get to you," he said. "That was dumb." He held Abby away from him. "Are you all right?"

"I feel a little warm."

"I bet you do." He shook his head, then with a chuckle, drew her back into his arms.

For a moment, she resisted, but when the room started to spin, she hung on to him. He'd been wearing a jacket earlier, but he'd taken it off when they'd come into the bar. His Western-style shirt was clean and crisp, and it smelled of soap—and of him.

The hand against her back was warm; everything was pleasantly, hazily warm. Through half-closed eyes, she looked around and wondered why she hadn't liked it here at first. The music was nice, and so were the people. Except for Merilee.

"Is she your girl?" she asked.

"Merilee?"

"Of course, Merilee," she said, and then in a softly off-key voice, she began to sing, "Merilee, Merilee, Merilee, Merilee, life is but a dream...."

"You're bombed, Miss Sedgewick."

"Bombed? Bombed?" Abby looked up at him. "Sedgewicks do not get bombed, Mr. Fitz—Fitzwonderful." She looked up at him, and it seemed to her that she had never seen eyes so green or hair so black. Black as a crow's feathers, she thought, and she reached up to smooth a strand of it off his forehead. With another sigh, she closed her eyes and snuggled her body closer to his.

Close enough for him to catch the scent of springtime apples when her hair brushed his cheek.

Walk her back to the table, he told himself. Make some kind of excuse and get the hell out of here.

But if he did, Jake would more than likely want to walk her back to the hotel. Nick wasn't sure how he felt about that. Abigail Sedgewick was his partner and his responsibility. He'd take her back.

He tucked her hand against his chest and held it there. She murmured something, sighed again and moved closer.

He could feel the heat of her small breasts as they pressed against his chest, and he knew if he moved his fingers down an inch and a half, he could touch the softness there. He felt the press of her legs, the line of hip, the brush of her inner thigh against his. And he felt his body grow taut with unexpected—and certainly unwanted—desire.

The music stopped, but still he held her. She stood there for a moment, her head still against his shoulder. Then a sigh shuddered through her and she stepped back and looked up at him.

He said her name, "Abby?" and taking her hand, he led her back to the table.

## Chapter Four

"If we head out of here Thursday morning, I reckon we ought to make it back by Sunday night. Might be our last chance before the weather—" Jake McClinton looked up and when he saw Abby, he said, "We're talking about a pack trip into the mountains next week—Merilee, Mr. and Mrs. Crimms, Nick 'n' me." He stood up to pull her chair out, and with a smile added, "Say, why don't you come along with us? Nothing like a pack trip to give you a taste of the real outdoors."

"Miss Sedgewick's a city girl, Jake," Merilee said before Abby could answer. "Two hours on a horse and she wouldn't be able to walk for a week."

"I've ridden before," Abby said. But she did not add that her ride, at age eight, had been for about five minutes and on a pony, not a horse.

"Then it's settled." Jake covered her hand with his. "A trip like that can be pretty rugged." Nick frowned. "Are you sure you're up to it, Abby?"

She looked at him, then at Merilee, and when she saw another challenge in the woman's eyes, she said, "Of course, I'm up to it."

The hour grew late. Abby's drink had mysteriously been replaced by a cup of black coffee. The coffee helped, but her head was still swimming, and every five minutes, she tried unsuccessfully to smother a yawn.

Nick got up and took Abby's arm. "I'll walk you back to the hotel."

Blanche Crimms kissed Abby's cheek, Jake squeezed her hand, and Merilee gave her a look that almost sobered her up.

When they were outside, Abby took a breath of fresh air. "I'm not accustomed to drinking," she said, and hiccuped.

The hiccup embarrassed her. The whole evening embarrassed her. She stole a sidelong glance at Nick and felt her face flush, thinking how it had been when they'd danced, the way she had clung to his hand and brought her body close to his.

He took her arm to help her step off the curb. "You shouldn't have let Merilee goad you into drinking if you weren't accustomed to it."

"I know."

She sounded so miserable that Nick smiled and said, "No harm done, but you'll probably have a bangaroo of a headache tomorrow." He stopped at the entrance of the hotel. "Can you get in all right?"

"Of course." She sounded indignant.

He hesitated. "Maybe I'd better walk you up to your room."

"I assure you that isn't necessary. I'm..." A wave of dizzyness caused her to falter, and she braced a hand against the side of the building.

"You're feeling rocky, aren't you?" Nick asked. And before Abby could protest, he put his arm around her waist and took her into the hotel.

When they reached the stairs, she said, "I'm all right, really," but he kept his arm around her and guided her up.

At her door, he asked for the key and when she gave it to him, he opened the door, then turned the light on and led her to the bed.

Abby pulled away from him. "If you think for one minute that you're going to come in here and take advantage of me, you're wrong," she said indignantly. "You're not going to stay. We're not going to—to..." She took a deep breath. "You are *not* going to make love to me, Nicholas Fitz—"

"You ought to wait until you're asked." Nick pushed the Stetson back on his head, crossed his arms over his chest, then gave her a long, slow look before he turned away from her and started toward the door. But at the door, he hesitated, gave her another long, slow look and went back into the room.

He towered over her, threatening in his power and masculinity. "Maybe a kiss will sober you up," he drawled, and before Abby knew what he was going to do, he pulled her into his arms and kissed her.

Like she'd never been kissed before.

She squeaked a protest and tried to pull away. But his arms tightened, and he pressed her closer.

Heat zinged like small electric shocks through Abby's body, and her knees went weak. She slipped her hands up around his neck, then down over his broad shoulders to feel the sheer power and the strength of his muscles.

The kiss deepened. He put his hand against the small of her back to urge her closer and suddenly, she wanted to be closer. Her body felt heated and hungry for more. For so much more.

She sighed against his lips and fitted her body to his.

"Abby?" His voice was a hoarse, surprised whisper. He kissed her again, deep and hard, then with a strangled sigh, he let her go, so abruptly that she staggered and would have fallen if he hadn't put his hand out to steady her.

"Sorry," he said. "I shouldn't have... Sorry."

Before Abby could respond, he turned and hurried out the door.

She stood in the middle of the room, fingertips against her trembling mouth. Her arms felt empty, and she dropped them to her sides. A low moan escaped her lips, and with a sigh, she sank onto the bed and closed her eyes.

Nick Fitzgerald had kissed her, and in a way she could not explain, she did not think she would ever be the same again.

Nick walked quickly down the hall. He took the stairs two at a time and didn't stop until he was outside on the sidewalk.

What in the hell had come over him? he asked himself angrily. He hadn't meant to kiss her. He shouldn't have kissed her. She'd had too much to drink, and a decent man didn't take advantage when a lady was in that condition.

And Abigail was a lady.

But she wasn't his type. He was a go-to-hell man, and she was as proper as a Baptist Sunday-school teacher. He gulped in a great breath of the cool night air to steady his nerves...and wondered why her mouth had tasted sweeter than any honey he'd ever sampled, and why he hadn't noticed before now how incredibly feminine she was.

He'd only meant to shock her, but he was the one who'd been shocked. When he'd felt her trembling against him, when he'd sensed her inexperience and uncertainty, a fire had ignited inside him and he'd felt an excitement unlike anything he'd ever known.

Her seeming inexperience puzzled him. She was thirty-three years old. There had to have been at least one or two men in her life. Her reaction intrigued him, and in spite of the fact that he knew she wasn't his type, he couldn't help wondering what would have happened if he had persisted. What would she have done if he had laid her down on that old-fashioned bed? What would it have been like to have felt her body warm and pliant under his?

His body tightened with painful intensity. He swore under his breath, clapped his hat firmly on his head and strode down the street as fast as his long legs would carry him.

The telephone's ringing jarred Abby awake. She tried to sit up, then moaned and fell back against the pillow and closed her eyes. But the phone kept ringing.

"H'lo," she mumbled.

"Abby?"

"I think so."

"This is Nick."

She opened her eyes.

"Are you all right?"

"Head aches."

"I bet it does," he said with a chuckle. For a moment there was only silence on the line. "About last night, Abby..." He cleared his throat. "I'm sorry. I made a mistake and I want to apologize. I hope it won't make a difference in our relationship, our business relationship, I mean."

She clutched the receiver tighter. "Of course not," she murmured. "I had too much to drink. I shouldn't have let you come into my room. Nice women..." What? Never let a man cross their threshold? Never felt their bodies warm and yearn as hers had yearned last night?

She sat up in bed. "Let's just forget it," she said crossly. "As far as I'm concerned, it never happened."

"Right." Nick cleared his throat again. "Well then, I'll see you tomorrow."

"Tomorrow?"

"Unless you've changed your mind about moving out to Jonah's."

"I haven't changed my mind."

"Seven o'clock all right?"

"Seven's fine." She closed her eyes and pinched the skin between her eyebrows.

"I'll see you then."

"Uh-huh." She put the receiver down, picked up a pillow and covered her head with it.

She tried not to think about Nick and the way she had felt last night when he kissed her. But the more she tried not to think about the kiss or about him, the more she did. He wasn't the kind of a man she would ever be interested in, of course, but, oh, she had never felt as alive as when his mouth had covered hers. His lips had been so firm, his arms had been so strong. She'd never known, had not even imagined she could feel the kind of emotion she had felt.

But it hadn't meant anything to him. He'd said it was a mistake, something to apologize for. Something...

A knock on the door interrupted her thoughts.

"Who is it?" she called out.

"Room service, ma'am."

"I didn't order anything."

"A gentleman did."

A gentleman? Abby sat up and reached for her robe. Pushing her disheveled hair back from her face, she padded barefoot to the door and opened it.

"Good morning."

She stared at the too-cheerful young man, then gestured to the nightstand and said, "Put it there."

"Yes, ma'am." He set the tray down, told her to enjoy her breakfast and went out, closing the door behind him.

Abby slumped down on the bed and looked at the tray. There was a pot of coffee—black, thank goodness—a tall glass of tomato juice, a bottle of Worcestershire sauce, a stack of toast, a small pot of orange marmalade and a nosegay of columbine. Under the tomato juice was a note that read, "Maybe this will help."

A smile softened Abby's face. She picked up the flowers and held them to her nose.

It doesn't mean anything, she told herself. He's just being nice. But when she finished her breakfast, she took a sprig of the columbine and put it carefully between the pages of the book she had been reading the day before.

Nick was waiting for her when she came downstairs at five minutes before seven on Monday morning.

"Let me have that," he said, and he took the suitcase out of her hand. "What about your other things?"

"They're all ready." She looked around the empty lobby. "I tried to call down to have someone help me, but nobody answered the phone."

"Give me your key. I'll get your things."

"Then I'll help."

Nick started to object, but she'd already turned and headed back up the stairs.

It took them two trips to load the rest of her suitcases and boxes into her car and his Jeep. When she started to put a box of books in the back seat of the Jeep she saw that it was already stacked with bags of groceries.

"I picked up a few things I thought you might need," Nick said. "And before I forget . . ." He handed her a key. "This was Evie's. She wanted me to give it to you, and she said she'd be calling you."

Abby looked at the groceries. "It was thoughtful of you to get the things, Nick. How much do I owe you?"

"Consider it a housewarming present."

"But—"

"Hot dogs, a couple of steaks, fresh bread, some fruit and a sack of dog food. Cheaper than flowers."

She thought of the columbine on the breakfast tray. "Thank you," she said. "And for breakfast yesterday."

"You're welcome." A grin softened his mouth. "I figured you'd need a tomato-juice transfusion."

"Yes, I did," she said as she got into her car.

She followed him out of town, and when he pulled into the parking lot of a small restaurant, she parked the station wagon next to his Jeep.

"I thought we'd better have some breakfast so you won't have to worry about it when you get out to the house," he said when he opened the door for her.

"I'm glad you thought of it. I didn't realize I was hungry until I saw the restaurant sign."

He ordered steak and eggs and hash browns. She asked for a dish of bran and rye toast.

He looked at her dish of bran. "Is that all you ever eat for breakfast?"

"Most of the time."

"You'd better start eating a lot more than that once the weather gets colder." He looked at her across the table. "Besides," he said, "you could use some more meat on your bones."

Bones? Abby's lips pursed. "You think I'm too thin?"

Actually, he thought she was just about right, but he was damned if he was going to tell her so.

"What I meant was that the winters out here can get pretty rough. You're going to need the extra strength that more food will give you."

"I assure you, Nick, I'm quite strong. If you're worrying about me carrying my share of work once we start the mine, you can forget it. I'm more than able to do whatever has to be done."

He glared at her across the table and wondered what in the hell they were fighting about and what it was about her that made him want to take care of her.

They finished the rest of the meal in silence, then got back into their respective vehicles and drove out to the mine.

Jasper, looking as well fed as ever, raced out to meet them. Nick ruffled the top of the dog's head with his fingers, but Abby knelt down and hugged him, glad that he remembered her.

She insisted on helping Nick carry her suitcases, boxes and all of the groceries into the house. They stacked the boxes in the big living room, and he carried her suitcases into the bedroom.

"You sure you're going to be all right out here all by yourself?" he said when he left.

"Quite sure." She put her hand out. "Thanks for all your help, Nick."

Her hand looked small and pale in his and for a reason he didn't understand, he hated to let go of it.

But he did. And said, "Call me if you need anything. I'll see you Thursday."

"Thursday?"

"The pack trip up into the mountains. Don't you remember?"

The pack trip? Horses? Abby stifled a groan. "Oh, sure," she said. "I'd almost forgotten."

"I'll pick you up at five."

"In the morning?"

Nick laughed. "Of course, in the morning. We want to get an early start."

"Right."

She wondered, after Nick left, if there was any way she could get out of it. She had three days to think of a reason she couldn't go. But by Wednesday night, she hadn't thought of one, and she'd already telephoned Evie, although she hadn't met her yet, to ask if she would look after Jasper. The only thing she could do would be to tell Nick that she'd stretched the truth when she'd said she knew how to ride and to admit she'd never been out on a real horse.

But somehow, whether from pride or a need to prove that she could do anything Merilee Beals could do, Abby simply could not bring herself to call Nick. And, after all, she told herself before she went to bed Wednesday night, how hard could it be? She liked animals. Surely she could get along with a horse. Couldn't she?

At five minutes before five on Thursday morning, Abby stood on her front porch and waved a hello to Nick. She was wearing blue jeans, a long-sleeved, tailored, white shirt, a sweater, boots and a wide-brimmed felt hat.

She'd bought the clothes the day before, along with a knapsack in which she carried an extra pair of jeans and another shirt, a Windbreaker, pajamas and slippers, and a small cosmetics bag with a toothbrush, soap, a washcloth and towel.

When she had showered and dressed this morning, she had started to pin her hair back into its usual twist, but she'd changed her mind and pulled it into a ponytail instead.

She was relieved to see that Nick had Blanche and Henry Crimms with him, and she was oddly pleased when Nick looked at her approvingly, and said, "'Morning, Abby, I like your outfit."

He looked more like a cowboy than ever this morning. His jeans were well worn and looked like they had been poured over his flat stomach, narrow hips and long, muscled legs. His crisp blue-and-white-checkered shirt was open at the neck, and his throat was as tan as his face.

"We're meeting Merilee and Jake at White River Forest," he explained after good-mornings had been exchanged. "We'll pick up the horses there."

He glanced at Abby when he got into the Jeep. "When's the last time you went riding?" he asked.

"It's been . . . quite a while," she answered truthfully.

"Well, don't worry, honey," Blanche said from the back seat, "Nick will pick out a nice, gentle mare for you. This is going to be fun, you just wait and see. The mountains are beautiful this time of year."

Abby looked out at the shadowed mountains in the distance. Fun? she thought. I'll bet!

She still wasn't sure why she had come or why she had found it necessary to prove that she could do anything Merilee Beals could do. Was it because of Nick? Had she accepted Merilee's challenge to go along today because she wanted to prove to Nick that she was just as much a woman as Merilee was?

The thought made Abby uncomfortable. She didn't have to prove anything to anybody, certainly not to Nick Fitzgerald. Nevertheless, Merilee had thrown out a challenge and she had accepted it. And since she had, she was going to do her best not to make a fool of herself.

They stopped for a breakfast of pancakes and bacon—that is, the others did. Abby had bran. By the time they reached White River Forest, the first light of dawn had pinked the sky.

The horses were ready. Abby took one look at the horse she would ride and began quaking in her brand-new boots.

It was a *big* horse, a *very* big horse. She had no idea how she was going to get up on it, let alone stay in the saddle.

Jake and Merilee pulled up in Jake's pickup while Blanche was explaining to Abby how gentle Blaze was.

Blaze? Abby thought. As in blazing along the trail at breakneck speed?

She turned away from the horse and summoned a smile for Jake and nodded to Merilee, who raised one finely arched eyebrow and said, "I bet you're really looking forward to this."

"I certainly am," Abby replied.

Merilee linked her arm through Nick's. "So am I," she murmured, snuggling closer. "There's nothing like mountain air to get the hormones working, is there, Nicky?"

Nicky? Abby wondered. *Nicky?*

Jake introduced Abby to the two men who would be in charge of the pack mules and the setting up of the camp sites. "Abel Gentry and Sam Crocket," he said. "This is Miss Abby Sedgewick, boys. Jonah's niece from back in Ohio."

"How do?" The two nodded. "Your uncle was a mighty fine man, Miz Sedgewick," Sam said. "Him 'n' me used to go hunting together. Nobody had a keener eye than old Jonah. He could spot a pheasant a mile away. He was a mighty fine man, and I don't reckon anybody who knew him would be likely to forget him.''

''I know I never will,'' Abby said softly.

Nick swung around and looked at her, surprised by the tone of her voice and the expression in her eyes. Except for the day she had said she wouldn't think of selling the mine because Jonah had wanted them to work it for a year, this was the first time since he'd known her that she had expressed any real feeling about her uncle.

Jonah had told him about her, of course. ''She was such a solemn little thing,'' he'd said, and Nick remembered that even as a boy, he hadn't liked it when Jonah talked about her because he'd been jealous. She was an honest-to-goodness blood relative of the man he so admired, while he was only an outsider, the son of a father who drank too much and of a mother who had left him when he was eight.

''Lord, I hated to leave her,'' Jonah had often said. ''She was only a little bit of a thing, a lot too young to have the responsibility of taking care of her ailing mother and keeping house for her father.''

Nick had always thought that maybe one of the reasons Jonah had taken him in was to make up for Jonah's wishing Abby had been his.

He'd loved Jonah, and when the older man got sick, he'd been there for him. It had been he and Evie who'd taken care of Jonah. Abby, the one Jonah had loved the most, hadn't even come to Cripple Creek for the funeral. He'd thought it had been because she hadn't cared, but he'd heard something in her voice just now that made him less sure.

He watched her as the morning progressed. It was obvious she hadn't been on a horse for a long time, if, in fact, she'd ever been on a horse before at all. She gripped the reins too tightly, and the way she was trying to clutch the horse's belly with her legs, he knew she'd probably rub the skin off the inside of her knees by the day's end. But though she was having a hard time of it, her back was straight and her mouth was firm. She was spunky as hell, and he admired her for that.

They stopped to rest two hours after they had started. As soon as he reined his horse in, Nick hurried over to help Abby dismount. But Jake reached her first, put his arms around her waist and said, in that damned rustic cowboy way of his, "Here now, Miss Abby, let me help you down."

Nick glowered, turned away and went to help Sam start a fire, while Abel got a few supplies off the mules. Blanche headed for the trees, and Merilee came up behind Nick and put her arms around his waist.

"I'm glad we decided on the pack trip, Nicky," she said, nuzzling his neck. "I've missed you."

"I've missed you, too, but I've had a lot to do this week."

"Helping Miss Ohio of 1929 settle in?"

"That's not nice, kiddo. But, yes, I helped her move in on Monday. She's my business partner. She and I are going to be working together for the next year."

"And after that?"

"The will only stipulated that she stay in Cripple Creek for a year. When the year's up, she'll go back to Ohio."

"A hell of a lot richer, but I hope not a lot wiser." Merilee pushed a strand of red hair out of her face. "She's not your kind of woman, Nicky. She looks like she's got ice in her veins and a ramrod up her spine. And I'll bet you a nickel beer that she's never been on a horse before in her life."

"No bet." Nick laughed, then his face sobered and he said, "Go easy on her, will you, Merilee? She's trying to keep up. No jokes. Okay? Don't try to pull anything funny."

Merilee gave him a look of pure innocence. "Me? Pull something? Why, Nicky, you positively offend me."

She turned, but before she could move away, he swatted her across her fanny. And when he did, she threw him a kiss.

Watching, Abby frowned and wished she hadn't come. Her legs ached, and her back felt as though she'd been hit by a two-by-four.

"Let's have a cup of coffee, Miss Abby," Jake said. "You look a little done in."

Done in, out, backward and sideways, Abby felt like telling him. Instead, she forced a smile and headed slowly and carefully toward the camp fire and the waiting pot of coffee.

"Come sit next to me." Blanche patted the large rock she was sitting on.

"Thanks, but I think I'll stand." Abby looked around, noting the nearby trees and the lovely autumn fields spread out below. "Is this where we're going to camp?" she asked hopefully.

Henry, who really looked quite dapper in his tailor-made jeans and matching jacket, shook his head. "We've got another five or six hours ahead of us today," he said. "We've only stopped here to rest a spell and have a cup of coffee."

Five or six hours? Abby thought. By then, they'd have to throw her dead body over the saddle to haul her on down the mountain. She wasn't a quitter, but she honestly didn't think she could get back on her horse again.

"If it's too much for you, either Abel or Sam could take you on back to town," Merilee said.

"It isn't too much for me," Abby said testily. "I'm a little tired from settling into Uncle Jonah's, that's all. I'll be fine after a good night's sleep."

"Have you done much camping out?" Merilee asked.

Abby hesitated. She wanted to say that, of course, she had, but in a way, it seemed to her that if she lied, she'd be playing Merilee's game, and that wasn't what she wanted to do.

"Actually, I've never camped out," she said. "It's something I've always wanted to do, though, and I'm looking forward to it."

"You're going to love it," Blanche said. "There's just nothing in the world like sleeping out under the stars." She stood up and dusted her hands off against the sides of her jeans. "Let's mount up," she said, and perhaps sensing the sigh that Abby barely managed to suppress, she put an arm around Abby's shoulder. "We'll stop again in a little while for lunch," she whispered. "Just hang on, it's going to be all right."

Abby gave her a grateful smile, but when she reached the mare named Blaze, her smile faded because she knew it would be at least another two hours before they stopped again. She'd hang on, though. By *God*, she'd hang on if it was the last thing she did in this world.

By four o'clock that afternoon, she was pretty sure that today's ride probably was the last thing she'd ever do in this world. She was so saddle sore she could barely walk. Her back and shoulders ached, and the insides of her knees were rubbed raw. Three more days of this and she'd be begging for mercy.

She didn't join in the conversation around the camp fire that night. In spite of her aches and pains, she was so tired, she couldn't hold her head up. All she wanted to do was crawl into the sleeping bag Sam had laid out for her and go to sleep. Merilee would be sleeping on one side of her, Blanche on the other. Henry would be sleeping next to Blanche. Jake and Nick, along with the two guides, would sleep near the camp fire.

After lunch, she'd managed to get Blanche aside to ask what they did about bathroom facilities.

"Pick a tree," Blanche had said. "One big enough to hide behind."

Gritting her teeth, that's what Abby had done and what she did now. She also pulled off her new—and probably too-tight—boots and changed into her pajamas.

The others were still sitting around the camp fire, laughing and joking, when she emerged from the trees, but as soon as he saw her, Nick stood up and came toward her. He handed her a jar of salve and said, "Rub this on the inside of your knees. It'll help."

"How did you...?" Abby took the jar. "Thanks," she said.

"How long has it really been since you've been on a horse?"

She debated about telling him the truth, but it was too late for a lie now because anybody with a brain in his head would know she'd never ridden before. "I sat on a pony for about five minutes once when I was eight," she said.

"Then why in the hell...?" Nick shook his head. "Why didn't you tell me, Abby? If you'd really wanted to come along, I could have at least given you a few riding lessons, maybe got you a little more used to being on a horse." He shook his head. "You're going to feel terrible tomorrow."

"I don't think I could feel any worse than I do right now."

"Wait till you try to get up in the morning."

"Thanks a lot," she said. "That's something to look forward to."

"Try to let the horse do the work," he told her. "Don't grip so hard with your knees. If you'll relax, you'll do better."

She knew he was trying to be kind, and though she didn't for a minute believe that anything could make it better, she summoned a smile, and said, "Thank you, Nick. I'll try."

He rested a hand on her shoulder, wishing he could help ease some of the discomfort she was feeling. But because he knew that only time would do that, he told her goodnight and went, reluctantly, back to the others.

Abby crawled into her sleeping bag, stretched her legs out and groaned because it felt so good to be flat. It was wonderful to lie down and stretch—

Something slithered across her bare foot. She yipped in fright, bounded out of the sleeping bag and reached for the flashlight Sam had placed next to it.

The snake was a foot and a half long. She grasped it behind its head and picked it up. The bag had been zipped up. How in the world had it managed to get inside? How had it . . . ?

Of course.

Keeping her eye on the group around the camp fire, Abby slowly unzipped Merilee's bag and dropped the snake inside. "Sleep well, little fella," she whispered.

Later, when Merilee crawled into her sleeping bag and screamed, Abby smiled and went back to sleep.

## Chapter Five

It took every ounce of Abby's willpower to crawl out of the sleeping bag and stand up the next morning. She felt ninety years old. Every bone in her body ached, and she was so cold, she could barely keep her teeth from chattering.

"'Morning," Blanche said from her own sleeping bag. "Did you sleep okay?"

Abby nodded. "I only woke up once," she said.

"That'd be when Merilee found the snake in her sleeping bag." Blanche chuckled. "Hollered like a banshee and said words I didn't know she knew. Surprised me, her letting a snake get into her bag like that. She knows better than to leave her bag unzipped."

"I guess we all get careless once in a while." Abby looked over to where Merilee was standing with Nick and the other men near the camp fire. Merilee would know that

Abby had put the snake in her sleeping bag and would probably be mad as a hornet and ready to sting.

But I'll be ready for her, Abby thought as she picked up the clothes she'd folded beside her bag last night and put a sweater over her shoulders. "It's cold this morning," she said.

"Probably going to rain." Blanche crawled out of her bag. "Often does this time of year up here in the mountains."

"Then we'll be going back?" Abby asked hopefully.

But Blanche shook her head. "A little rain's good for the complexion," she said cheerfully, then stretched and suggested they head for the trees.

Abby bathed as well as she could in the pan of hot water Abel Gentry had given her, and she tried not to whimper when she touched the insides of her knees. The salve that Nick had given her had helped, but she was still bruised and sore.

In spite of her aches and pains, Abby found that she was hungry. A folding table and camp chairs had been set up near the fire. Sam was cooking pancakes on a griddle, and Abel busied himself frying what looked like three dozen eggs and enough sausages to feed an army.

"Biscuits'll be ready in a minute, Miz Abby," he said. "Just set yourself down and have some coffee while yer waitin'."

"Thank you, Abel." She said good morning to the others, and when Jake asked if she'd slept well, she said, "Yes, indeed," and smiled at Merilee, who glared back at her and looked mad enough to spit tenpenny nails.

What the hell is going on? Nick wondered. Last night, Abby had been miserable. She had to be feeling her aches and pains this morning, but she actually seemed cheerful.

Testing her, he said, "I'm sorry we haven't got any bran for breakfast."

"Bran's fer mules," she said, remembering that long-ago morning when Uncle Jonah had first fixed her breakfast. She held her plate out for the three eggs, pancakes, sausages and biscuits Sam piled on.

Maybe it was the fresh air that made her feel good. Maybe, as Merilee had said, mountain air did something for the hormones. Or maybe it was because she had bested the other woman. Whatever it was, Abby was more aware of the beauty all around her this morning. Tall Ponderosa pine and blue spruce covered the mountains. The wind whispered through the quaking aspen. Fields of wildflowers, of daisies and Indian paintbrush, carpeted distant meadows. A bluebird sang a song from the pine tree above the campsite, and two inquisitive and hungry squirrels sat on their hind legs watching them eat.

She looked across the table at Nick. "It's beautiful here," she said. "I'm glad I came."

"So am I." She looked pretty and fresh this morning. The blush in her cheeks, unlike the blush that Blanche and Merilee had on their cheeks, was natural. Her brown eyes, that really were the color of fine Spanish sherry, sparkled in the faint morning sunlight. It suddenly occurred to Nick that maybe she wasn't so plain after all, that she had her own style, her own particular kind of beauty.

When he'd met her in Toledo, she'd looked as spinsterish and as severe as his Great-aunt Elvira, who thought all men were worthless debauchers headed straight for hell. But something had happened to Abby in the few days she'd been in Colorado. She'd softened somehow; she looked a lot more human, a little vulnerable and certainly attractive.

It was pretty obvious from the way Jake was looking at her that he found her attractive, too.

Nick wasn't sure how he felt about that. After all, Abby was his partner. Before Jonah had died, he'd said, "When she comes out here, I want you to keep an eye on her. She's all alone now. Keep her safe and don't let her get into any trouble."

He intended on keeping an eye on her, and that meant keeping an eye on Jake McClinton, too.

When they finished breakfast and the horses were saddled, Nick made sure that he was the one who helped Abby onto Blaze.

"Remember," he said as he rested a hand on the calf of her leg, "easy does it. Relax your legs. Don't hold your body so rigid. Follow the motion of the horse and try to go with her." He looked up at her and in a voice so low that none of the others could hear he said, "I know you're hurting, Abby. If you don't want to go on, I'll take you back. It's up to you."

"I want to go on."

"You're sure?"

"Absolutely."

"We're going to be climbing, and some of the mountain trails are narrow and dangerous. But don't worry, Blaze has crossed the trail dozens of times." For the briefest fraction of a second, his hand tightened on her leg. "And I'll stay close to you, Abby. Okay?"

She looked down at him. "Okay," she said.

The rain began after lunch, a slow, chilling drizzle that made the trail even more dangerous. Abby followed close behind Sam Crocket, and Nick followed her. She tried to do what he'd said, tried to let her body relax and follow the motion of the horse. Most of all, she tried not to look down.

The trail was no more than three feet wide in places, with a sheer drop of what looked like thousands of feet.

At one point, a rock just ahead of her clattered down the mountainside and over the edge. Abby pulled back on Blaze's reins, and behind her, she heard Nick say, "Steady, Abby. We'll be over this pass in a little while. From there on, it's even terrain."

She did her best to unclench her jaw and concentrate on following the motion of the mare. Rain dripped off the rim of her hat and ran down her neck under the plastic poncho that Sam had given her before they'd started out this morning. She was cold and wet and hungry, and she couldn't believe that people did this for fun, that the others might actually be enjoying this. As for her, if she ever got back to civilization, she'd never leave. She certainly would never get on a horse again.

A little before noon, the rain slackened and stopped, but the skies were still heavy and threatening. And though the trail widened, the terrain was rough. When they stopped for lunch, Abel said, "'Fraid it's still too damp for a fire, folks. We'll have to make do with sandwiches."

Blanche groaned, and her husband put his arm around her shoulders. "Things are going to dry out soon, hon," he said.

"But I'm cold and I'm hungry," Blanche complained. "I want some hot coffee, dammit."

"Now Blanche—"

"Don't 'now Blanche' me, Henry Crimms." She shrugged off his arm and walked angrily away from the others.

Merilee smiled at Abby. "Having a good time?" she asked.

Abby ignored her and started after Blanche. When she caught up, she said, "Hey, I'm supposed to be the tenderfoot."

Blanche gave her a rueful smile and shook her head. "It's just that I'm so darn cold," she muttered. "The weather bureau forecasted a great weekend, and look at it. We'll reach the place where we're going to camp in another hour or two, but I'm all for giving up and heading back home. How about you?"

"I just came along for the ride," Abby said. "I'll go along with whatever everybody else wants to do, but I won't yell uncle until everyone else does."

"Especially Merilee?"

"Especially Merilee."

"She put that snake in your bag last night, didn't she? And then you put it in hers."

"Who, me?" Abby widened her eyes and looked innocent. "I'm just a city girl, Miz Crimms. I'd plumb be scared outten my skin to touch a snake."

"Uh-huh." Blanche nodded approvingly. "You know, I think you're going to do all right, Abigail Sedgewick. There's more to you than meets the eye. A whole lot more."

They were both smiling, their arms around each other, when they went back to join the others. They ate ham-and-cheese sandwiches. The others had beer; Abby drank a diet cola.

"How are you doing?" Jake asked her.

"I'm still a little damp around the edges. Blanche said we'd reach the camp in an hour or two." She looked around at the wet ground. "Will we put up tents?"

"No, Abby, there're cabins where we're going. They're rustic, but they've got fireplaces and camp beds." He shook his head. "I'm sorry the weather's been so rotten. I don't suppose you're enjoying this."

"I'm enjoying part of it," she protested.

"Which part? The cold lunch or the rain?"

She laughed, and with a shake of her head, she said, "I can't believe people do this on purpose, Jake. That anybody would ride for hours for the fun of sleeping on the ground, going to the bathroom behind a tree and trying to wash in a teacup full of hot water."

"I reckon you're just not into camping," he said with a grin.

"Partner, my idea of camping is a hotel with clean sheets and room service. That's just about as rugged as I want to get."

They smiled at each other and before she could step back, Jake reached up and tucked a damp strand of hair back from her face. "The weather's going to clear," he said. "It'll be better tomorrow."

Nick, watching, tightened his hands on the reins and called out in a voice one decimal below a roar, "Let's go! We've got another two hours ahead of us before we reach the camp."

Abby looked up at him, surprised, then hurried over to Blaze, and with Jake holding the horse's reins, she swung up into the saddle. "Ready," she said as Nick pulled his horse around.

What in the world is wrong with him? she wondered. He was acting like a trail boss, "Round 'em up and head 'em out." She shifted in the saddle, trying to get comfortable, and when she did, the mare reared back, bucked and, with a startled whinny, broke loose and started running.

"Wait!" Abby screamed. "Stop! Whoa! Slow down!" She tried to pull back on the reins, but the simple act of holding on seemed more important. Sore knees or not, she gripped the horse's belly, squeezed and hung on. A tree limb slashed her face. She saw another, bigger limb just ahead and ducked.

Behind her, she heard Blanche scream. Jake shouted, "Hold on, Abby."

Somebody else yelled, "Pull back on the reins."

Blaze broke through the trees. Ahead of her, Abby saw a stretch of grassy plains and more trees beyond that. Maybe the horse would stop now that she was out in the open. Maybe she'd—

Blaze broke into a full gallop, ears back, nostrils flaring. The wind whipped Abby's hat off and blew her hair about her face. Blinded by her hair and by the wind, she could barely see. She crouched low over the horse's neck and gripped the pommel as well as the reins.

Her whole life didn't pass before her, but flashes of memory did: Her father and her mother. Her bedroom back in Toledo. Uncle Jonah and the Ferris wheel. She knew she was going to die.

"Abby!"

She glanced over her shoulder and saw Nick five yards behind, coming fast.

"Hang on!" he shouted.

Blaze headed for the trees.

Nick came abreast of her, and Blaze, aware of the stallion bearing down on her, sprinted ahead. Nick tried to grab the reins. Abby saw his face close to hers for a moment. He reached out for her at the same instant Blaze stumbled.

Suddenly, Abby was out of the saddle and flying through the air. She had a fleeting impression of gray sky, dark clouds, then brown earth before she hit, hard.

Nick was off his horse before it stopped. He ran to where Abby lay at the foot of a tree, facedown on a bed of pine needles, arms flung above her head, not moving.

Heart racketing hard in his chest, Nick dropped to his knees beside her and gently turned her over. Her eyes were closed. He brushed the hair back from her face. There was a bump on her forehead and a long, red scratch on her cheek. He felt under her shoulders, her neck and her back. He ran his hands down her arms, her legs, across her ribs.

"Abby?" he said urgently. "Abby?"

Her eyelids fluttered. "Where...?" She opened her eyes and tried to focus. "What happened?"

"Your horse ran away with you. Are you all right? Do you hurt anywhere?"

"Everywhere." She tried to sit up, but when she did, the ground tilted and she slumped back.

"Easy does it." Carefully, Nick brought her up across his lap and into his arms.

"Dizzy," she whispered, and she leaned her head against his chest.

"You've had a nasty fall, but I'm pretty sure nothing is broken."

"Why did she run away like that?"

"Something spooked her. It wasn't your fault. I don't think an experienced rider could have stopped her." Very gently, he began to massage the bump on Abby's forehead. "Are you feeling better?"

"I—I think so. I can get up now."

"Give it a minute or two, honey."

Abby leaned back against his chest and closed her eyes. His fingers felt cool and good on her forehead. They took the hurt away.

He brushed the damp tendrils of hair back from her face. "You've got beautiful hair," he said almost to himself. "Why do you always pull it back?"

"Practical," Abby murmured without opening her eyes. "I'm a practical woman. Sensible, too."

"Are you?"

Abby opened her eyes. His face was close to hers. If she raised her hand, she could touch him the way he was touching her. She could stroke the black hair back off his forehead and rest her hand against his cheek and across his mouth.

His mouth.

"We'd better get back to the others," she said.

"In a minute." He drew her closer, supporting her shoulders with his arm. "I want to make sure you're all right."

She sighed. "You feel so nice and warm," she murmured. "I feel so safe with you."

The breath caught in Nick's throat. He whispered her name, "Abby?" and kissed her.

He felt the small intake of her breath, and one hand came up to push him away. But when it did, he took her hand and held it to his chest. "No," he whispered against her lips. "Don't fight me. Kiss me back, honey. Kiss me."

He covered her mouth with his, kissing her like he had that other time, and though she tried to fight it, the same feeling she'd had before enveloped her.

He said, "Part your lips for me, Abby, I want to taste you." And when she tried again to pull away, he took her bottom lip to bite and tease, and when she gasped, his tongue found hers and he kissed her deeply, softly.

Under the hand that he held so tightly against his chest, she felt the hard beating of his heart. And her own heart began to pound because she had never been this close to anyone before, had never felt another's heartbeat.

He trailed a line of kisses down her neck. He nibbled her ear and licked the smooth skin behind it.

"Let go of my hand," she said, and when he did, she encircled his neck and drew him even closer because she wanted his mouth again.

But he held back, making her wait while he kissed the corners of her mouth and took her bottom lip between his strong white teeth to lick and to suckle.

It wasn't enough. He wanted more. Her lips were honeyed, her body softly vulnerable in his arms. He curved his hand around the fullness of one breast and felt her gasp. She gripped his wrist to push him away, but he said, "No," and covered her mouth with his so that she couldn't protest. And though she struggled in his arms, he unbuttoned her blouse and slipped his fingers inside her bra.

"You mustn't," she whispered. But his hands were warm against her skin and his fingers were tender as he stroked her, softly, gently. And all the while, he kissed her mouth.

Abby moaned deep in her throat, not even aware that she had lifted her body closer to his or that she whispered "Nick, oh, Nick." Or that he had thrust her bra aside so that he could more freely caress her.

He gently squeezed, then rubbed her nipples, and a flame unlike anything she had ever known burned through her veins, heating her body, warming and readying her so that she was barely aware when he shifted and laid her back against the damp earth. Still holding her, he cradled her in his arms and began to kiss her breasts.

Abby gasped and tried to break free, but he held her with his mouth and with his body half over hers.

He wanted to take her here on this damp ground beneath the pines. Wanted to feel her naked and vulnerable beneath him. Wanted—

"Please," she gasped. "I can't. Not here. Not like this. The others . . . Nick, please."

He looked at her for a long moment, his face tense and hard, his green eyes dark with desire. And she was afraid, 'sure that he was going to do as he wanted.

But he didn't. With a sigh, he rested his head against her breasts and waited for the terrible tightness of his body to slacken, the heat to cool.

He wasn't sure what had happened to him. He wasn't a boy, a teenager with raging hormones who had no control over his emotions. What was it about this woman, this one woman, that had made him behave like this?

He let her go and helped her to sit up. "I'm sorry," he said, and he remembered that was what he'd said the last time he had kissed her. He waited while she adjusted her bra and buttoned her blouse and sweater, but before he took her hand and helped her to her feet, he said, "Something's happening between us, Abby. I'm not sure what it is, but I know that the next time—if there is a next time— I won't stop." He put a finger under her chin and lifted her face. "Remember that," he said. "Be careful of me."

It was Jake who discovered the burr under Blaze's saddle.

"What the hell?" he said when the others had gathered around Abby. "Look at this, Nick. Somebody deliberately put a burr under the saddle. No wonder Blaze took off like she'd been shot out of a cannon."

Abby, her hands cupping a mug of hot tea, looked up. They were gathered around the fire that Sam had built. Blanche was sitting next to her. The rest of them were standing and looking down at Abby, concern written on their faces.

"Jake's right," Nick said. "Somebody put the burr there."

Merilee looked down at her boots. Her face was so white, every one of her freckles showed. She looked at Abby, defiance in her eyes, and fear.

Abby tightened her hands around her cup. "I helped Abel saddle up this morning," she said. "Maybe I was careless. I mean I—I think I rested the saddle blanket on the ground. That's probably how I picked up the burr."

Blanche shot her a look. She opened her mouth to say something, then snapped it shut.

"That's what must have happened," Henry said. "Nobody'd do anything like that deliberately, Jake. Abby probably picked up the burr before Abel put the saddle on and maybe it slipped down to where it hurt the horse." He patted Abby's shoulder. "No harm done," he said.

"No harm done!" Hot color crept into Nick's face. "She could have been killed."

"Nobody wanted...would want anything like that to happen," Merilee said in a small, tight voice. She looked at Abby, then quickly away. "I've known people who did something like that as a joke, but I'm sure they didn't mean any harm. Any real harm, I mean."

"Something like that isn't a joke," Blanche said. "It's pure viciousness."

"I'm all right," Abby said. "Why don't we forget it."

"You think you're up to getting back on Blaze?" Nick asked.

Abby got to her feet. She didn't want to get back up on the horse, but she didn't see any other way to get on with the trip.

"We'll take it nice and slow, Abby," Jake assured her. "I'll ride right alongside you."

He held the mare's head, and Abby approached Blaze. She stood beside the horse for a moment, uncertain, remembering her terror of only a little while before.

"It'll be all right." Nick rested his hand on her shoulder. "The horse is calmer now, she won't give you any trouble. Let me help you up."

Abby took a deep breath, then with a nod, she put her foot in the stirrup and vaulted into the saddle.

They reached the cabins a little over an hour later. Though sparsely furnished, they were adequate. There were four bunk beds in each of the three cabins, as well as a table and chairs and a fireplace.

The women would have one cabin, the three men, another. Abel and Sam would take the third.

"There's a fresh-water pond down yonder where you-all can bathe," Abel said. "Ladies first, then the gents."

Blanche and Abby went first. "I'll go later," Merilee had said, which suited Abby just fine because the less she had to do with the other woman, the better she was going to like it.

She still wasn't sure why she had protected Merilee. Maybe it had been the fear and, yes, the shame she'd seen in the other woman's face. Maybe it was because she knew that if Nick found out what Merilee had done, it would hurt their relationship. Abby didn't want that. Nick and Merilee had been friends since school. Their friendship, or whatever it was, very likely meant something to both of them. Abby couldn't forgive or excuse what Merilee had done, but she couldn't bring herself to expose the other woman.

But from now on, she would be careful of her.

When they came back from the pond, Abby stretched out on one of the bunks and went to sleep. Blanche awakened her in time for a dinner of steaks cooked over an outdoor grill, beans and biscuits. For dessert, there were fresh strawberries.

The clouds had lifted. A half moon shone in the night sky, and the air was rich with the scent of pine when they gathered closer to the camp fire, hands around their coffee mugs.

Abby looked across the fire at Nick and saw that he was watching her. Try as she might, she couldn't pull her gaze from his. This afternoon, he had said that the next time, if there was a next time, he wouldn't stop. He had told her to be careful of him in a way that hadn't been a threat but a simple statement of fact. Nick was a man. Sooner or later, if she was not careful, she would succumb to his charm.

But she would be careful, Abby vowed. They were partners; it wasn't smart to mix business . . .

A smile tugged at the corners of her mouth. With what, pleasure? And the breath caught in her throat because what she had felt this afternoon had been a pleasure unlike anything she'd ever known.

When the hour grew late, Henry said, "I'm planning on getting up early to do some fishing in the morning so I think I'll turn in. He kissed Blanche's cheek.

"Sleep well, Henry," she said, and looking at Merilee and Abby, asked, "Are you two ready for bed?"

Merilee, who had been silent all evening, nodded and, without a word of good-night to anyone, headed for the cabin.

But Abby, more relaxed than she'd been all day, lingered near the fire, listening to Jake and Nick talk about Cripple Creek and the way it had been at the turn of the century with all the mines operating and fifty trains coming in and out every day. They talked about the men Nick had hired to work Uncle Jonah's mine, and whether or not they could keep operating during the hard winter months. Finally, Nick stood up and said that he was about ready for bed. Turning to Jake, he asked, "What about you?"

"I thought I might like to take a stroll down toward the pond." Jake looked at Abby, hesitated, then asked, "Would you like to come with me, Abby?"

"Well, I—"

"Abby's tired," Nick said quickly. "She's been through a lot today. She needs to get some sleep."

Abby raised one eyebrow, but not wanting to make an issue of it said, "Another time, Jake. Nick's probably right, I'd better get to bed." She smiled at both of them, and with an "I'll see you in the morning," turned and went into the cabin.

Blanche was already asleep when Abby came in, but Merilee was sitting on the edge of her bed waiting for her.

"Okay," she said in a low voice, "why did you do it?"

"Why did I do what?"

"Don't play games with me, Abby. Why did you tell them you might have picked up the burr they found under the saddle."

"I might have," Abby said calmly.

"But you didn't."

"All right, I didn't."

"You knew I put it there."

"Yes," Abby said, "but I don't know why."

Merilee pushed her red hair back off her face. She was pretty, Abby thought, but she wore too much makeup and her clothes were too tight. Well, at least for my taste, she amended. God knows I'm not an expert on makeup or clothes or much of anything else. If Merilee wants to dress the way she does, that's none of my business.

But it was Abby's business to find out why Merilee had tried to harm her. "Why did you do it? I could have been badly hurt today. I could have been killed."

"I didn't mean for you to get hurt. I just wanted to pay you back for putting the snake in my sleeping bag."

"But you'd put it in mine first," Abby said reasonably. "Why do you dislike me, Merilee? Is it because I'm not from here; or is it because of Nick?"

Merilee's eyes narrowed in anger.

"Because if it's about Nick, then you don't have any reason to dislike me," Abby went on. "Nick is my partner. We're going to be working together, reopening and operating the mine. I have to stay in Cripple Creek for a year, but when the year is out, I'm going back to Ohio."

"You're certain of that?"

"Yes, I'm certain," Abby said. "Colorado isn't my home. I don't belong here."

Merilee studied her for a moment. "Nick is special to me," she said at last. "He always has been." When Abby didn't respond, Merilee said, "I'm sorry—about today, I mean. You won't say anything to Nick, will you?"

Abby shook her head. "No, I won't say anything."

Merilee stood up. "You want to use the bathroom first?"

"No, you go ahead."

When the door closed, Abby stood up and began to undress. She was buttoning her pajama top when Blanche, without opening her eyes, said, "You're going to let her get away with it?"

"This time," Abby answered.

"You're making a mistake." Blanche opened her eyes. "You ought to tell Nick."

"I don't think so." Abby looked down at the other woman. "She's in love with him, isn't she?"

Blanche nodded. "Has been for a long time. Does that bother you?"

"No," Abby said too quickly. "Why should it?" But because she could not help herself, she asked, "How does Nick feel about her?"

"I don't know. He's a funny guy, Abby. I don't think he's ever really been serious about a woman. As far as I know, he and Merilee are just good friends." Blanche yawned and pulled the blanket up under her chin. "I'm going to sleep," she murmured. "We'll talk in the morning."

"Sure," Abby said. "In the morning."

When she was in bed and the light had been turned out, she thought about Nick and what Blanche had said about his never having been serious about anybody. A slight smile curved the corners of her mouth, and just before she drifted to sleep, she touched her lips. "Nick," she whispered. And with his name on her lips, she went to sleep.

## Chapter Six

Evie Montgomery came to call a few days after Abby returned from the camping trip. She telephoned to ask if she could stop by, and Abby invited her for lunch.

Abby was in the kitchen when the car drove up and Jasper began to bark. By the time she dried her hands and went to open the door, Evie was on the front porch and Jasper was jumping up all around her and wagging his tail.

A small woman in her middle sixties, Evie Montgomery had short, curly, white hair that framed a friendly, attractive face. Her eyes were a clear gray; she had a turned up nose and a wide and friendly smile. She was slim enough to carry off the blue jeans and red flannel shirt she wore.

She handed Abby a plant. ''Philodendron,'' she said. ''Jonah didn't like plants in the house, but I thought you might. Women usually do.''

''I always had plants back home in Toledo,'' Abby said. ''Philodendron and African violets.''

"I'm no good with African violets. After one look at me, the poor little things just clutch their throats and die."

Abby laughed and accepting the plant, she held the door open for Evie to come in. "I've been wanting to thank you for taking care of the house," she said.

"I was afraid I might be overstepping because the house belonged to you once Jonah was gone. But it didn't seem right, somehow, leaving it all alone and empty. Besides, Jasper wouldn't leave and somebody had to feed him. I guess he kept thinking Jonah was coming back." Evie rested her hand on Jonah's comfortable old chair, unconsciously smoothing her fingers back and forth against the well-worn leather.

"I'm glad you're here," she told Abby. "Jonah would have been pleased that you decided to move in."

"I knew as soon as I saw the house that this was where I wanted to be, but everybody tried to discourage me."

"Everybody'd be Nick and Henry Crimms. The two of them think a woman without a man can't take care of herself." Evie raised an eyebrow. "How're you getting along with Nick?"

Abby motioned the other woman to sit in Uncle Jonah's chair before she answered. "We get along all right," she said. "Would you like a drink?"

"Scotch, straight up, no ice."

"Scotch it is." Abby went to the sideboard that Uncle Jonah had kept well stocked. She poured a splash into one of the short, round glasses and handed it to Evie, then fixed a cola for herself.

"I heard in town that Nick's been hiring men to work the Lucky Lady," Evie said. "When do you think you're going to get started?"

"Next week."

"I also heard you went on a pack trip up into the mountains, you and Nick, Jake McClinton, Merilee and the Crimmses. Heard you put a snake in Merilee's sleeping bag. Bet she'd put it in yours first."

Abby laughed. "News travels fast in Cripple Creek."

"A person can't sneeze in the lobby of the Imperial Hotel without folks knowing about it down at city hall five minutes later." She took a sip of the Scotch. "I don't imagine Merilee's too happy about your being here. She's always thought of Nick as her private property."

"Is he?"

"Lord, no! Nick's fond enough of her, the way he'd be fond of a sister, but he sure as shooting isn't serious about her. Never has been, never will be. Matter of fact, Nick's never been serious about any woman that I know of."

Abby thought of the way he had kissed her, the tenderness and the urgency when he had touched her. And his warning her that the next time he kissed her, he wouldn't stop. "That's a little strange, isn't it?" she said. "For a man like him, I mean."

"Maybe not. Nick's a rugged man, more of a chauvinist than he ought to be. He likes women, but he's skeptical of them, Abby. Has been ever since his mother ran out on him and his father."

Evie stared down into her drink. "Nobody ever blamed Louise for leaving Ernie. He was as mean a son of a bitch as ever set foot in Cripple Creek. But Nick was only eight. She shouldn't have left him behind. Once she was gone, Ernie took to beating Nick, like it was the boy's fault his mother had left."

Abby felt a sudden sickness in her stomach.

"One day, Jonah and I were coming back from town when we spotted Nick. He couldn't have been more than ten or eleven, but he was trudging along the road with a knapsack over his shoulder. Jonah stopped, and I knew he was planning to pick the boy up and take him back home. He said, 'Where you off to, son?' and that's when we saw that both Nick's eyes were blackened and that he had a bump on his forehead the size of a golf ball.''

Abby tightened her hands in her lap.

''Jonah took Nick home with him. We took care of his cuts and bruises, but there wasn't much we could do with the marks on his back where Ernie'd been beating him for God knows how long. Nick didn't say anything or cry the whole time we were tending him. Jonah didn't say anything, either, but after we put Nick to bed, Jonah went out to the shed where he kept the firewood, picked up a piece of wood and got in his old pickup. I knew where he was going and what he was going to do, and I knew I couldn't stop him even if I'd wanted to, which I didn't.''

She looked over at Abby. ''Jonah kept Nick all that next winter. Then Ernie died, and it just seemed like Nick became the son Jonah'd never had and Jonah became the father Nick had always wanted. They gave each other a lot, and I know that Nick misses him as much as I do.''

For a long time, the two women didn't speak. In the silence, Abby thought about the little boy who hadn't cried, and she knew how hurt he must have been, not just physically, but way down inside, and ashamed for himself and for the father who had done this to him.

In a little while, she put the lunch on and they went into the kitchen to eat.

After they'd eaten, Abby washed the dishes and Evie dried them. They continued their table talk about plants and gardening, and about how it would be when the mine was operating again. But they didn't talk about Jonah or Nick.

As Evie was leaving, Abby said, "I'd like it a lot if you could come to dinner on Sunday. I thought I might invite the Crimmses, too."

"And Nick?"

"And Nick," Abby answered with a smile.

"It's the friendly thing to do." Evie patted Jasper's head and went out to her two-year-old Lincoln Continental. Grinning over her shoulder at Abby, she said, "Birthday present from Jonah. Gave it to me on my sixtieth birthday. Sure cheered me up."

With a wave of her hand, she got into the car and drove out of the yard.

Henry and Blanche said they'd be happy to come to dinner on Sunday, and so did Nick. Abby went into town on Friday to shop, which was a good thing, because on Saturday afternoon, it started to rain.

Thunder rolled in over the mountains and lightning flashed. The temperature dropped, and when it kept dropping, Abby built a fire in the fireplace and let Jasper in. She was debating about whether or not she ought to get out the candles and light the oil lamp when all of the lights went off.

She found matches, and with Jasper following close on her heels, she got out the lamp and put the candles on the coffee table.

"There," she said, more to herself than to Jasper. "Now we'll listen to some music, okay? She put a cassette of classical music into her portable stereo and had just settled down on the sofa with Jasper at her feet when over the sound of thunder and rain, she heard a car door slam.

Jasper barked. Abby got up from the sofa, wondering who had driven way out here on a night like this. She opened the front door just as Nick made a dash for the porch.

"What a night," he said, sluicing water off his raincoat and slapping the Stetson against his side. "Your road's flooded. Good thing I had the Jeep. Another few hours, nobody'll be able to get through."

Abby, not sure why he'd come, held the door open for him. "You better take your boots off and come over by the fire," she said.

He took his raincoat and boots off by the door and in stockinged feet, padded to the fireplace. "Feels good," he said with his back to the fire. He rubbed his hands together. "It's cold out there."

"I was just going to have a sandwich and make some cocoa," Abby said. "Have you eaten?"

Nick shook his head. "I had a hamburger about noon. I guess I forgot about dinner." He looked around the room, thinking how warm and welcoming it looked, and remembering other nights like this when Jonah had been alive.

"How long have the lights been out?" he asked.

"Not long. Just a little before you came." Abby picked up the oil lamp and led the way into the kitchen. "I'm still trying to get used to the gas stove. I burned the rice yesterday, and the chicken today. I'm hoping I'll do better tomorrow." She set the lamp down. "You're a little early for Sunday dinner," she said.

"Yep, I reckon I am," Nick drawled. "Always did like to be on time for things. But as a matter of fact, Miss Abby, I came out to make sure you were all right."

"That was nice of you." She turned and smiled at him. "I'm glad you came, Nick."

He watched her make a salad, then start on ham-and-cheese sandwiches—man-size sandwiches, not little bread-

and-butter things. He liked the way she moved, the efficiency with which she cut the bread and sliced the tomatoes and cucumbers.

He made the cocoa, and when the food was ready, they carried it, along with the plates, napkins, knives and forks, into the living room, to the coffee table in front of the fireplace.

Nick had debated about coming out here tonight, but now he was glad that he had. He'd tried to tell himself that since Abby had been determined to move out here, she could very likely take care of herself, that a little thunder and lightning weren't going to hurt her. But somehow, he'd found himself putting on his raincoat and getting into the Jeep.

He was glad he had. The storm had turned into a real gully washer. He'd have hated the idea of her being out here all by herself.

But that wasn't the only reason Nick was glad he'd come. He liked the way Abby looked tonight. He was seeing another side of her that he knew he wouldn't have seen if she'd known he was coming. But she hadn't known and so her hair was down, loose and pretty about her shoulders, and she was wearing a blue sweatsuit and fluffy, blue slippers.

"Is classical music all right, or would you prefer something else?" she asked.

"I like what you're playing." He poured more coffee into her cup. "This is nice, Abby," he said. "I'm glad I came."

"So am I."

"You were right to want to be out here. It suits you."

She looked around the room, softened by the glow of the fire and by the candles, and at Jasper curled up next to the hearth. "I love it here," she said softly. "I wish I had come sooner, when Uncle Jonah was alive, I mean."

"Why didn't you?"

"I don't know, Nick. For a long time, I couldn't have. I took care of my mother for years, and after she died, I took care of Papa. By that time, I suppose I was so used to the routine of daily living that it never occurred to me that I could take a few weeks off and come out here."

She took her slippers off and curled her bare feet under her. "I'd only known Uncle Jonah for that one month when I was ten. I never forgot him, but I suppose my image of him faded over the years, along with the memory of that long-ago summer. But everything came back to me when I got the telegram saying that he'd died." She looked at Nick over the rim of her cup. "I was sorry that I couldn't have been here for him."

"You should have been."

"Yes," she said, "I should have."

"He loved you. He never forgot you."

"He had you," she said. "You were the son he never had."

"Evie told you?"

Abby nodded. "She came out a few days ago. I like her, and I'm glad she was a part of Uncle Jonah's life." Abby looked at Nick, her eyes level, honest. "I'm glad you were a part of his life, too."

"I loved him," Nick said. "I miss him."

Abby reached out and touched his hand, and when he turned his hand so that he could hold hers, she didn't pull away.

"I came here to live when I was eleven," he said. "I had the room that you have now, without the lacy curtains." He smiled and then his face sobered. "This was the only real home I'd ever had, Abby. I love every piece of furniture, every book—"

"It should have been yours," she said. "It *should* be yours."

Nick shook his head. "I left here when I went away to college, and afterward, I traveled halfway around the world on different jobs." He tightened his hand on hers. "Jonah wanted you to have it because it was part of him, of the way he lived. I thought you were wrong when you said you wanted to move in out here, but now I know how right it is."

"It's only for a year," she said. "The house really belongs to you, Nick. When I go back to Ohio, we'll sign whatever papers we have to so that the house will be yours legally."

"Maybe you won't go back."

"I'll go back. It's where I belong." She began to stack the dishes, but when she got up to take them into the kitchen, Nick said, "No, leave them." He took her hand again and drew her back down to the sofa. "Stay," he said. "Enjoy the fire."

He put his arm around her and brought her closer. For a moment, she hesitated, then with a sigh, she settled back against his shoulder.

Rain slashed hard against the windows and the thunder rolled ominously. It was nice to be here like this, she thought. In a few minutes, she'd get up and go into the kitchen, but for now, it was pleasant to be in this room she'd grown to love, to gaze into the fire and, yes, to have Nick's arm around her.

"Tell me about Jonah," she said.

Nick drew her closer. "He came to Cripple Creek when he was a young man. The gold boom had happened fifty years before, but Jonah was convinced there was still plenty of it left in the ground. Henry told me that for the first few years, Jonah worked at whatever job he could get. He worked in a mine over at Squaw Gulch for a couple of years, then went over to Midway and worked at the Wild Horse Mine. Eventually, he scraped up enough money to buy the Lucky Lady.''

"And that's when he discovered gold?" Abby asked.

"Not right away. There were a lot of lean years. He only had one or two men working for him and finally, because he couldn't pay them, he had to let them go. But he kept working the mine by himself.'' Nick rubbed his chin over the top of her head. "I worked the mine with him after school and summers from the time I was twelve. I learned a lot from him, Abby, just about everything there is to know about mining. Sure I went on to school, and I've got a graduate degree as a mining engineer, but most of my good, solid, practical training came from Jonah.''

Abby leaned back on his arm so that she could look up at him. "When did he discover the gold?" she asked.

"The summer I was fifteen. We were down on one of the lower levels, just the two of us, and suddenly he said, 'Hot damn, boy, I think we've found her.' And there it was, Abby, a whole, beautiful, rich vein of gold." Nick took a deep breath. "I'll never forget it or the way Jonah looked when he knew he'd finally found it.

"There were a lot of good years before that vein ran out. But no matter what the experts said, Jonah was always convinced there was another vein. He kept trying to find it until he got too sick to work.'' He tightened his arms around Abby. "Now we're going to find it for him.''

Abby took a deep breath. "Yes," she said, "we're going to do it for him.''

Her face was close to his, and because he had wanted to so badly all the time they'd been sitting here together, Nick cupped her face between his hands and kissed her.

For a moment, she didn't respond, then her lips softened and she answered his kiss.

"I've been wanting to do that all evening," he said when he let her go. "You're a strange and complex woman, Miss Abby Sedgewick. You're strong and opinionated, and most of the time, you give the appearance of being so in control, you almost scare me. But there are other times, like now, tonight..." His eyes searched her face. "I'm not sure who you are, Abby. I only know that I want to kiss you again and keep on kissing you."

"Nick, I . . ." But whatever protest she'd thought to offer was lost in the wonder of his mouth on hers. His tongue touched hers and with a half-smothered gasp, she touched his back. And when she did, he sighed with pleasure and eased farther down onto the sofa, taking her with him.

They were lying side by side, his arm beneath her head. He kissed her eyes, her nose and the sensitive corners of her mouth. He stroked back her hair and whispered a kiss against her ear.

I should stop, Abby thought, right now, before it goes any further. Just one more kiss and I will. One more . . .

But, oh, his mouth was so warm, so gentle, yet so demanding.

He slid his hand under her sweatshirt. "You don't have on a bra," he said, surprised.

"No, I—I didn't know anybody was coming. I—"

"Don't apologize!"

He curved his hands around the fullness of her breasts and began to caress her, and when she whispered a protest, he said, "Just for a minute, Abby. Let me touch you this way, honey. Just for a little while."

He took her mouth again, and she knew that if she didn't stop him soon, she would be lost.

But when Nick said, "Sit up," she obeyed. "Raise your arms," he said, and she raised them so that he could pull the sweatshirt over her head.

He looked at her for a long and breathless moment before he said, "You're beautiful, Abby. You really are beautiful." Then he lay down with her and cradled her in his arms. It was heaven to be held by him like this, to feel so warm, so protected. He touched her with such gentle hands, and though she told herself she should resist him, she did not. She hadn't known she could feel this kind of emotion, this warm, wonderful, sexual emotion.

Abby knew now that she would not stop, that she had to go on and that she wanted to go on.

But when he put his hand against the small of her back and pressed her closer and she felt the hardness of his manhood against her thigh, she stiffened and tried to pull away.

"No," Nick said. "No, Abby." He came up to claim her mouth again, to say against her lips, "It's going to be fine, sweetheart. It's going to be good between us." He tugged the sweatpants down and cupped her through the thin protection of her panties.

"I want to stop," she whispered. "I want to . . ."

He eased down the silk and lace and began to caress her there, and, oh, his fingers were so hot and smooth against her flesh.

"Abby." He breathed her name against her lips. "You feel so good, sweetheart, so soft, so warm and ready."

"No, I—"

He took her protest into his mouth and while he kissed her, he touched her, touched her until her body burned and she moaned little whimpers of protest and of pleasure, and tried to lift her body to his.

"Wait, love." He sat up and quickly took his clothes off and tossed them aside.

Abby squeezed her eyes shut, wanting, needing, but afraid to even look at him.

He gentled her beneath him and kissed her again, and the whole length of his body was on hers. "It's going to be fine," he said again, and gripping her hips, he thrust himself into her.

She gasped and cried out in pain.

Nick froze. "Abby? Lord . . . why didn't you tell me? I didn't know. I didn't. . ." He groaned, trying to hold back his terrible need.

She kissed the side of his face. "It's all right, Nick. I want to. Really, I want—"

"Oh, Abby." He kissed her, and because he could not help himself, he began to move very slowly and carefully against her. Only when her body began to accommodate him did he move deeper.

He had never known this kind of a feeling from another human being before, this total yielding, this giving. He hadn't even suspected that she was a virgin. If he had, he wouldn't have— Liar, he told himself. You would have. You love it that this is her first time. You love it that she isn't sure of what to do or how to respond. You love knowing that it will be you who teaches her.

"Put your arms around my shoulders, Abby," he said. "Raise your body to mine, honey. That's it, Abby. That's it, sweetheart."

He moved slowly against her, reveling in the pleasure of her body. Because it was so good for him, he wanted it to be good for her, too. He quickened his pace. She whispered his name in a surprised little gasp and when she pressed him closer, he felt himself swell almost to the bursting point. But still he made himself wait because he wanted this to be special for her, wanted her to experience everything he was feeling.

He leaned to kiss her breasts and grasped one tender peak between his teeth to lick and to suckle, and when he did, she cried out and her body began to move under his.

"Yes," he whispered. "Yes, Abby. This is the way it's supposed to be. Let yourself go, sweetheart. For me, Abby. For me, sweetheart."

She clung to him, gasping in pleasure. She hadn't known, hadn't even guessed she could feel this desperate wanting, this need to be a part of him. She was out of control, climbing higher and higher to a place she'd never been before, into a whirlpool of feeling, a small dying.

Nick's arms tightened around her and he thrust hard, once, twice. He found her mouth. "Yes, oh, yes," he cried, raining kisses on her face. He held her until her breathing evened. He caressed her and told her how sweet she was, how fine, how wonderful.

Later, when the room grew cool, he picked Abby up and carried her into the bedroom.

She had never slept with a man before, and though she protested, he pulled back the blankets and when he had laid her down, he came in beside her and gathered her into his arms.

"Why didn't you tell me it was your first time?" he asked.

Abby wouldn't look at him, so he put a finger under her chin and raised her face to his. "Tell me," he said.

"I was embarrassed," she admitted. "I mean, I'm thirty-three years old and I'd never..." She turned her face into his shoulder. "I was afraid if I told you, you wouldn't want to make love to me."

He kissed the top of her head. "I've wanted to make love to you since that first night in the hotel restaurant when you were wearing that blue dress with the white collar and cuffs. You looked so ladylike and prim, Abby. And you made me want to find out if you were always so proper." He moved lower so that he could nuzzle his face against her throat. "Maybe if I had known you were a virgin, I would have backed off tonight," he said. "Maybe I would have stopped. I'm not sure, Abby. I only know how badly I wanted to make love with you and that I'm glad we did."

He stroked the hair back from her face. "I know I hurt you tonight, but I won't again. It will be better next time, I promise you."

Next time? She took a shaking breath, but before she could say anything, Nick said, "Go to sleep now, Abby. Go to sleep, sweetheart."

He began to stroke her back, and though she was sure she wouldn't, her eyes drifted closed and she slept.

It didn't matter that the rain slashed hard against the windowpanes or that thunder rumbled across the autumn sky. She was warm and safe here in the circle of Nick's arms.

## Chapter Seven

She was gone when Nick awoke. In the clear cool light of day it seemed impossible to him that he had made love to Abigail Sedgewick.

He knew what Jonah would have had to say about what he'd done.

Jonah had always been tolerant of Nick's affairs, though once in a while, as Nick got older, Jonah had said, "Sowing a few wild oats is one thing, making a career out of it is something else. For a lot of folks, making love doesn't mean much more than having one heck of a good time. And if that's the way both people go into it, then I reckon it's okay. But it goes deeper than that for some, women more'n men, I think. I wouldn't like you hurting a woman, Nick. I wouldn't like that at all."

A few months before Jonah died, he'd gripped Nick's hand and said, "You're the son I never had and I'm grateful to God for letting you come my way. I wish I coulda' had Abby, too, wish the both of you coulda' been mine. She had a mighty tough time of it when she was growing up, Nick. I'm going to try to make things better for her, but I won't be here to watch out for her. She may be book smart, but I got a feeling she doesn't know beans about what makes the world go 'round. When she comes out here, I want you to look after her until she gets her feet on the ground. You see somebody sniffing round her with bad intentions, I want you to step in, same as I would if I was here.''

Nick squeezed his eyes shut but it didn't help. He could still see Jonah looking at him, and he could still hear Jonah saying, ''I wouldn't want you hurting a woman, boy.''

Especially Abby.

She wasn't like the other women he'd known, women who could enjoy lovemaking without thinking it meant a lifetime commitment. Almost all of the women he'd known had understood from the very beginning that he wasn't interested in a permanent relationship. He had liked the women he slept with, and with the exception of one or two of them, he had stayed friends with them long after the relationship had ended.

But he knew it would be different with Abby. She wasn't like the others.

That scared the hell out of him. He'd made a mistake last night, a mistake he wouldn't make again.

Abby wasn't the kind of love-'em-and-leave-'em woman he was used to. Last night when he'd heard that first muffled cry of pain and known that it was the first time for her, he'd been overcome by a feeling of tenderness he'd never known before. He'd wanted to hold her, to kiss and comfort her, and, yes, he had wanted it to be good for her.

And when it had begun to be good for her and he'd heard her small gasp of pleasure and the whisper of his name, he had been overwhelmed by a feeling he had never before experienced. She had touched him in a way no one else ever had.

But last night had been a mistake and he would apologize. He'd say it had been the storm and the fact that the two of them had been alone, that it had been his fault and that he was sorry.

And he would not, he absolutely would not, make the same mistake again.

With a muttered curse, Nick went in to shower, and while the hot water cascaded over his body, he rehearsed what he'd say. *I hold you in the highest regard,* he would tell her. *I would never do anything to hurt you. I hope we can be friends, and because we are friends, as well as partners, I honestly don't think what happened last night should happen again.*

He would be firm, but gentle. And he would try not to think of how it had been in that final moment when she had cried out against his lips.

He found Abby in the kitchen. Her hair was pulled tight back off her face into a twist. She wore a high-necked blouse, a calf-length tweed skirt and sensible shoes.

"Good morning," she said in a crisp, no-nonsense voice. "Your breakfast is ready, and there's fresh coffee on the stove."

She was all Abigail; there wasn't a trace of the woman he had made love to last night.

"Aren't you going to eat?" he asked.

"I had breakfast earlier."

Nick poured himself a cup of coffee while she dished up a plate of eggs and bacon. "Sit with me," he said.

Her mouth tightened, but she sat down opposite him. He cleared his throat, ready to launch into the speech he'd prepared in the shower. But before he could, Abby said, "We need to talk about last night."

"Yes, that's what I—"

"It was a mistake. It should never have happened."

"I—"

"I'm not that kind of a woman," she said. "I don't believe in or approve of casual relationships."

"I didn't think you did, Abby. But—"

"We're partners, Nick, and I hope we're friends."

Son of a bitch! She was making *his* speech! She was putting *him* on the defensive. Even though it had been wrong, last night had been special—at least, it had been for him, and it made him mad as hell that she could sit there so calmly and act as though nothing important had happened.

"It was my fault," she said as he took a bite of his eggs. "It's the woman who controls the situation, and obviously, I wasn't in control."

Nick swallowed and took a sip of coffee. "You're making too much of this," he said quietly.

Delicate eyebrows raised. "I beg your pardon?"

Male pride shot all to hell, his anger growing like a bright hot knot in his stomach, Nick carefully placed his knife and fork across his plate. "We made love," he said. "It meant something to me. I was hoping it meant something to you, but obviously it didn't."

Color rose in Abby's cheeks. "I—I didn't say it didn't—"

"But I agree that what happened was a mistake. We're business partners, and if we intend to maintain a businesslike relationship, then what happened last night shouldn't happen again.'' He looked at her across the table. "Agreed?"

She looked back at him and firmed her jaw. "Agreed," she said.

She got up and began to clear the table, back straight, as prim and proper as the first time he'd seen her in Toledo. She banged the pans, shot water into the dishpan and plopped the dishes into it so that the water splashed over the side.

Nick cleared his throat. "I'm going out and have a look at the mine," he said.

"Dinner's at two." She turned around and looked at him. "I wouldn't want anybody to know you spent the night."

"No one will know."

"I'm not like Merilee. I wouldn't want them to think that I was."

Nick's face darkened. "You're right," he said in a slow and dangerous drawl. "You aren't anything like Merilee. She's woman enough not to be ashamed of her emotions." He opened the door, but halfway out, he turned back. "Not that it matters," he said, "but I've never been to bed with Merilee."

Abby stared at the closed door. She told herself it didn't matter to her whether or not Nick had slept with Merilee, but she knew that it did matter and she was glad that he had told her. She didn't blame him for what had happened last night, for surely she had been as much a part of it as he had, but she had wanted him to understand that it must never happen again.

She'd felt such a mixture of emotions when she had awakened this morning—chagrin because of what she had done, embarrassment because of what Nick must think of her, and shocked-out-of-her-socks surprise because of the way she had responded.

She hadn't known making love would be like that. She had expected the pain, and when that had come, she had been surprised by Nick's tenderness and by the gentle way he had touched her. But what had surprised her most of all had been the pleasure that followed the pain. Suddenly, unbidden, a small flame kindled in her midsection and snaked like a slim line of fire down to her loins. Lord, she thought, what's happening to me? I'm not like this. I'm not...

The dish that she'd been holding slipped from her fingers and fell with a crash. She closed her eyes and leaned against the sink. "Nick," she whispered, then she took a deep breath and began picking up the pieces.

Henry and Blanche arrived promptly at two, and a few minutes later, Evie drove up.

Nick went to the door with Abby. "I came a little early to have a look around," he explained as she greeted them. "The workers will be here in the morning and I wanted to be sure that everything was set."

Evie handed Abby two apple pies. "I made them this morning," she said. "Thought you might like to have them for dessert."

"That's wonderful," Abby said. "I'd planned on baking something last night, but the lights went out and I—I couldn't have seen to bake, I mean to measure the ingredients." Her face flushed. "With just the oil lamp I mean."

Evie raised one eyebrow. She looked from Abby to Nick, but offered no comment.

That's the way the rest of the day went. Nervous as a cat, Abby put chili powder in the gravy instead of salt, cut her finger when she tried to slice the turkey and let the cranberry sauce slide off the plate when she went to put it on the table.

She couldn't help it. She was sure that Blanche, Henry and Evie knew exactly what had happened last night. She wasn't the same person she had been yesterday. She hadn't suddenly grown a wart on the end of her nose, and she certainly didn't have a scarlet letter emblazoned on her chest, but she wasn't the same. Couldn't they see that? Wasn't it obvious?

It seemed to Abby that the day would never end, but at last, when the hour grew late and the sky began to darken with the threat of more rain, Henry said, "I guess we'd better be heading back to town."

Blanche kissed Abby's cheek. "It's been a lovely afternoon, dear. Thanks for inviting us. The dinner was delicious."

"Yes, indeed," Evie said. "I kind of liked the taste of chili powder in the gravy." She took Abby's hand. "Maybe you can all come out to my place for dinner next Sunday. I've got some old pictures of Jonah you might like to see, Abby." She looked at Nick. "You leaving, or you figuring on staying for a while?"

"I'm leaving." He picked up his Stetson, then put his hand out and when Abby took it, he said, "The men will be arriving at eight tomorrow morning. You don't have to, but it would be nice when I bring them in to meet you if you had a pot of coffee ready."

"Of course," she said in a voice as formal as his.

"Well then…" He took Evie's arm. "I'll walk you out," he said.

Abby stood on the porch, Jasper beside her, waiting until the two cars and the Jeep headed down the road and out of sight.

When she went in and closed the door the house seemed very empty.

Nick kept thinking about the way Abby had looked when they'd all left. Alone except for the dog at her side, there in the glow of the porch light, her hand raised in a goodbye wave.

He hated the thought of her all alone. The watchman he'd hired to guard the mine would start tomorrow night. Nick would make sure the fellow kept a watch on the house, as well. But that was tomorrow, what about tonight?

He told himself that Abby had been alone other nights. Just because he'd spent last night... No, he wasn't going to think about that.

But he couldn't help thinking about it and he smiled, remembering how flustered she'd been all day, how sure that everybody must somehow have known that they'd spent the night together.

A couple of times when she'd looked at him, a soft blush of color had crept into her cheeks and her mouth had gone all quivery and tremulous. He'd wanted to tell her that making love wasn't something to be ashamed of or sorry about. He wanted to say how special it had been for him, how making love with her had made him feel.

He wished he could have said something to her tonight before he had left, to ease the words they had spoken that morning. It didn't seem right, leaving her without a touch, a hand on her shoulder, a word. He wanted to tell her that he valued her and that he valued what had passed between them.

He wanted...

With a muttered curse, Nick slowed the Jeep and pulled off the road. He sat there in the dark, the Stetson pushed back on his head, and drummed his fingers on the steering wheel.

"Damn," he muttered under his breath. And swinging the Jeep around, he headed back the way he'd come.

Jasper started to bark as soon as Nick got out of the car and started toward the house. There was a light on in the bedroom, and he saw the bedroom curtains move as he ran up the steps to the porch.

He knocked and waited. In a minute or two, he heard Abby call out, "Who...who is it? Nick?"

"Yes," he said over the noise of Jasper's barking. "I'd like to speak to you for a moment, Abby."

She shushed Jasper, then opened the door and stood there, hand at the throat of her long, flannel gown.

"What is it?" she asked. "Is something wrong? Something with your car? Did you have an accident? Did—"

Nick shook his head. Jasper scooted around him and bounded off the porch. "No, I..." Nick saw her shiver. "It's cold," he said. "May I come in for a moment?"

"Yes, of course. I'm sorry. I... Just let me get a robe."

"No." Nick put a hand on her arm to hold her back. "I won't stay. I just wanted to..." He looked down at her. She was barefoot. Her hair was loose about her shoulders, and her face in the glow of firelight was open, vulnerable.

"N-Nick?" His name trembled on her lips.

He slipped his hand around to the back of her neck and brought her closer. Though he had told himself he wouldn't do this, that this was not why he had come back, he took her into his arms.

He whispered her name against the spill of her hair and knew that he had lied to himself, that this *was* why he had come back. He had needed to hold her like this, to feel her warmth, her womanliness. He traced his fingers down her spine, down to the fullness of her rounded bottom and urged her closer.

"No," she whispered. "You can't—"

He took her mouth and her lips trembled under his. He felt the resistance of her body, the fists doubled against his chest, but he wouldn't let her go. He wanted to hold her and kiss her, just for a moment, he told himself. But then the hands she had made into fists opened and spread against his chest, and the lips that trembled under his parted. With a strangled half sob, half sigh, she moved closer, and Nick knew that he wouldn't let her go.

She opened the buttons of his shirt and slipped her hands inside. They were warm against his skin, and he said, "Abby. Oh, Abby," before his mouth found hers again.

She clung to him, afraid if she didn't, she would surely fall. He cupped her face between his hands. He kissed the corners of her mouth and nuzzled a trail of kisses down her throat and around to her ear. "I want you," he whispered, "I want you, Abby."

She tried to pull back from his embrace, from the lips that teased and tortured and made her yearn for more.

"Listen," she said. "We agreed . . . We said—"

He picked her up and held her against his chest. "I don't care what we said or what we agreed." He kissed her again and with his mouth on hers, with their tongues seeking and tasting, he carried her into the bedroom and laid her down on the bed.

Her heart was beating so hard it was difficult to breathe. She watched him pull his boots off, his shirt and his trousers. She looked at him, at the black, hip-hugging briefs that covered him, and from somewhere in her almost-forgotten past, she remembered her grandmother telling her that a lady never looked below the second button of a gentleman's vest.

He hooked his thumbs under the elastic of his briefs and pulled them down over his hips. She lowered her eyes.

"Abby?" When she didn't respond, he said, "Look at me, Abby."

She took a deep breath and complied. A jolt of embarrassment shivered through her, a tremor of fear, a zing of excitement.

He came into bed beside her and drew her into his arms. He began to stroke her breasts through the flannel gown, and when he felt her relax, he said, "Sit up, Abby. I want to undress you."

"Turn off the light first," she whispered.

But he said, "No, I want to see you, Abby. I didn't last night. Everything was too fast." He pulled the blankets back and helped her to sit up so that he could draw the nightgown over her head. When he did, she lay back quickly and pulled the blankets back up to her chin.

Nick smiled down at her, then slowly, he took the blankets and lowered them. For a long moment, he didn't say anything. He only looked at her.

Her skin in the soft glow of light was a perfect ivory rose. Her breasts were small and high, the tips the color of ripe peaches. Her waist was narrow, her stomach was flat. He touched the spring of brown-red hair at the apex of her legs and though she quivered beneath his touch, she did not try to move away.

He stroked the legs that she disguised with the too-long skirts and sensible shoes. If you were mine, he thought, you would wear high heels. I would dress you in—

"Nick . . . ?"

He took a deep breath and pulled the blankets up to cover her. He lay down beside her and began to kiss her, and to stroke and pet her. She sighed with pleasure, and he folded the blankets back so that he could kiss her breasts. The tender tips were poised and waiting and he took one between his teeth to scrape and tease and lick. He felt his excitement grow when she moaned and stretched a long cat stretch and lifted her body to his.

When he cupped the apex of her legs, she tried to draw away, but he held her there and touched her there, and when he couldn't wait any longer, he brought his body up over hers.

She stiffened, remembering the pain, and he said, "It won't be like that now. I know I hurt you last night, but I won't again. I promise you, Abby. I won't hurt you."

He kissed her, and lifting her hips, he slowly, gently entered her.

She held her body rigid, waiting for the pain. But there was no pain, there was only the sense of being filled by that throbbing part of him that she had been so reluctant to even look at. He moved against her, slowly, deeply, and she was suffused by a delicious warmth, a wondrous creeping heat that spread and grew until it seemed as though every part of her body became thrillingly alive and sensitive to his touch.

"Put your legs around my back," he said, and when she did, he whispered, "That's it, Abby. That's it, sweetheart."

He caressed her breasts with his lips and with his tongue. And when she lifted herself to him, he said, "Yes, Abby. Oh, yes."

He sought her mouth and kissed her. She felt the quickening of his breath and the thud of his heart against her breasts, and because she knew that she was pleasing him, his pleasure became her pleasure, his excitement became her excitement.

His thrusts went deeper, harder. "So good," he said. "So good."

Abby clung to him, whispering incoherently, lost, reaching as she had last night for that distant, unobtainable place.

Nick took her mouth and kissed her, and when he let her go, she buried her face against his shoulder, afraid of all of the urgencies that surged and trembled through her body.

He plunged against her, again and again, until she was writhing under him, out of control, lifting herself to him, crying aloud in her terrible need. "Oh, please . . . I can't stand . . . Oh, please."

"Yes, Abby. Now, Abby . . . now."

And it came to both of them at the same time, shattering and explosive in its intensity, rendering them helpless, breathless.

Abby clung to Nick, her face against the hollow of his shoulder. He held her and stroked her hair and told her how fine she was, how beautiful and good. He kissed her eyelids, her nose and her cheeks. He caressed the breasts that quivered at his touch, and he ran his hands over all the curves and hollows of her body.

At last, her breathing evened and though he knew that she slept, he kept stroking her because he loved to touch her this way, to feel her skin so soft and smooth beneath his hands.

He told himself that he hadn't meant this to happen again, but knew that he could not be sorry that it had. He kissed her brow and she murmured in her sleep. "Sleep, my precious girl," he whispered.

But it was a long time before Nick slept, and when he did, it was to dream of Jonah, Jonah who had said, "I want you to look after her, same as I would if I were here."

Nick tightened his arms around her and murmured a prayer that wherever Jonah was, he would understand.

*Chapter Eight*

Nick knocked on the back door at eight the next morning, freshly shaved, dressed in jeans, a blue, open-neck shirt and a worn, brown leather jacket. Behind him were Sam Crocket, Abel Gentry and three other men.

"Good morning, Miss Sedgewick," he said in a politely formal voice.

"Good morning, Mr. Fitzgerald," she answered, equally formal.

"I thought you'd like to meet our crew. You already know Sam and Abel."

Abby put her hand out. "It's nice to see both of you again." She smiled at the other men.

"Paco Sanchez," Nick said. "Joe Hart and Moe Brady."

"Gentlemen." Abby shook hands with all of them, then held the door open and said, "Please come in and have a cup of coffee before you start work."

She'd set out coffee mugs on the red-checkered table-cloth along with a heaping plate of the oatmeal cookies she'd baked this morning. When the men pulled their chairs up to the table, she poured the coffee.

"Long time since I was in this kitchen," Sam said. "Don't look much different than it did when Jonah was here." He bit into a cookie. "But you're a better cook than he was, Miz Abby. 'Bout all he ever cooked were those guldurn hardtack biscuits."

"He fixed them for me when he came to Toledo," Abby said with a smile. "Hardest things I ever ate, but I loved them."

"He was good at Mexican food," Paco said. A tall man with a shock of white hair that was in marked contrast to his tanned face, he smiled shyly at Abby. "He made good *sopa de frijoles,* bean soup, and his salsa was so hot, *el diablo* himself wouldn't have touched it." Paco put a tea-spoon of sugar into his coffee. "He was a good man, Se-ñorita Abby. It would make him happy to know that you and Señor Nick are going to open the mine."

"How soon do you think we can get it going?" Abby asked Nick.

"Maybe by the first of next week." He indicated the tall black man sitting next to him. "Joe's an engineer, too. He and I will go in first this morning. If there isn't any trou-ble then Moe—" he nodded to the short, dark-haired man across the table "—and the others will come in and we'll start shoring up."

"When can I go in?" Abby asked.

"Maybe next week."

"But I'd like to see—"

"When we know it's safe," Nick said, cutting her off.

"Nick's right, Miz Abby." Abel reached for a cookie. "Soon's we know everything is shipshape I'll be glad to take you in myself."

"Down the shaft," she said.

"Women don't do that." Moe scratched his chin whiskers and frowned at her. "It's pure bad luck for a woman to go down a mine shaft. If your uncle was running things, wouldn't be no woman going in, let alone going down the shaft."

"But my uncle *isn't* running things, Mr. Brady," Abby said. "Half of the Lucky Lady belongs to me, and though I don't know anything about mining right now, I intend to learn."

"From books?" he scoffed.

"From books, from Nick and from the rest of you." She snapped off a bite of cookie. "I may not be from Colorado, and I may not know anything about mining, but I can learn the same as the rest of you did. I'm not afraid of the dark. I don't swoon at the sight of a mouse or a *moose*. And if you think I'm going to spend my time in the kitchen baking cookies, you've got another think coming!"

"I'll be damned," Abel said. "She sounds just like old Jonah did when he'd get his tail up." He patted Abby's shoulder. "Like you said, it's half yours and you got a right to know what's going on."

Nick didn't say anything, he just watched what was happening. The men sat straighter in their chairs. Paco smoothed back his white hair, Sam ran a finger across his drooping moustache and Joe brushed a speck off his vest. There was a grudging admiration in their expressions and appreciation of the fact that they were sitting with a woman who, though opinionated, was as fresh and as pretty as a Colorado morning.

He wasn't sure when he'd started thinking of Abby as pretty. A month or so ago, she'd been plain Abigail Sedgewick. Now, here she was in Jonah's kitchen, asserting herself, letting five, hard-bitten, rough-talking men know who the boss was.

She'd said she wasn't afraid of the dark, but he knew that was a lie because he'd seen her come streaking out of the mine white-faced and shaking. She'd probably keep on being afraid, but nobody would ever know it because that's the kind of woman she was.

When he woke up early this morning, she had been asleep, curled onto her side, burrowed in close, one arm across his chest. He'd known he had to leave to get back to town before daylight so he could pick Joe up by seven-thirty, but he'd been reluctant to move away. He had leaned his face against her throat to feel her warmth and her softness and watched the rise and fall of her breasts. At last, he had made himself get up because he'd known if he didn't, he would want her again.

On the way back this morning, Joe had asked him what kind of a woman Abby was. And Nick had answered truthfully. "I'm not sure I know."

There were as many facets to her as there were to a perfectly cut diamond. But diamonds, though beautiful, were hard. Abby wasn't hard, but from what he'd seen of her so far, she was strong, feisty, determined and spunky as hell. Most surprising of all, she was all woman.

As he watched her clear the table, he thought of all the things he would teach her, of all the varied ways of love he would delight in showing her. With the thought of how it would be, he felt himself tighten with need and so he made himself push his chair back from the table.

"Let's get going," he said to the men. "We can't sit here all day gabbing and eating cookies like a bunch of bridge-playing women."

Joe Hart looked up at him, startled, but he, like the other men, shoved back his chair. "Thanks a lot for the coffee and cookies, Miss Abby," he said. "By the end of the week, we'll have checked the mine out enough so you can have a look around."

Paco said, "My brother, Jacinto, will be here every night, *señorita*. He'll be guarding the mine but he'll also be making rounds and keeping an eye on the house too. You need not worry about anything."

Abby had told Nick that she didn't need a bodyguard, but this wasn't the time to say anything. She thanked Paco and shook hands with him and with the other men as they filed out the door.

Nick stayed behind for a moment, and when the others were out of earshot he said, "About last night, Abby, I had to come back."

"I'm glad you did," she whispered.

"Would you like to go over to Colorado Springs for dinner tonight? Seven o'clock?"

"Seven's fine."

He rested his hand on her shoulder for a moment before he turned away. And she wondered as she watched him go down the path to the mine how she could possibly wait until tonight to see him again.

The telephone rang late that afternoon. When Abby answered, a man said, "Miss Sedgewick? My name is Taylor. Perhaps Mr. Fitzgerald has mentioned my name."

"Not that I recall, Mr. Taylor."

"I'm representing a group of people interested in buying the Lucky Lady. I understand you're Mr. Sedgewick's niece. I'd like to talk to you about an offer for the mine that we made to Mr. Fitzgerald.''

"I'm sorry, Mr. Taylor, but my answer will be the same as Mr. Fitzgerald's.''

"But it wouldn't hurt to talk to the people I represent, would it, Miss Sedgewick? We made Mr. Fitzgerald an extremely generous offer, and we might be willing to go a little higher.''

"I'm afraid I'm not interested, Mr. Taylor.''

"You're making a mistake, Miss Sedgewick. A very big mistake.''

The connection was cut off and Abby stood there, staring at the phone. There had been an unspoken threat in the man's voice. She'd tell Nick about the call, she decided. Tonight.


The restaurant Nick chose was high up over Colorado Springs. The city below twinkled like Christmas tree lights in a darkened room. Thick, red carpets and polished wood lent a feeling of understated elegance.

Abby liked it immediately, especially when the maître d' led them to a cosy table close to the stone fireplace.

In a high-necked, ivory silk blouse and an ankle-length black crepe skirt, she looked ladylike and elegant. Her only jewelry was a pair of pearl earrings. Her face was devoid of makeup, and she'd pulled her hair back into a twist.

He would take her hair down tonight in front of the fireplace, Nick decided. He would undress her there, and watch the flames warm her body. He would—

"Would you care for something to drink?''

Nick looked up at the waiter. "White wine for the lady,'' he answered. "I'll have a Scotch and soda.'' To Abby, he said, "No boilermakers for you tonight.''

She made a face. "Or ever." And because she could not help herself, she said, "How *is* Merilee?"

"Okay, I guess. I haven't seen her in almost a week."

Abby unfolded then refolded the linen napkin on her lap. "You said the other day that you and she...that you hadn't...you know."

"Made love. No, we haven't."

"She's in love with you."

Nick smiled. "Merilee's in love with love."

"No," Abby said. "She's in love with you, Nick."

"Merilee is a friend, Abby. She helped me through some rough times, and I'm fond of her. But I'm not in love with her. Okay?"

"Okay."

"You know she put the burr under your saddle, don't you?"

"Yes, I know."

"Then why did you try to protect her by saying it was your fault, that you'd been careless?"

"Maybe because I understood why she did it." Abby concentrated on buttering her roll. "Maybe being in love with you isn't an easy thing."

Nick's eyebrows came together in a frown. "*Love*'s an overused word," he said. "People say 'I love' about almost anything. 'I love French fries. I love your car. I love Paris.'"

Abby's mouth tightened. "I admit that the word is overused, Nick, but surely the emotion of love isn't. I don't think you should make fun of it, or of Merilee because she cares about you."

"I'd never make fun of Merilee," he said quietly. "But I didn't ask for whatever it is she feels. I've never mentioned the word *love* to her or any other woman. I'm not sure that I believe in love."

"Then what do you believe in?"

"In being honest, Abby. In a relationship, I believe that both the man and the woman should be honest and up front with each other. No lies, no lasting declarations, no broken promises."

His face was intent, his eyes never left hers.

"I believe in mutual respect, Abby. In being totally aboveboard for as long as a relationship lasts."

"I see." She folded her hands over her napkin. And because it was important to her she made herself ask, "What about marriage, Nick?"

"Marriage is a trap, Abby, for both the man and the woman. Maybe one out of twenty turn out all right. But the others..." He shook his head.

The waiter brought their drinks. Abby took a sip of her white wine.

"I have a picture of my mother and father when they were in their early twenties," Nick said. "They had their arms around each other. They looked happy and in love. They didn't have a lot of money, but they were doing all right. My father was a miner. My mother had finished two years of college, but the only job she could get was at Zeke's. Everybody said they'd never seen a couple who seemed more in love than my mother and father.

"They did all right for a few years, but then the mines closed and my father lost his job. Maybe that's when he started drinking." Nick looked down at his drink, started to pick it up, then shoved it away. His mouth was tight, the corners bunched and hard.

"He beat my mother. I was young, but I remember the sound of the blows, and I remember my mother screaming, begging him to stop. I—"

"Don't," Abby said. "Nick, don't."

But he'd gotten started and now he couldn't stop. "She ran away," he said. "I don't blame her, I've never blamed her. But she should have taken me. I was only eight years old, Abby. Why didn't she take me?"

Abby reached across the table and covered his hand with hers. She wanted to weep for him and for the child he had been. But she knew that she couldn't, that he would hate it if she did.

"Is that what love is?" he went on in a low, bitter voice. "A man who tells a woman he loves her and then beats her until she screams. A mother who tells her son she loves him, then leaves him?"

"Nick, I—"

"If that's what it is, then I don't want any part of it." He turned her hand over in his and rubbed his fingers across her palm. "I've never lied to any of the women I've ever gone with, Abby, and I won't lie to you. I like you a lot, maybe more than I want to. As long as we're together, I'll be completely faithful to you, but I honestly don't believe in love or that there can ever be any permanency in a relationship. I wanted you to know—up front, I mean."

"I see." She took a deep, shaky breath and withdrew her hand.

She tried to tell herself that she appreciated Nick's honesty, but she couldn't. For the first time in her life, she had become emotionally and sexually involved with a man, and she knew that for her, the two things had to go together. Nick had changed her. He had come into her life and she would never again be the woman she had been before.

Making love with Nick—and that's what it had been for her—had not been a casual thing. It had been a beginning. Could she accept the fact that he had no intention of allowing their relationship to develop into anything permanent?

The decision was hers to make.

He had said *As long as we are together*... Could she go on knowing that someday it would be over and he would walk away from her?

She knew that she couldn't; that's not who she was.

She ate automatically, fork to plate to mouth, forcing the food down with sips of wine, making herself eat enough so that he wouldn't know how difficult this was for her, how much she was hurting.

When they left the restaurant, he put her coat over her shoulders and asked if she would like to go dancing. When she said no, he said, "How about a movie?"

"It's late," she said. "We should be getting back to Cripple Creek."

And when, in the car, Nick pulled her closer, she did not resist. Nor did she speak, not because of anger, but because there was such a coldness in her heart.

On the edge of the city, they saw the lights of a carnival. When they drew closer, Nick said, "I don't know why they allow things like that in the city."

Abby rolled down the window so that she could hear the music of the carousel. "Uncle Jonah took me to a carnival the night before he left, the night before my father came home from the hospital. We rode the Ferris wheel and the carousel. He bought me cotton candy."

"Terrible stuff," Nick said. "Pure sugar."

Abby gazed out at the glittering lights, fighting back tears that threatened to fall because she wanted so much to tell him about that night, the last night of her childhood. But she couldn't, not now.

She moved away from him and, closing her eyes, she leaned her head back against the leather seat.

But the music was still in her ears; the taste of cotton candy was on her lips.

\* \* \*

Nick did not go into the house with her.

"I'm tired," Abby said. "I think I'd just like to go to bed."

"So would I." Nick smiled. But when Abby didn't smile back, his face sobered. "I didn't mean to hurt you tonight," he said. "But I had to be honest, Abby." He took her hand. "I love making love with you," he told her. "I care about you."

She nodded, unable to speak.

"I'll see you in the morning."

"Of course."

"Good night, then." He kissed her cheek, and as awkward as a teenage boy on his first date, went down the steps to his car.

Abby watched until he drove away. She had just started up to the porch when she saw the beam of a flashlight and heard a voice call out, "Señorita Sedgewick? Is that you?"

Beside her, Jasper growled. "Steady, boy," she cautioned as she placed a hand on his collar.

"It is I, Jacinto Sanchez." The man, a heavier, younger version of his brother, stepped into the light. "I heard the car," he said. "I wanted to make sure it was you."

"Thank you, Señor Sanchez." Abby came down the steps and offered her hand.

"I'm here to keep an eye on things, *señorita*. I'll come by every hour or so all night. If there is ever anything you need, don't hesitate to call me."

"I won't, Señor Sanchez. Thank you. Would you like Jasper to make your rounds with you?"

Jacinto shook his head. "It's better he stay here with you, *señorita*."

A smile tugged at the corners of Abby's mouth. She now had a bodyguard as well as a watchdog, and though

Jacinto seemed like an agreeable man, she really did not think she needed him.

It wasn't until she went into the house and closed the door that she remembered the phone call she'd had this afternoon. She had forgotten to tell Nick about it.

## Chapter Nine

"*Ernie, no! Oh, please, no! What did I do? I'm sorry. Whatever it was... I won't do it again.*"

The sound of blows. Muttered curses. A muffled scream.

"*Oh, God, Ernie...*"

His mother's sobs. Her sobs...

Nick groaned in his sleep, struggling, fighting his way out of the dream.

"*I'm going away,*" his mother said. "*I love you, Nicky. Remember that I love you. Love you....*"

"*Don't leave me...! Mama... Mama...*"

Nick sat up in bed, his body covered with sweat, his heart pounding hard against his ribs. He hadn't dreamed that dream in years. Why now? Lord, why now?

He tried to blot out the childhood memories. He didn't want to remember anything, not even the good times.

Like that perfect summer's day when he and his mother had taken a picnic basket up into the foothills. There had been fields of daisies and columbine. They had bologna sandwiches, a little jar of sweet pickles and cupcakes with chocolate frosting his mother had made that morning.

She'd spread an old blanket under a cottonwood tree, and after they had eaten, they had lain on their backs and made up pictures out of the clouds. Butterflies had darted around them. He'd fed bologna to a pair of squirrels. His mother had clasped his hands and they'd danced around and around through the field of daisies and columbine. 'Here we go 'round the mulberry bush...''' they had sung.

She had been so young, so pretty. He had thought his heart would burst from loving her.

Nick fell back against the pillows, one arm over his eyes. It was a long time ago, he told himself. It doesn't matter now. It just doesn't matter.

But there were shadows under his eyes the next morning, and when he lifted his razor to his face, he saw that his hands were shaking.

Nick didn't see much of Abby during the next few days. He was sorry that he had hurt her, but he told himself that for both their sakes, he'd had to be honest with her. She wasn't a child and life wasn't all Ferris wheels and cotton candy. People didn't always live happily ever after; they took what happiness they could, when they could.

He had told her that he loved making love with her, and he had. He'd felt a giving, a total yielding and a loving tenderness in Abby that he'd never felt ·in a woman before. He wanted to make love to her in a dozen different ways. He wanted to lie with her in front of the fireplace on cold winter nights and watch the play of flames against her skin. He wanted to be with her . . . for all the time that she was here.

But he was not, by God, about to commit himself to a long-term relationship.

But the dreams continued. He lost his appetite, and he wasn't sleeping well. He was irritable with the men, working them as hard as he worked himself. Walls had to be shored up. Tunnels had to be inspected for loose rocks or slides. Every piece of equipment had to be checked. Cables, winches and hoisting equipment had to be tested.

Nick went over every inch of the mine with Joe Hart. One at a time, they lowered themselves down the quarter-mile-deep shaft in the narrow, steel cage, into a darkness Nick had all but forgotten. A darkness as black and as still as death.

Abby did not come near the mine, nor did he go to the house. He had telephoned her twice in the evening to ask her if she would have dinner with him. The first time, she had said, "I'm sorry. I'm having dinner with Evie tonight."

The second time, she had offered no excuses, she'd only said, "I don't think so, Nick."

On Saturday, after the other men had left, he went to the house to tell her that the preparatory work had been completed and that the men would begin mining operations on Monday. But that wasn't the only reason he wanted to see her. He wanted to talk to her, to sit across the table and drink coffee with her. He wanted to touch her hair and hold her hand.

He went to the back door, hat in his hand, and knocked.

When she came to the door, she said, "I was in the living room. Come in, please."

"I wanted to talk to you . . . about the mine."

She held up a cautioning hand. "I'm not alone." Before Nick could answer, she turned and led the way into the living room.

A man was sitting in Jonah's old leather chair, a black Stetson on the hassock next to him. He was tall and slim. His porcine face was smooth and unlined, his hair patent-leather slick. Well dressed in a black suit, white shirt with a string tie and polished, black boots, he gave the appearance of a wealthy rancher.

But Nick knew better. "What are you doing here, Taylor?" he asked.

The tall man stood. "Nice to see you again, Mr. Fitzgerald."

"I asked what you were doing here."

"I came to speak to Miss Sedgewick, to talk to her about the Lucky Lady."

"I've told you, we're not interested in selling."

"You told me *you* weren't interested. I didn't know you spoke for Miss Sedgewick. She might be interested in what the people I represent have to offer."

"You're wasting your time. She feels the same way I do."

Taylor smiled. "Is that true, Miss Sedgewick?"

Abby hesitated. She did feel the same way Nick did, but she didn't like him speaking for her. "What kind of an offer are your people talking?"

"Dammit, Abby—"

"I want to hear the offer," she said.

"Five million," Taylor said. "For the mine and the house."

She looked at Nick and knew suddenly where the expression Black Irish had come from. His eyes were like shards of hard, green glass. His dark eyebrows were drawn together, and his lips were pulled back in a snarl. "No!" he said. "Absolutely not!"

Hands on her hips, as angry as he was now, Abby faced him. "Look," she said, "the house is mine. I can do whatever I want with it. I own half of the mine—"

*"Half,"* he said in a dangerously quiet voice. "You can sell the house because it's yours, but you can't sell the mine unless I say so."

They stared at each other, their gazes unbroken until Taylor said, "Five million dollars is a lot of money."

"We don't want your money," Nick told him. He swung his gaze away from Abby. "Now get the hell out of here."

Ignoring Nick, Taylor said, "You'll be hearing from me." And picking up the black Stetson, he left.

They both spoke at the same time. "How could you . . . ?"

"I had no intention of . . .

"Of course, I wouldn't sell," Abby said. "Uncle Jonah gave us the mine. He trusted us to get it running again."

"Then why—"

"I wanted to hear what he had to say, but you came storming in here like Mr. Macho, telling me what I could or couldn't do, like I didn't have sense enough or honor enough to turn him down." She took a step closer to Nick. "I'm not stupid, and believe me, I can spot a phony ten miles away. I've taken care of myself for a long long time, and I don't need you or anybody else telling me what I can—" she paused to take a deep breath "—or can't do. Is that clear?"

He wanted to shake her till her teeth rattled. Instead he made himself step away from her. "It's very clear," he said. "I—"

The phone interrupted him. Abby murmured, "Excuse me," and picked it up.

Nick turned away and glared out of the window at the distant mountains.

She said, "Hello? Oh, hi. Yes, of course. Seven is fine. I'll see you then, Jake. Bye."

"Jake?" Nick said when she put the phone down. "You're going out with Jake McClinton?"

"Yes, I am. For dinner."

"Why?"

It was her turn to raise an eyebrow. "Why?"

"Yes, dammit. Why?"

"Because I want to," she said.

"How long has this been going on?"

"This *what?*"

"This thing with Jake?"

"There isn't any 'thing.' I'm going out to dinner with him, that's all." She raised her chin. "What I do or who I go out with isn't any business of yours, Nick. You've made that pretty clear."

His jaw tightened. "You misunderstood what I said. I wanted to be honest with you. I—"

"And you were. Now if you don't mind, I'd like to start getting ready for my date."

He wanted to tell her not to go. *I don't want you going out with Jake McClinton or any other man,* he wanted to say. But he didn't have the right, he didn't want the right. So instead, he said, "I came to tell you that the mine is in pretty good shape and that we'll begin operations on Monday. If you'd like to go down into the shaft, I'll take you."

Abby nodded. "I'll look forward to it."

"Fine." He picked up his Stetson and slapped it hard against his thigh. "Until Monday, then," he said.

He went on out to his Jeep, jumped in and slammed the door. He drove out of the yard, hell bent for leather, and didn't look back.

It hadn't been the best evening in Abby's life, nor the worst. She liked Jake. He was nice, he was attentive and he was fun. But he wasn't Nick.

They went to Victor, which, like Cripple Creek, lay in the great gold-mining district of years past.

"At the turn of the century, Victor was a boom town," Jake told her when they were driving over. "By 1900, there were over twelve thousand people living there. Four hundred and seventy-five mines were operating and shipping gold out. Seventy trains a day came in and out of town back then."

"What happened?"

"Union troubles mostly. World War I changed things, and people moved on. The government closed all the gold mines down during the Second World War, but with the rise in gold prices, a few mining companies have started bringing out gold again. They're doing the same thing in Cripple Creek." He slowed his pickup for a curve. "Like the Lucky Lady," he said. "I sure hope you and Nick strike it rich, Abby."

"Yes, so do I." She debated about telling him about the man named Taylor, and finally said, "We've had an offer to sell the mine. A man by the name of Taylor—"

"Simon Taylor? He's with that bunch over in Denver that are buying up every piece of mining property they can get their hands on." Jake slowed the car for a curve. "Are you and Nick planning to do business with him?"

"No, of course not."

"He and his buddies are a bad bunch, Abby. There have been rumors, but nothing anybody can prove, that if they don't get what they want, they can get pretty nasty. Five or six months ago, Taylor paid a visit to old Malcolm Tate, wanting to buy the Nellie Jane. Tate ordered Taylor off his property with a twenty-gauge shotgun. Fired once to get him moving. A week later, there was an accident in the mine. Tate and another miner were killed.''

Abby stared at the sheriff in disbelief. ''Did it have anything to do with the offer? With Taylor?''

''I've got a hunch he and his people were behind it, but I can't prove anything. I want him and his kind behind bars so bad I can almost taste it. If he even spits on the sidewalk, I'll lock him up and maybe scare him into letting something slip. But he's slick and he's careful.'' Jake shook his head. ''He's a no-account skunk, Abby. Don't have anything to do with him.''

She finally understood Nick's anger and wished that he had told her how dangerous Taylor and the people he represented were. Of course, she wouldn't sell, and she certainly wouldn't have anything else to do with Simon Taylor.

But she didn't want to think about Simon Taylor or about Nick.

The restaurant Jake took her to was rustic, but the food was good. They had inch-and-a-half-thick steaks, French fries and salads. Though Abby said she didn't want dessert, Jake insisted she taste the homemade pumpkin pie, and she was glad she did because it was the best she'd ever had.

They lingered over coffee. Abby told him Nick and the other men had been working on the mine and that on Monday, she was going down the shaft.

''You won't be scared?'' Jake asked.

"Probably," Abby said with a laugh. "But I want to learn about mining, Jake, and the only way to do it is to go down into the mine."

"Nick knows what he's doing. He wouldn't let you set foot in the Lucky Lady unless he was sure it was safe." Jake looked down at his coffee. "Are you and Nick ... ?" He hesitated. "Are you seeing each other?"

"We've had dinner a couple of times."

"I shouldn't have asked. It's just that you're a mighty nice woman and ..." Jake cleared his throat. "Nick's just about the best friend I've got, Abby, but when it comes to women—" he shook his head "—I've seen a lot of them come and go, and he hasn't been serious about any of them. Maybe someday he'll settle down, but I kinda doubt it. I guess what I'm trying to say is that I'd hate to see you get hurt because I—I think you're a special kind of a woman, and I ..." He blushed to the roots of his hair. "Forgive me for talking like this, Abby. It isn't any of my business and I apologize."

"There's no need to apologize, Jake." Abby took a sip of her coffee. "But Colorado isn't my home. I'm only here for a year and when the year is over, I'll go back to Ohio."

"Maybe you'll decide you like it here and stay."

Abby shook her head. "I don't think so," she said. And thought, because there isn't anything to keep me here. Not now.

It was almost eleven when they left the restaurant, and though the air was cold, they walked around the town. Jake pointed out the Lowell Thomas Museum, the library, the post office, the curio shops and the old Midland Terminal Railroad station.

"There are a lot of things to see around these parts," he said. "A lot of old mines up on Battle Mountain I'd like to show you, whenever you have time."

"I'll make time," Abby said with a smile.

On the way back to Cripple Creek, Jake didn't attempt to put his arm around her or to take her hand. When they drove up in front of the house, he walked her onto the porch and shook hands with her.

"I had a mighty fine time," he said. "I'll call you next week, if that's all right with you."

"That'd be fine."

"Well then . . ." He let go of her hand. "I'll be seeing you. You take care."

"I will, Jake. Thank you for a lovely evening."

"The pleasure was mine, Abby. From start to finish. I can't remember when I've had a better time."

She thought then that he was going to kiss her. But he didn't. He shook her hand again, then ran down the steps to his car.

When she went into the house, Jasper padded over to her. She bent to scratch him behind his ears and that's when she saw the long legs stretched out from Uncle Jonah's old leather chair.

"About time you got home." Nick, a brandy glass in his hand, pushed himself up out of the chair. "You and Jake have a good time?"

"What are you doing here?" Abby said indignantly. "What right do you have coming into my house like this?"

"I wanted to make sure you were okay." He set the brandy glass down on the table nearest the fireplace. "Actually, I wanted to make damn sure that Jake didn't try anything."

Abby slammed her purse down and shrugged out of her coat. "Whether or not Jake tried anything, and whether or not I let him, isn't any of your business," she said.

"No?" He opened the door and called to the dog. "Go on out and chase a couple of rabbits, Jasper." When the dog scooted out, Nick, hands on his hips, took a step toward Abby. "I'm making it my business," he said.

"You can't..." She started to say, and gasped when he cupped the back of her neck with one hand and drew her closer.

So close, it seemed to her she could see every one of the raven black eyelashes on his half-closed eyelids. So close, that she could see the danger in his Irish green eyes.

"No," she whispered more to herself than to him. "I won't let you. I—"

His mouth crushed on hers, and his arms came around her, so quick and hard that the breath woofed from her body. She stiffened, resisting him, lips compressed, hands against his chest to hold him away.

But he wouldn't let her go. He held her, his mouth insistent on hers, his arms so tight around her, she could barely breathe.

Abby fought him—and the sudden flare of heat that grew and spread like the insidious fingers of a forest fire. But her mouth was unrelenting, her body rigid.

He forced her lips apart and plunged his tongue past them. With one hand around her shoulders, holding her so she could not escape, he pressed his other hand against the small of her back, forcing her even tighter against him.

His body was hard, masculine, unrelenting, and suddenly, Abby was afraid because there was no tenderness in him, only this terrible, unyielding force. She wanted to beg him to stop, but his hungry mouth held her silent.

The heat of the fireplace was at her back. She couldn't retreat, but she struggled against Nick, trying to get away from him.

"No!" he muttered against her lips. Then he pulled her down onto the hearth rug so that they were kneeling together in front of the fireplace. He put his hands in her hair and tugged at the pins that bound it, scattering them on the floor in his haste. He shook her hair loose, and his fingers were hard against her scalp. "Why do you bind it?" he said angrily. "This is the way it should be, this is the way I want it, soft and silky and loose so that I can get my hands into it." He rubbed a handful across his face. "Oh, yes," he whispered. "Yes."

"Let me go," Abby said. "Let—"

But he took her mouth again, and his hands found her breasts. When she resisted and tried to push him away, he brought her down to the rug, and with his body half over hers, he held her there while he tugged at the buttons of her blue silk blouse. One popped off. She heard it hit the stone fireplace. He had his hands on her breasts and when she tried to slap him away, he took both of her wrists and held them above her head.

He opened her blouse and yanked it down off her shoulders. She felt the heat of the flames on her bare skin.

"This is what I wanted," he whispered. "To see your breasts like this. Because they're mine, Abby."

She tried with every bit of her strength not to give in. But, oh, his mouth was warm, and oh, his tongue was soft.

"You want this as much as I do," he said against her skin.

"No!" She twisted her body from side to side, trying to get away from him. But all the while, her body burned with the need to have him inside her.

The breath came fast in his throat. She could feel him hard against her thigh, and not even knowing that she did, she moved her legs apart.

He let go of her wrists. "Abby," he said. "Oh, Abby, honey..."

"No!" The cry tore from her mouth. "No!"

She rolled away from him, onto her side, breathing hard, fists clenched against the terrible need that threatened to destroy her.

Nick started to reach for her. She wanted this as much as he did. He wasn't going to let her stop, wasn't going to let her deprive both of them....

"No," she said again, and this time the word became a sob.

He hesitated. A shudder ran through his lean hard body. He took a deep, shaking breath and tried to quell the terrible urgency that made him ache with the need to possess her. He had never wanted a woman the way he wanted Abby. He could... No, he could not. No matter how fierce the need, he could not force himself on her.

Her shoulders shook with the force of her sobs.

"Don't," he said. "Abby, don't."

The anger he had felt earlier because she had gone out with Jake, because he could not stand the thought that Jake had touched her, faded.

He stroked the hair that spilled across her bare shoulders. "I'm sorry," he said. "Don't cry."

With an effort, he made himself get up. He stood over her but she didn't move. She lay huddled, her back to him, her face damp and flushed from weeping.

He put his key on the table. "I'm sorry," he said again.

Abby heard the door close, but still she did not move. She lay where she was, her face against her forearm, feeling more empty, more lonely than she had ever felt in her life.

## Chapter Ten

Abby stayed in the house all day Sunday. The phone rang several times but she didn't answer it. After breakfast, she put on a sweater and a heavy jacket, and went out for a walk.

The weather had turned cold during the night. Hoarfrost covered the ground, and low, gray clouds hung low over mountains already capped with early snow.

It was the kind of a day that suited her mood.

With Jasper beside her, Abby went through the barren fields and down past a dry creek bed of flat, gray stones. Once, a covey of quail flew out of a clump of bushes in front of her and Jasper bounded after them.

She watched a cast of hawks soar high into the gray, October sky, and she tried not to think about Nick or of what had happened between them last night. She wished that like the hawks, she could fly away. She didn't want to think or feel. She felt empty and cold and more alone than she had ever felt before.

All of her life, she had been reaching out for something or for someone, but she had not really understood the many faces of love. When she had seen love happen to other women, younger women, she had found it difficult to empathize or to understand what was happening to them or why they were so changed by that first glow of love. Nor had she understood the pain that came with love.

And while she had envied the emotion that other women experienced, she hadn't quite believed it, hadn't been convinced that what they were experiencing was real. Surely, she had thought, there were not so many highs and lows of love. How could it be possible that one moment, you were more alive than you'd ever been in your life, more aware of everything around you, feeling as though you had discovered an absolutely delicious secret, and the next moment, you could feel so totally bereft?

But if, indeed, that was the way of love, she had thought, then it happened to other people, not to sensible and strong-minded Abigail Sedgewick.

Tears stung Abby's eyes and she told herself not to be foolish. Love didn't just happen. It didn't come unbidden to clutch at your heart and make you want to cry out with anguish unlike anything you'd ever known before.

She had thought that if—and it had been a very large and doubtful if—she ever fell in love, it would come slowly, with time, with someone she had known for months, even years. Friendship would blossom into an undemanding relationship. He would tell her that he loved her and ask her to marry him. It would all be quite proper: engagement, marriage, honeymoon, children. In that order.

She had thought love would be pleasant. Yes, that was the word that had come to mind when she'd thought about love. But, my God, what a Milquetoast word for all of the emotions she'd felt from the very first time that Nick Fitzgerald had kissed her.

She groaned aloud. She didn't want to be in love with a man to whom a long-term relationship meant a few weeks or a few months. Nick didn't believe in love or need love, he only wanted to *make* love. And so did she, but only with him. Forever with him, because she was that kind of a woman, a forever woman.

But Nick wasn't a forever man. She could take him the way he was, enjoy this time with him on his terms, or she could turn and walk away.

No, she couldn't even do that. She would have to see him, every day, for all of the time she was here. And that would be hard, so hard.

When the air grew cooler and the skies darker, Abby headed back to the house...to find Evie Montgomery sitting on the steps of the front porch.

"I called and you didn't answer," Evie said when Abby drew closer. "I was afraid something might have happened to you, so I drove on out."

"I'm all right. I just went for a walk."

"You okay?"

"Of course." Abby took the key out of her pocket and opened the door. "How long have you been sitting out here?"

"Long enough to get cold as a witch's britches."

"Would you like some tea?"

"If I can spike it."

"You can do anything you want to with it. I'll put the kettle on."

She was glad that Evie was here because it would be nice to sit in front of the fire— No, not the fire. That would make her think about last night, and she didn't want to do that.

Evie came into the kitchen with a half-filled bottle of brandy. "I'd better buy you a bottle next time I come," she said. "This was about full when I was here last Sunday. I didn't know you liked brandy."

"I don't. Nick was here last night, and I guess he drank some of it."

"Nick? I thought you had dinner with Jake last night. I saw him this morning at church, and he said he'd had a date with you."

"Yes, but Nick..." Abby clasped her hands around the mug of tea. "Nick was here when I got home," she said.

Evie raised an eyebrow.

"He was angry, and we...we quarreled."

"Because you went out with Jake." Evie poured a dollop of brandy into her tea. "You want to talk about it?"

"No."

For a minute or two, Evie didn't say anything. Then she said, "I suppose Nick told you your uncle and I were together for a long time."

"Yes, he told me." Abby looked at Evie over the rim of her mug. "Why didn't you marry him?"

"I'm not sure. I guess when it started between us, I thought maybe Lou—that was my husband, Louis Alfred Montgomery—might decide to come back. He never did. So Jonah and I settled into the way we'd been living, half out here, half at my place in town. It was working out so good that after a while, we were afraid to change anything."

Evie turned and gazed out of the window at the distant mountains. "I never in my life loved a man the way I loved

Jonah," she said. "A preacher saying words over us wouldn't have made it any different. We were true to each other all those years, and now that he's gone, there'll never be another man for me."

"I'm glad he had you, Evie."

"Thank you, Abby. I appreciate that." Evie took a sip of her brandy-laced tea. "You know, I had you dead wrong. I figured from what I'd heard about you, about how straitlaced your folks were, that you'd be shocked when you heard that Jonah and I had been living together all those years."

"I wasn't shocked," Abby said, trying to hold back the tears that stung behind her eyelids. "On the contrary, I envy you having somebody to love, somebody to love you."

"Honey...?" Evie put her hand on Abby's shoulder. "Are you all right, honey?"

"No," Abby said, "I'm not all right."

"It's Nick, isn't it?"

Abby nodded.

"Oh, Lord."

"Oh, Lord, indeed."

"I couldn't love him more if he were my son..." Evie hesitated.

"But?" Abby asked.

"But I don't envy the woman who falls in love with him."

"I'm not..." Abby took a deep breath. "I'm not..." But the rest of the words wouldn't come. She looked at the other woman and shook her head. "I don't want to be," she whispered. "It just happened."

"He was here last night because he was jealous about you being out with Jake?"

"Maybe. Yes, I suppose he was jealous."

"I hope you told him what you did wasn't any of his danged business."

"That's exactly what I told him."

"Men!" Evie took another swig of her tea. "What're you going to do about him?"

"Danged if I know," Abby said.

Evie laughed, then her face sobered. "Those first couple of years Nick came to live with us were hard for him. He had this look in his eyes, like a wounded deer. If you moved sudden like, he'd jump and bring his hands up like he had to protect himself." Evie shook her head. "I'm not sure you ever get over being hurt real bad when you're young, Abby. And Nick was hurt by that no-good, low-down-rotten skunk of a father, and maybe even more by Louise running off and leaving him like she did. I'm not sure that he has it in him to trust a woman enough to love her."

Evie got up and went to stand by the back door, looking out at the gathering clouds. For a long time, she didn't speak, but when she turned back to Abby, she said, "Maybe Nick needs somebody to teach him how to love, Abby. Maybe if the right woman loved him enough, he could forget all the hurting that's gone before."

She walked back to the table and downed her drink. "You want to go out for some barbecued ribs?" she asked.

Abby took a deep breath. "I . . . All right."

"There's a place over near Saddle Mountain that Jonah and I used to go sometimes. Nothing fancy, so you don't need to change. Just put on a warm coat, because it's going to get cold tonight."

Abby knew that for now at least, they weren't going to talk any more about Nick. But all the way into the mountains, she kept thinking about a young boy with wounded eyes, a boy who had shielded himself at any sudden movement. And Evie's words... *maybe if the right woman loved him enough, he could forget all the hurting that's gone before.*

The right woman.

The adobe-type restaurant was almost half a mile off the main road. It looked rustic and unpretentious, but the parking lot in the back was filled with expensive, foreign-made cars.

The ribs were the best Abby had ever had. The salad was crisp, and the baked beans were seasoned just right. While they ate, Evie told her stories of what Cripple Creek had been like forty years before, and Abby told her about growing up in Toledo, about her parents and about the look on Eloise Zircle's face when she'd told her she was quitting.

It was cold by the time they left the restaurant. The ground was covered with snow, and thick flurries beat against the windshield.

Evie, who hadn't had anything to drink in the restaurant, drove carefully down from the over-eleven-thousand-foot elevation, creeping along, trying to see through the snow.

"Isn't it early in the season for a storm like this?" Abby asked.

Evie shook her head. "We almost always have snow by Halloween. But don't worry, I know this road. I've been over it a thousand times before."

"I'm not worried," Abby said. "But when we get back, I want you to spend the night. I don't want you driving back to town by yourself."

"I don't want to impose."

"You won't be imposing. On a night like this, it will be nice to know that I'm not alone in the house."

"Do you ever worry about that?"

"Not really," Abby said. But when they turned onto the road leading to the house, she was glad that Evie would be with her tonight. Glad, too, that they were friends.

She gave Evie one of her flannel nightgowns. "If there's anything you want, you probably know where to find it better than I do," she said. Then, with a sudden impulse, she hugged Evie. "I'm glad you're here. Sleep well."

Evie smiled and hugged her back. "You, too, Abby. I'll see you in the morning."

That night, although she hadn't thought that she would, Abby went immediately to sleep.


They were having breakfast the next morning when Nick knocked at the back door. Because Abby was at the stove, it was Evie who answered.

"Hi, you rascal," she said when she saw him. "Abby and I are having breakfast. Want some?"

"No, Evie, thanks." He stood at the door, holding his Stetson, looking uncomfortable.

"I stopped by to see if Abby would like to have a look at the mine later." He shot a quick glance her way, but he didn't quite meet her eyes. "Would you?" he asked.

"Yes, I would, Nick. Thank you." She poured coffee into a mug, and handing it to him, said, "Come in and sit down."

He stamped the snow off his feet. The snowfall had stopped during the night, but a light coating still covered the ground, and the temperature was in the low thirties. The kitchen was warm and welcoming, but he didn't have any right to be here, not after the way he'd acted on Saturday night.

It wasn't up to him to object to Abby going out with Jake or anybody else, and the fact that he'd acted like a jealous fool, that he had almost forced her into making love, had left him so ashamed he could hardly look at himself in the mirror when he shaved. He'd never done anything like that before, and he hated facing her this morning. If she'd thrown him out of the kitchen, he wouldn't have blamed her. That's what he'd been prepared for, and her attitude surprised him. She wasn't angry or cool as he'd expected. She seemed composed, at ease with herself and with him.

She was dressed in wool pants and a dark blue turtleneck sweater. Her eyes were clear, her cheeks were pink. She looked rested.

He'd barely slept since Saturday night.

He stood in the middle of the room, feeling as though his arms were too long and his hands were too big. All he wanted to do was drink his coffee and get the hell out of here.

"Abby and I drove on over to Battle Mountain for ribs last night," Evie said. "Snow caught us by surprise. I stayed here instead of going back to town." She dished bacon and eggs onto Abby's plate, then onto her own. "Sure you won't have anything to eat?" she asked Nick.

"No, thanks. I have to get back to the mine. I could take you down later this morning, Abby." He looked at her. "If that's convenient."

"Ten o'clock all right?" she asked.

"Yeah, ten's fine. I . . . we'll show you around."

"I'll be looking forward to it, Nick."

Her smile was warm. He couldn't figure her out.

"Well, then," he said, trying to sound hearty, "I'll see you later." And as an afterthought, he asked Evie if she'd like to go into the mine, too.

"Lord, no," she said. "Jonah took me down once and I had a panic attack. It was all he could do to get me in the cage and keep me from going berserk on the way up." She looked at Abby. "I hope you're going to be okay," she said. "Maybe you're a better woman than I am."

"Nobody's a better woman than you are, Evie, but Uncle Jonah left part of the Lucky Lady to me, and I want to have a look at her." She nodded to Nick. "I'll be over at ten," she said.

And she promised herself that no matter how afraid she might be, she wouldn't let him see her fear.

Abby met Nick in the mine office. He was impersonal and businesslike. He gave her a hard hat with a light attached to the front, then put a belt with what looked like a cassette player around her waist. "The battery will operate your light," he said.

"There's no electricity down below?"

Nick shook his head. "This is what all the miners use. But don't worry, the battery lasts a minimum of eight hours." He switched her lamp on and off, testing it. "You don't have claustrophobia, do you?"

"No," she answered too quickly. "Don't worry about me, I'll be all right."

"If you're having any trouble when we get down, don't try to brave it out. Tell me and we'll go back up."

"I'll be okay."

"All right," he said. "This is what we're going to do." He reached for a map and spread it on top of the desk. "There are fourteen tunnels that branch off from both sides of the shaft. You see here, these are the tunnels. So far, we've only checked out the first three on the right side of the shaft." He pointed to a section of the map. "Today, we're going to start here, at a level of three hundred and sixty meters."

Abby swallowed. "What about air?" she asked.

"It comes down from the shaft."

"And there's enough of it to ventilate the mine?"

"There's enough," Nick said. "Are you ready?"

"I'm ready."

The other men were waiting at the entrance of the mine. Joe shook hands with her. Abel gave her a hug, then blushed and stepped back.

Sam said, "There's nothing to worry about, Miz Abby. The first time's kinda scary, but it's perfectly safe. Besides, you've got Nick to take care of you. You're going to do just fine."

Only Paco frowned and shook his head, and she knew he didn't approve of a woman going into a mine.

She wasn't sure she did, either, but now wasn't the time to chicken out. "Ready when you are," she told Nick.

He nodded. His face was grim, his expression almost angry. They started into the mine, the same way Abby had gone the first day. The men came behind them. Nobody said anything. She saw the tracks, then ahead of them, the wire cage.

"Go ahead, get in," Nick said. And when she did, he nodded to Joe. "All set," he said.

The cage began to descend.

Abby tightened her hands around the iron bar that Nick had snapped closed when they'd entered.

A darkness unlike anything she'd ever known closed in around her.

"We're down to the first level now," Nick said. "We go down six more." His voice, in this narrow, closed in space, sounded strangely hollow. He took a flashlight out of his back pocket and turned it on. "There's a ladder that runs up the side of the shaft to the surface," he told her. "It's an escape route in case something happens underground and the men have to climb out."

"How—how far down does it go?"

"All the way down. More than a thousand feet."

"Has anybody..." Abby took a steadying breath. "Has anybody ever had to do it?"

"Not that I know of. I know I wouldn't want to try it."

Abby's hands were clammy. All of a sudden, she couldn't seem to get enough air. She made herself take slow, deep breaths and vowed that no matter what happened, no matter how afraid she was, she wouldn't let on. She'd wanted to go into the mine. She'd insisted on going down. She wasn't going to make a fool of herself now.

The cage stopped. Nick said, "Here we are," and led the way out of the cage.

Here we are where? Abby wanted to ask. But didn't.

"It...the cage, I mean...it will stay here? I mean it won't go back up? Without us, I mean?" She swallowed hard. "How do we get back up?" she asked.

"I signal." Nick looked at her. "Are you all right?"

"I'm fine," she lied. "Show me what you're going to be doing."

"We'll start over here, where the pneumatic drills are."

"I thought miners used picks and shovels."

"They did years ago." Nick started ahead of her. "This way," he said. "The tunnel goes back about thirty feet. We'll start from the back and work toward the shaft when we begin—"

Suddenly, a piece of shale and a tumble of rocks clattered down just in front of him. He threw his arm out behind him to stop Abby.

"What is it?" she asked. "What...?"

Nick froze. The breath clogged in his throat. He couldn't speak. It was like Ecuador. He and Steve had been alone in number ninety-eight. There hadn't been any warning, just the clatter of shale and rock before everything caved in on them. They had been trapped, buried alive, two thousand feet underground.

Steve's legs were broken, his chest was crushed.

"Holy mother," he said. "There's no way in hell we're ever going to get out of this alive."

"I'll get you out," Nick said. "The boys up top will know. They'll find us."

"Not in time. I hurt real bad, Nick. My legs...my chest... Can't breathe, pal. Can't..."

And Nick had been alone with the body of his best friend.

"Nick?"

He looked at Abby through the eerie blackness.

"What is it?" she said. "What's wrong?"

He didn't answer. He couldn't.

She put her hand on his arm. Once, years ago, she had taken a neighbor's child to the dentist. "She's scared to death of going," the child's mother had said. "Maybe she'll do better if I'm not along."

But the little girl hadn't done better without her mother. She'd gone deathly pale as soon as she'd seen the dentist's chair, and her skin had been cold and clammy.

"She has to get over this silly fear," the dentist had said.

But Abby had known that the fear hadn't been silly, it had been a real and a terrible problem. She'd taken the child out of the office and later she had told the little girl's mother that the child needed some kind of professional help, that she shouldn't be forced to do something that frightened her so.

Nick wasn't a child, but his fear was as great as the child's had been. She took his hand and said, "Can we leave, Nick? Can we go back up now?" She moved closer to him. "I'm sorry, but honestly, I really hate it down here. Maybe I could try it again some other time."

He looked down at her. His face was pale. She saw the sweat on his upper lip.

She leaned her head against his chest. "I'm frightened," she whispered. "Help me, Nick."

A shudder ran through him. "It's all right," he said. "I'll take care of you, Abby. I'll get us out of here."

He led her back through the narrow tunnel, back to the cage. He gave a signal, and they started up. When she clutched the iron bar, he put his hand over hers.

The other men were waiting for them.

"That sure was a fast trip," Sam said. "I guess it was pretty scary for you, Miz Abby. Maybe next time, it won't be so bad."

"Maybe not, Sam."

"What happened?" Joe asked.

"Loose shale and rock," Nick said.

"You all right?"

Nick jerked a nod.

They walked out into the sunlight. Nick's face was still pale under his tan.

"We've got to go back down," he said to Joe. "The walls and the top have to be shored up again."

Abby looked at him. She had seen his fear. She knew what it would cost him to go back down.

She wanted to help him, but she didn't know how.

## Chapter Eleven

Late that afternoon, Nick knocked on Abby's back door and asked if he could use the phone. "I need to order a new drill," he told her. "If I wait until I get back to town to call, the place will be closed."

Abby held the door open for him. "Come in, Nick," she said.

He followed her through the kitchen into the living room and when he saw that she had built a fire, he said, "I'd better bring some more wood in before I leave. It's supposed to get colder tonight."

"Thanks, I'd appreciate that."

He made the call and went back to the kitchen. "They have the drill," he told her. "I'll send Sam to Denver tomorrow to pick it up."

"Good." Abby took the lid off the pot that was cooking on the stove. "I'm making chili," she said. "Why don't you stay for dinner?"

"Uh, no. I'd better not. I'll just bring in the wood."

"Do you have other plans for dinner?" she said, persisting.

Surprised by her question, Nick hesitated a moment before he answered. "No, I don't, but I thought—"

"Then stay and eat with me."

"All right, Abby. Thanks. I'll just bring in the wood, then."

She smiled as she reached for the cornmeal to make corn bread, and hummed while she beat the batter and poured it into a round pan. When Nick came back with the wood, she said, "We've got a few minutes before dinner. Come in by the fire and have a drink. Is Scotch all right?"

"Scotch is fine." His expression was uncertain, puzzled.

She poured his Scotch and a small sherry for herself. "How's the work going?" she asked, motioning him to Uncle Jonah's worn leather chair.

"Better. We've shored up the tunnel where you and I were this morning. It's safer now." He took a pull of his drink. "I'm sorry about what happened," he said. "About the rocks falling."

"I'm sorry I panicked."

Nick put his drink down. "Let's get one thing straight," he said. "You weren't the one who panicked, it was me. I know what you did, so don't try to deny it."

Abby took a sip of her sherry. "Everybody is afraid of something, Nick. It isn't anything to be ashamed of."

"Isn't it?" Nick got up and stood in front of the fireplace. "I'm a mining engineer. It's my profession, it's what I do." He turned away from her and looked down into the fire. "It doesn't happen every time I go down," he said. "It was the rocks today, when they fell, I mean. It was almost like the other time."

"What other time?"

Nick shook his head.

"Tell me," she said.

And he did. He started talking, and he told her all of it, about Steve, about how they'd met at school and how they'd become friends. "I got him through math," Nick said, "and he got me through physics. After graduation, we worked a mine in Bogotá together. After Bogotá, I went to work for a company in England, and Steve came back here. When I heard about the job in Ecuador, I called him. I told him they wanted two engineers and that the pay was terrific." Nick turned and faced Abby. "He came because of me, and it killed him."

Abby put down her glass and went over to Nick.

"We knew it was bad as soon as we got there," he went on. "But we'd signed a one-year contract, and the money was good. We raised hell with the management and we did everything we could to improve the safety conditions." He shook his head. "But it wasn't enough. The men were spooked. They refused to work one of the tunnels, so Steve and I went down to inspect it. A couple of rocks fell, like they did today, then everything...everything just caved in on top of us."

He looked away from her, but not before Abby saw how ravaged his face was, how tortured his eyes. She wanted to touch him, but knew, somehow, that she shouldn't. Not yet.

"I dug us out. Steve's legs were broken, his chest was crushed." Nick looked away. "He died that night."

She put a hand on his arm and felt a shudder run through him. "What about you? How did you get out?"

"The men dug us out two and a half days later."

"Two and a half days?" Her eyes went wide with shock. He'd been there that long with his dead friend? No wonder he'd panicked today.

"Joe knows what happened in Ecuador," Nick said. "He's the only one except you who's seen me freeze the way I did today."

"Why do you do it, Nick? Why do you go down the shaft, I mean. You're an engineer. You've got men to do the work. You didn't have to go down today. Why did you?"

"I was afraid to trust anybody else to take care of you in case something happened." He ran a hand across his face. "I took care of you, all right," he said bitterly. "I freaked out."

"No," Abby said, shaking her head, "you didn't freak out. Maybe you froze for a minute or two, but that's all it was, Nick."

He rested his hands on the mantel and again looked down into the fire. "Before Jonah died, he asked me to take care of you," Nick said in a low voice. "I haven't done a very good job of it so far, have I?" He turned and faced her. "I apologize for what happened last Saturday night, Abby. I had no right to do what I did. My behavior was inexcusable. You have the right to go out with Jake or anybody else you want to go out with. I don't know what happened to me. I've never behaved that way before. I don't know why I did what I did. I—"

The ring of the phone cut off his words. "I'm sorry," Abby said. "I'll only be a moment." She crossed to the desk and picked up the phone.

"Hello? Oh, uh, hi, Jake. Yes, I'm fine. Friday night?" She looked over at Nick. He returned her gaze, then looked away.

"I'm sorry," she said, "but I'm afraid I can't. Yes, you, too. Yes, of course. I'll be talking to you. Thanks for calling."

She put the phone down.

For a moment, the only sound in the room was the crackling of the fire. "Why did you do that?" Nick said.

"You know why," she answered. And before he could say anything else, she said, "The corn bread's ready. Let's eat, shall we?"

Nick followed her into the kitchen and sat at the table while she dished up big bowls of chili and put the hot corn bread on the table.

"I like buttermilk with chili," she said, "but maybe you'd rather have coffee."

"Buttermilk's fine."

He kept watching her, trying to figure out what was going on. Last Saturday night, she had been weeping and vulnerable and he had been sure she'd never want to see or speak to him again. But tonight, she was perfectly at ease with herself and with him.

He barely touched his food; she finished her bowl of chili, ate three pieces of corn bread and drank two glasses of buttermilk.

When it was time for dessert, she cut two pieces of the cherry pie she'd made that afternoon and suggested they take it, along with their coffee, into the living room.

Nick put another log on the fire. "It's turning colder," he said. "There'll be more snow tonight. I'd better be getting back to town."

"If the weather's too bad, you can spend the night."

A muscle twitched in his cheek. "In Jonah's room?"

Her smile was enigmatic. "If that's where you want to be."

What in the hell was going on? The woman sitting on the opposite end of the sofa from him wasn't the Abigail Sedgewick he knew. If he didn't know better, if she hadn't made it clear how she felt about an affair without a commitment, he'd say she was trying to seduce him.

She looked pretty tonight, infinitely feminine and desirable. She'd pulled her hair back, but it wasn't as severe as it usually was. Tendrils of it drifted about her face and down the back of her slender neck. The rosy pink sweater—just a little bit tighter than she usually wore her sweaters?—did nice things for her breasts. She leaned forward to put her coffee cup down on the table and he could have sworn she wasn't wearing a bra.

And though he had vowed after last Saturday's fiasco that he would never again lay even a pinkie on her, he found himself wanting to pull her over onto his lap, to hold her and to kiss her. He wanted to curl the soft tendrils of her hair around his fingers, to stroke her ears and to kiss the back of her neck. He wanted to slide his hands up under the pink sweater and fondle her breasts. He wanted... Lord! He had to get out of here!

He stood up so abruptly, he spilled his coffee. "I've got to get back to town," he said.

Abby didn't move. "I don't want you to go," she said.

Nick stared down at her. "Do you know what you're saying?"

"I know."

"Do you want me to spend the night?"

"Yes, Nick."

"In Jonah's room?"

"No, Nick."

He took her hand and brought her up beside him. "Are you sure, Abby?"

"Yes," she said. "I'm sure."

"Are you ready for bed, then?"

She moved closer and rested her head upon his chest. She felt the beating of his heart against her cheek. A sigh trembled through her, and she said, "Yes, Nick, I'm ready."

Outside, the wind howled, and snow and sleet beat hard against the windowpanes. But it didn't matter. Nothing mattered because she was here with Nick and it was a home-coming, a welcome joy to be with him again.

She still wasn't sure why she had decided to accept what Nick had to give. She only knew that she loved him. It was as simple and as complex as that. Somewhere in the back of her mind there was the hope that by loving him, by giving him all the love she had, she could make up for the love he had missed. And perhaps someday, from her loving, he would learn to love.

He held her so gently, he kissed her so tenderly, and when he covered her body with his, she tightened her arms around him and whispered, "I like to feel your weight on me. I like the way you tease and move." She lifted her body to his. "Like this, Nick," she said. "Like this."

He gasped with pleasure. "Tell me," he whispered. "Tell me what else you like."

"I like you inside me," she said, and pressed her hand against the small of his back to urge him closer. "I like to feel you swell and grow and move against me." Their bodies merged, and she moaned against his mouth. "Like this, Nick. Like this."

She rose to meet his every stroke, his every thrust, glorying in a depth of feeling that threatened to overwhelm her.

"It's so good," he whispered against her throat. "Oh, Abby. I've missed you so." He rained kisses on her face, her throat and her breasts. And when it became too much, he cried, "Yes, now...yes...oh, yes," in a voice that was incoherent with passion.

And when she cried her own completion, he tightened his arms around her and held her as though he would never let her go.

There had never been a time in Abby's life as happy as this time. Joyous in the burgeoning love she felt for Nick, she did not think of what would happen tomorrow or the day after that. There was only today and the richness of the time they were with each other.

They had dinner together every night, sometimes in the coziness of her kitchen, sometimes in a restaurant. During the week, because Nick said it wouldn't be a good idea for the men to find out about their new relationship, he left her before midnight. But he was with her from Friday afternoon when the men had left until Monday morning when the mine opened. If the night guard Jacinto Sanchez was aware that Nick spent each weekend with her, he never gave any indication of it.

In the evening, they sat together in front of the fireplace, and sometimes, when the ground was white with snow and the windows were silver with frost, they made love there. Those were magic times for Abby. She was mesmerized by love and by the flames that crackled and reached like fingers of fire, casting shadows on the wall, shadows of their two bodies joined in love.

She would watch the subtle play of his shoulder muscles, the smooth, slim line of hip, the long, strong legs entwined with hers. She would run her trembling hands down his body, touching, tasting, luxuriating in him. Like a good and willing pupil, she delighted in letting him teach her the many ways of love.

When one night he set her astride his hips, she said, "Like this, Nick? Is this what you want, darling?" And, oh, how good it was to be with him this way. To look down at his face, to watch his eyes when she took him into her, to hear him whisper her name in the throes of his passion, and to know that she was pleasing him.

Pleasing Nick. Loving Nick. He filled her every thought, her every dream. She had never been so at peace with herself, had never been so sure of what she was doing. For the first time in her life, she understood what it was to love a man. Her body had never been more sensitive, more aware. She marveled at the sparkle of sunlight on snow, the shadowed purple mountains, barren now in the cold of winter, the smell of wood smoke in the clear, morning air. Food had never tasted better. Music had never sounded sweeter. All of her senses, her very pores, tingled with life.

Nick had only to look at her in a certain way to kindle the fire that lay smoldering within her. He had only to hold out his hand and say, "Come here, Abby," for the spark to become a flame.

She was his without reservation, totally, completely his. And Nick responded. He was a tender, caring lover who took her to the heights of an ecstasy she had not even dreamed existed. When he left her on the nights he had to return to town, he kissed her so tenderly, so lovingly that sometimes, tears came to her eyes. "I'll see you in the morning, sweetheart," he always said, and he would kiss her cheeks and her lips, and then, because they both knew that if he lingered he would not go, he would tuck the blankets close around her and leave.

One morning, dressed in jeans and boots, bundled in a heavy sweater and a mackinaw, a red, knitted stocking cap pulled over her hair, Abby took a big thermos of hot coffee out to the men.

"I want to learn everything I can about mining," she said. "I want to know what the daily production is, how the tracks and the cars work, how you separate the gold from the rock or quartz or whatever it is. How you know which tunnel to work, which tunnels have already been worked. I want to know everything."

"Lord a'mighty," Abel said, "you sure hidey are kin to Jonah."

"You're right about that." Abby glanced at Uncle Jonah's watch on her left wrist. "It's seven-thirty," she said. "Shouldn't we be getting to work?"

"You've created a monster, Nick," Joe said.

And Nick, barely suppressing a grin, answered, "I've always wondered what it would be like working for a woman."

"With," Abby said. "Not for."

She listened carefully to everything Nick told her. She made notes, she asked questions. A week later, she insisted on going into the mine. When she picked up a hard hat, Sam, who was going to take her down, said, "That one won't do," and when Abby raised a questioning eyebrow, he handed her a hat that had Miz Abby written on the front of it.

Inordinately pleased, Abby thanked him and fastened the battery belt around her waist.

"You sure you want to do it again?" Nick asked.

"I'm sure."

"Take the watch off and leave it here," he said. "It's too big on your wrist. You might catch it on a piece of shale." He squeezed her shoulder. "I know Sam will take good care of you," he murmured, "but I hate the thought of you going down again."

"But I want to learn about mining, Nick, and the only way I can do that is to see for myself how everything's done."

"You do exactly what Sam tells you to do. Stay with him, don't go off in any direction by yourself."

"Don't worry, I won't."

Sam poked his head in the office door. "You ready?" he asked.

"Ready," Abby said.

She went out with him and stepped into the cage. Though she hated the dark eeriness of the descent so far below the surface of the earth, she made herself ask what she hoped were intelligent questions.

Once they were in the narrow, low tunnel, she listened to everything Sam said.

"When we're drilling, we use a face mask," he told her. "We got water dripping in to help with the dust, but we still need the masks to filter out the bad stuff." He guided her forward. "This here's the tunnel we were working on before Jonah took sick. He was sure there was more gold, that's why he kept working till he almost dropped, and that's why me'n the boys are glad you and Nick have got the Lucky Lady going again. Jonah'd be pleased." Sam looked at her through the darkness. "Ain't many women would go into a mine the way you're doing, Miz Abby. If Jonah was alive, I don't guess he'd want you down here, but, Lord, he'd be proud that you were."

Sam showed Abby how the pneumatic drill worked, and he explained how the ore was loaded into the cars and sent up to the surface. Every now and then, he'd ask her if she wanted to go back up, and each time he did, she said, "No, not yet."

He led her toward the far end of the tunnel. "Tomorrow, we're going to open up this end," he said.

"How?" Abby wanted to know.

"Dynamite."

"You're going to dynamite down here? Isn't that dangerous?"

"Not if you know what you're doing and how much to use. If we didn't use dynamite, we'd be here a month of Sundays."

"Who'll do it?"

"Me'n Nick most likely."

Abby's hands curled into fists in the pockets of her mackinaw. She thought of Nick's fear. And of the danger.

In a little while, she and Sam got into the cage and rode back to the surface, where Nick was waiting for her.

"How did it go?" he asked. "You didn't get spooked?"

"She was a real trooper," Sam told him. "Didn't hardly bat an eyelash all the time we were there. Jonah would'a been proud of her."

Nick nodded. "You're a hell of a woman, Miz Abby," he said with a smile. And even though the other men were watching, he picked her up off her feet and kissed her.

* * *

That night when Nick rose from the bed to leave, Abby said, "No, don't go. Stay with me tonight."

"I shouldn't," he said. "The men—"

"You can be there before they arrive. They won't know. Please, Nick?"

He hesitated, then he came back into the bed with her. They made love again, and when it was over, he curled himself around her back and went to sleep.

But it was a long time that night before Abby slept. She lay in the dark and thought about Nick, and that tomorrow, he would go into the mine with dynamite.

## Chapter Twelve

Abby hadn't known how painful waiting could be. She sat at the desk in the mine office and listened to the men. None of them would go down until Nick and Sam had finished dynamiting.

"Nothin' much to it," Abel reassured her. "What they do is, they drill some holes in the wall and stick a cartridge of dynamite in. Then they attach a powder explosive to the cartridge and run that out aways. That's injected into the dynamite and lighted. So long as they don't use too much, it's perfectly safe."

"Dynamiting's never safe." Moe Brady stuck a piece of gum into his mouth. "I remember a few years back a fella over at that mine near Squaw Gulch used too much of the powder explosive and it blew him to kingdom come. Wasn't enough of him left to—"

"¡Cállate!" Paco said. "Shut up! What are you trying to do, scare the Señorita Abby to death?"

"I was just talking, making the time go," Moe said.

"You've talked enough," Joe snapped. And to Abby, he said, "Nick knows what he's doing. Both he and Sam have done the same thing dozens of times. There's no need to worry."

Then why did Abel light one cigarette after another? Why did Joe pace back and forth across the office floor and keep looking at his watch?

"How long will it take?" Abby asked.

"A couple of hours," Joe said. "They've got to drill the holes before they can do anything else. Then they have to string and inject the powder explosive."

"They'll be in the other section of the tunnel when they set off the dynamite?"

"Not really in another section," he said. "But they'll be well back."

"I see." Abby rubbed wet palms against the sides of her jeans. It was useless to pretend that she wasn't worried because she was. The thought of Nick so far below ground with dangerous explosives terrified her. She thought of his fear, of the two and a half days he'd spent trapped underground with a dead friend. If anything like that should happen again... She tried not to think about that. There wasn't anything she could do. She had to wait. Wait.

Two hours went by. Two and a half.

She paced up and down in front of the mine, and finally, she and the other men went down to the cage. They were silent now. Not a one of them said anything while they waited for Nick and Sam to come back up.

"How much longer?" Abby asked Joe.

"They should be up anytime now." His face was as tense as hers. "Why don't you go on up to the house? I'll send one of the men over as soon as they're up."

"I couldn't do that," she said.

Another half hour went by before they heard the creak of the cable and saw the cage ascending. Thank God, Abby thought. They're all right. They...

Sam was alone in the cage.

"Where's Nick?" Joe's voice was strained, anxious.

"Patching up and clearing out some of the rock. He told me to come on up. Said I should send Moe and Abel down to help."

Abby started toward the cage. "I'm going down," she said.

Joe took her arm. "What they're doing now is man's work. You'd only be in the way."

Abby glared at him, hands on her hips, ready to defy him and every one of the other men if she had to. She wanted to be with Nick, and Joe couldn't stop her.

"I want to make sure he's all right," she said.

"Nick wouldn't like it." Joe's voice was firm. "He wouldn't like it at all."

Abby swallowed hard. Joe was right. If she went down, she'd embarrass him in front of the other men; he'd hate that.

"I—I just wanted to make sure everything was all right," she managed to say. "In the tunnel, I mean." She fought to summon a smile. "You'll have to forgive me, Joe, but this is all pretty new to me. I'll go on back to the house now, but I'll be back this afternoon to finish up some of the paperwork in the office."

She made it to the house on legs that were shaking so badly, she could barely walk. She sank down on the back-porch steps, put her head against her knees and wished she had fallen in love with a plumber, a bricklayer or a C.P.A. But she hadn't. She'd fallen in love with Nick, and there wasn't anything she could do about it.

Finally, she went into the kitchen and began to scrub the cupboard doors. When that was done, she took everything out of the refrigerator, cleaned it and put everything back. She had just finished scrubbing the floor when Nick came to the back door.

His clothes were dirty and so was his face; she'd never been so glad to see anybody in her life.

"I just wanted to let you know that everything went well," he said. "The men have knocked off for lunch, and I thought..." He stopped. "Abby? What—"

She launched herself at him, almost incoherent in her relief. "I was so afraid," she said as she wept against his throat. "I hate it when you go into the mine. I don't want you to ever do it again. Promise me, Nick. Please... promise that after this, you'll let somebody else do it. I can't stand it when you're down there. I don't want you going down again. I was so scared...." She clung to him, weak with relief now that he was safe.

"It's what I do," he said.

"But you hate it. You're afraid. You..."

He put his hands on her shoulders and put her away from him. "Yes, I'm afraid," he said coldly. "I'm ashamed that I am, and I'm ashamed that you saw my fear."

"Nick, I—"

He held up his hand, silencing her. "It's my profession, Abby, and I won't allow my fear or you or anyone else to keep me from doing what I do." His voice hardened. "Or ever tell me what to do. Is that clear?"

Stung, she pulled away from him. "It's perfectly clear."

"Joe said you'd wanted to go down after me. Is that true?"

Abby wet her lips. "I—I just wanted to make sure you were safe."

Nick's mouth tightened. "Don't you ever do anything like that again in front of the men. Ever!" He turned away and started out of the kitchen. "I've got to get back," he said. "Tonight, I have some things to do in town. I'll see you at the mine tomorrow."

"Very well."

He hesitated as though he were about to say something else. Instead, his face still tight with anger, he went out the door and down the path toward the mine.

Abby watched him leave. She had made a mistake. She wouldn't let it happen again.

It snowed that night, and the temperature dropped to the zero mark. When it was time for dinner, Abby opened a can of soup and had a sparse and solitary meal at the kitchen table.

She kept waiting for the phone to ring, but it didn't. A little after eleven, she put on a flannel nightgown and taking her robe, a pillow and a blanket, went into the living room. She'd sleep on the sofa in front of the fire tonight; her bed was too cold and empty without Nick.

But even there, with the dim glow of the flames to light and warm the room, and with Jasper so close by, Abby felt isolated and alone. It was strange, she thought, how quickly you could become accustomed to sleeping with someone. She and Nick hadn't been together long, but she missed him with an ache that was almost physical. And it came to her as she lay staring into the firelight, that as important as the sexual part of sleeping together was, the warmth and the comfort of that other person next to you was equally important. She had grown accustomed to hearing his whisper of good-night as she drifted to sleep, to reaching out and knowing that he was there next to her.

And to awaken with him beside her in the morning was a pleasure unlike anything she had ever known.

She had decided to accept Nick on his terms, without any promises on his part, any word of commitment. Now another condition had been added—she was never to tell him what he could or could not do. If she was afraid for him, she must sublimate that fear. "Stifle yourself," Archie Bunker used to tell poor Edith. And that's what Abby was supposed to do with her fear, and with her yearning for love and commitment. Stifle it.

Could she do it? That was the big question.

Finally, still troubled by her thoughts, Abby closed her eyes.

She didn't know how long she had been asleep when she heard the noise. She wasn't sure what it was that had awakened her, then she heard Jasper's warning growl.

"What is it, boy?" Abby sat up and reached for her robe. "What do you hear, Jasper? Is something out there?"

She got up, stepped into her slippers, put on her robe and went to the desk to get the flashlight. With Jasper beside her, she leaned close to the door. Everything was quiet and she was about to turn away when she heard a muffled cry, a thrashing about, then a sharp crack of sound, like a car backfiring or a firecracker...

Or a gun.

Jasper raced from the window to the door, barking, growling. He threw himself at the door, ears back, teeth bared.

Abby held his collar. "Easy, boy," she whispered, trying to fight the fear that gripped her. "Easy."

A car door slammed. An engine roared. She pulled back the curtain and peered out into the night in time to see the red taillights of a car disappearing down the road that led to the highway.

"It's okay," she told the dog—and herself. "Whoever it was has gone. He—"

Something thumped against the steps and the words died in her throat. Jasper began barking again, and this time, Abby didn't try to quiet him. She raced to the fireplace and standing on her tiptoes, reached for the rifle that hung on the wall there.

Gripping it, she went back to the door. She heard another thump, almost like someone knocking, not on the door, but on the steps. Her hands tightened around the rifle. She heard a feeble cry, and the words, *Ayúdeme... por... por favor. Ayúdeme.*

"Jacinto?" Abby called out. "Jacinto, is that you?"

There was no answer. She snapped the porch light on and slowly, cautiously, without taking the chain off the door, opened it a few inches.

"Jacinto?"

There was no answer. She hefted the rifle, took the chain off the door and stepped out onto the porch. Jasper pushed ahead of her, barking, then the bark turned into a whine, and she saw the body lying halfway up the steps.

She leaned the rifle against the side of the porch and ran to the fallen man. He was facedown. "Jacinto?" she cried, and when he didn't move, she tried to turn him over. He was heavy, but she managed.

He was unconscious, his face pale in the porch light. She felt for a pulse; it was slow, feeble. She opened his mackinaw and her fingers came away sticky with blood.

Abby sucked in her breath. The flannel shirt beneath the mackinaw was soaked with blood, too, but she made herself unbutton it, and then she saw the open wound six inches below his armpit.

Don't panic, she told herself. She could phone for an ambulance, but by the time it got all the way out here and back into town, Jacinto would very likely bleed to death.

The bleeding, she had to stop the bleeding.

She ran into the house, into the bathroom, grabbed a towel and tape, and raced back out to the porch. In the dim light from the porch, she saw the blood pumping out of the wound. She pressed the towel against it and held it in place with the tape.

Hurrying back into the house at a dead run, Abby shrugged out of her robe and pulled a pair of jeans and a sweater over her nightgown. Then grabbing her purse, not even bothering to get a coat, and wearing only her bedroom slippers, she ran out of the house and got into the station wagon.

She cursed in frustration because the engine was cold and she had to take the time to warm it up. She made herself slow count to ten before she put the car into gear. Then she drove around to the front of the house, as close to the steps as she could get.

Jasper started barking again when he saw her. Leaving the engine running, she got out of the wagon, lowered the tailgate and ran to Jacinto.

She tried to lift him under his shoulders, but he was a compact man, square and solid, and Abby moaned in frustration because she knew she couldn't lift him by herself.

"Jacinto!" she cried. "Jacinto, can you hear me?"

He groaned. His eyelids fluttered.

"I've got to get you to the hospital," she said. "You've got to help me, Jacinto."

He struggled to sit up. *"Un hombre,"* he whispered. *"Malo,* bad. Shot me."

"I know, I know. But you're going to be all right." She looped one of his arms around her shoulder. "I'm going to help you," she told him, "but I can't manage by myself. Try to stand. Try to get on your feet."

"*Si....*" He took a ragged breath and staggered up. He swayed, unsteady on his feet and leaned heavily on Abby.

"Only two steps down," she said. "You can do it, Jacinto. Come on. One step. Okay, now, one more."

When he slumped onto the back of the wagon, she climbed in and with her hands under his shoulders, panting with effort, she managed to drag him all the way in. She slammed the back door shut, then covered him with a blanket she kept in the back.

"You're going to be all right now," she said. But Jacinto didn't answer, and she knew he had lost consciousness.

She climbed into the front seat and when she started out of the driveway, Jasper began to bark, so she opened the door and said, "Get in, boy," because it occurred to her that whoever had shot Jacinto might be waiting on the dark and lonely road leading to the highway. She'd left the rifle on the porch and she didn't want to go back for it. Jasper would be some protection in case she was stopped.

For all the years Abby had driven, she had never exceeded the speed limit. But she did tonight. She had to be careful on the dirt road because of Jacinto, but once she reached the highway, she got the speedometer up to ninety and kept it there.

"Hold on," she kept saying under her breath. "Hold on, Jacinto."

She reached the hospital in a little under ten minutes, pulled up at the entrance with her horn blowing, and when she had brought the wagon to a stop, ran into the hospital crying, "Help me! I've got a wounded man in the car."

A nurse looked up from her desk, startled, eyes wide.

"He's bleeding to death!" Abby shouted.

The woman grabbed the phone and snapped an order. A young man with a beard came running from a room on the right and grabbed a gurney. "Where is he?" he said.

"In front." Abby ran out to the station wagon and yanked the tailgate down.

The nurse and the young man eased Jacinto onto the gurney. The blood had soaked through the makeshift bandage.

They wheeled him into the hospital just as an older man rounded the corner of the reception room. "What happened?" he asked Abby.

"He's been shot. Out at the mine. The Lucky Lady."

"Tell surgery I've got an emergency," the man said to the nurse. "Stat!" And to the young man, he said, "Let's go, Mike!"

They left Abby standing there in the hall.

When the nurse got off the phone, she asked Abby for information. Abby told her all that she knew.

"It's going to be a while," the nurse said. "Why don't you go on home. There's really no sense in your waiting around here. It'll be morning soon. You can come back then. Meantime, I'll call the sheriff. He'll want to talk to you."

"Jake," Abby said.

"That's right, dear. Jake McClinton." The nurse looked at Abby. "Are you all right?"

"I'm—I'm fine," Abby said. "Fine."

"You don't have a coat."

"I left in a hurry." Abby started toward the door. "Take care of him," she said. "I'll be back."

*Sam said, "You need a bigger stick of dynamite, boy. One big enough to blow the whole danged mountain."*

*As though in slow motion, the older man wired the sticks together—six, seven, eight, nine.*

*"No!" Nick tried to shout, but the words came out weak, whispered, faint. "No! You'll blow us up!" he tried to run toward Sam, but his feet were stuck in the shale and all he could do was watch in horror while Sam struck a match and held it to the fuse. He saw the flame, watched it sizzle slowly up the cord.*

*He had to stop it, had to yank the cord free before it reached the dynamite. Another three seconds... Oh, God, help. Help!*

*The alarm bell sounded, shrill, sharp, warning of the cave-in. He had to get out. Find Steve.*

*This time I'll get us out.... This time...*

Nick came awake with his heart pounding like a revved up engine, breath coming fast, every muscle so taut with strain that his skin hurt. He lay gasping, still caught in the throes of the dream, wondering why the alarm bell was still ringing. It took a minute or two to realize that he was awake and that it was his doorbell.

He snapped on the light and looked at the clock. It was a little after three. Who in the hell...? He grabbed the black terry-cloth robe off the foot of his bed and hurried into the living room.

"Who is it?" he called out.

"Abby." When she spoke, a dog began to bark.

He opened the door. "Abby? What...?" He saw her face, saw her shivering in just the sweater and the jeans. She wasn't wearing a coat. She had bedroom slippers on her feet.

Nick pulled her into the room and quieted Jasper down. "What's the matter, Abby? What...?" He saw the blood on her hands, on her sweater and jeans. "My God! You've been hurt. What happened?"

Her teeth were chattering, but she managed to answer, "I'm okay. It's Jacinto. Somebody...somebody shot him."

Nick stared at her. "Jacinto? Shot? Where is he?"

"In the hospital. I drove him in."

"But what happened? My God, Abby, what...?" He suddenly realized how cold she was, and he took his robe off, put it around her and led her to the sofa. When she was seated, he went to a cabinet and took out a bottle of brandy and poured a splash into a glass. "Drink this," he said when he went back to her.

"No, I—"

"Drink it."

She downed the brandy in one gulp and sputtered when the fiery liquid burned its way down to her stomach. "Better," she said. "Better now."

"Can you tell me what happened?"

"I was asleep...on the sofa, because you..." She looked at him, then away. "I heard a sound that woke me. Jasper was growling. Then I heard a noise. At first I thought it was a car backfiring or a firecracker. But it was a gunshot. I—I got the rifle down from above the fireplace and I went out, and Jacinto was lying halfway up the stairs. He was unconscious and I—I rolled him over, and he was bleeding—"

Nick stopped her. "Easy, honey," he said. "Easy."

Abby took a deep breath. "What time is it?" she asked.

"A little after three. Was the hospital going to call Jake?"

Abby nodded. "A nurse said I could talk to him in the morning."

Nick reached for the phone. "We'd better give him a call now. While I'm doing that, why don't you go out into the kitchen and make us some tea. The kitchen is past the dining room on your right. I'll call you if Jake wants to talk to you.''

"All right, Nick." So tired now that she could barely put one foot ahead of the other, Abby did as he said.

The kitchen, much larger than hers, was neat and utilitarian. There was a dishwasher, a microwave oven and all kinds of appliances that looked as though they had never been used. She put water on to boil, and found the tea, the sugar and the coffee mugs. She could hear Nick's voice from the other room, but she couldn't make out what he was saying. When the tea was ready, she took everything into the living room on a tray.

Jasper was curled up at the foot of the sofa. Nick had just put the phone down.

"The hospital had already called him," Nick said. "He'll meet us there at seven-thirty." He took the tray from her and put it on the coffee table. "I called Paco, too. He was going to call the rest of the family before he went to the hospital."

Nick handed her a mug of tea. "Drink this," he said, "then you'd better get to bed."

Abby shook her head. "I want to go back to the hospital. I want to know how he is. There . . . there was so much blood, Nick. I've—never seen anything like that before. I . . ." Her hands began to shake and the tea spilled over the side of the mug.

He took it from her and put it down on the table. "I'm putting you to bed," he said. And before she could protest, he picked her up off the sofa.

"No. I'm all right. I'm—"

"Shh." He held her against his chest and carried her across the room and down the hall to his bedroom, where he put her down.

She sat on the edge of the bed, and he helped her out of his robe, and when she pulled the sweater over her head, he saw that she had her nightgown on underneath. He took her slippers and her jeans off.

When she lay down, she looked up at him and said, "You were angry with me today."

"That doesn't matter now." He got into bed beside her and drew her into his arms. And it was true: nothing mattered except that Abby was here with him and that she was safe. What if Jacinto hadn't been there, guarding the mine and the house? What if Abby had been shot and was lying in the hospital now?

He held her close, one hand against the back of her head to press her tight against his shoulder because she was trembling with cold and with fear.

"It's all right," he said. "I'm here, Abby. You're safe, sweetheart. Go to sleep now. I won't leave you. I'm here, Abby."

And at last, too exhausted to keep her eyes open, warm in the shelter of Nick's arms, she slept.

But Nick didn't. Who had been prowling around? he wondered. What had they wanted? Why had they shot Jacinto Sanchez? Again and again, the thought came back, what if it had been Abby? What if they had broken into the house? And since there had been one violent attack, would there be others?

Nick tightened his arms protectively around Abby. She wasn't safe living out at the mine, not even with a guard. If she wouldn't move into town, then he'd move out to Jonah's with her. No matter what she said, he wasn't going to let her go back there alone.

When he woke her a few hours later, she stirred in his arms, unsure of where she was for a moment. Moving slightly away from him she asked, "What time is it?"

"Six-thirty. Go take your shower while I fix breakfast."

"Call the hospital first," she said.

Nick hesitated, but when she made no move to get up, he reached for the phone and dialed the hospital. "I want to ask about Jacinto Sanchez?" he said. "He was admitted early this morning." He looked at Abby. "About three?"

She nodded.

"About three," he said. "Yes, thanks, I'll wait."

Abby moved closer and put her hand on his arm because she needed the assurance of him beside her.

"Yes," Nick said into the phone. "I see. Thank you."

Abby's mouth went dry. "What—"

"He's in intensive care. It's too early to tell yet whether . . . whether or not he's going to live."

"Oh, God." Abby covered her face with her hands.

"Jacinto's a strong man, Abby. He'll make it. I know he will."

"I want to go to the hospital."

"Not until you've had something to eat." He kissed her, a light and friendly kiss, then pulled back the blankets and said, "Go take that shower."

She stood under the hot water for a long while. By the time she came out, Nick had the table set and the bacon was frying. "Coffee's on the stove," he said. "How do you like your eggs?"

"Over easy."

He cracked four of them into another frying pan. "I've called Merilee," he said. "I asked her to bring some clothes over for you."

"Merilee?" Abby resisted telling him that she'd rather walk barefoot through the snow than borrow anything from Merilee.

"She said she'd be right over."

"Wonderful."

Nick put a plate in front of her. "Merilee's a good kid. The two of you got off on the wrong foot, that's all."

"Sure." Abby took a bite of her egg. It was cooked just the way she liked it.

"Jake called a little while ago." Nick passed her a piece of toast. "He and a couple of his deputies had already been out to the mine. They checked it and the house but they didn't find anything. He's anxious to talk to you."

"I don't know what I can tell him. Everything happened so fast, Nick. Maybe Jacinto can tell him something. I mean, if he..." She shook her head and pushed her plate away.

Nick pushed it back. "Eat," he ordered. "I—" The bell rang. "That'll be Merilee," he said.

Abby frowned down at her plate when he went to answer the door, and she grimaced when she heard, "Hi, Nicky," and the sound of a kiss.

"We're in the kitchen," Nick said. "Come on out."

Abby forced a smile when they appeared. "Hi, Merilee," she said.

"Hi." Merilee had a package under her arm. "I brought you some shoes and a jacket." She put the package down on the table. "I hope the shoes fit. I have very small feet."

The tennis shoes were red with silver polka dots, and the fleece-lined jacket was hot pink. Abby looked inside one of the shoes. "They're a size larger than I take," she said, "but that's okay. I can pull the laces tight."

Merilee pursed her mouth and frowned. "How's Jacinto?" she asked Nick.

"He's in intensive care."

"That's terrible. He's such a nice old coot. I hope he makes it." She raised an eyebrow at Abby. "Couldn't you have done something? Jonah had a rifle. Couldn't you have used it?''

"By the time I got the rifle, whoever shot Jacinto had gotten into his car and was gone.''

"Abby managed to get Jacinto into her station wagon and get him to the hospital,'' Nick said. "She probably saved his life.''

"But whoever shot him got away.'' The way Merilee said it made it sound like it was Abby's fault that Jacinto had been shot and that his assailant had escaped.

"We're meeting Jake at the hospital.'' Nick glanced at his watch. "We'd better get going.''

"I'll go with you.'' Merilee looked at Abby. "If you don't mind, of course.''

"Why would I mind?'' Abby asked between clenched teeth. She put the tennis shoes on and picked up the hot pink jacket.

"Aren't you going to fix your face, dear? I mean...well, it isn't any of my business, but you really look pretty awful this morning. Maybe makeup would help.''

Abby put her arms in the jacket. "I doubt it,'' she said. "This is the way I usually look, Merilee.''

Merilee cocked her head to one side and her lips formed a small round O.

Nick cleared his throat. "Well,'' he said. "I guess we'd better get going.''

## Chapter Thirteen

Paco Sanchez was at the hospital, pacing up and down in front of the Intensive Care Unit when Abby, Nick and Merilee arrived.

Nick went to the other man and clapping a hand on his shoulder, asked, "How is he?"

"He's conscious. The doctors say that's a good sign. The sheriff is with him now."

"I'm so sorry about your brother," Abby said.

"The doctor told me that he's alive because you got him here so quickly, *señorita*. I thank you for that. He's *muy fornido,* a husky man. How did you manage to get him into your car?"

"Adrenaline," Abby said with a slight smile. "We all do what we have to in an emergency. And Jacinto helped. He's a strong man, Paco. He's going to make it."

The door to the ICU opened and Jake McClinton came out. He nodded to Paco, said, "Hi, Nick. Hi, Merilee," and put his arms around Abby. "Are you all right?" he asked. "When I heard what had happened, I thought you'd been hurt, too."

"No, I'm fine, Jake."

"But it could have been you, Abby. What if whoever shot Jacinto had broken into the house? You can't stay out there alone. You've got to move into town where you'll be safe."

"She won't be staying alone," Nick said. "I'm moving out there with her."

Jake's jaw dropped. "What?"

"I'm moving in with Abby."

"Wait a minute." Abby looked from Jake to Nick. "You can't do that. You—"

"Do you want to move into town?"

"No, of course not, but—"

"Then I'm moving in with you. That way, I'll be close to the mine if anything happens."

Jake's face was strained, his lips were tight and disapproving. "Let Nick stay out at Jonah's if he wants to," he said. "You can find an apartment in town, and if you can't, maybe you could move in with Merilee."

Move in with Merilee? I'd rather live with a two-headed cottonmouth with a nasty disposition, Abby thought. But all she said was "I don't think so, Jake. I like the house and I'm comfortable there. Besides, I refuse to be frightened away."

"Then it's settled. I'm moving in today." Nick frowned at the arm Jake still had around Abby's shoulders.

But Jake only drew Abby closer. "I'd like to ask you a few questions about last night," he said. "Let's go on down to one of the waiting rooms so we can talk."

"Of course, Jake."

"I'm going in to see Jacinto." Nick turned away, shoulders bunched, fists clenched. Jake McClinton was one of his best friends, but it was all he could do to keep from going after him. He wanted to pull him away from Abby, slam him up against the wall and yell, "What in the hell do you think you're doing with my woman?"

His woman? Dammit! What was wrong with him?

"Jake's been hot to trot from the minute he met her," Merilee said, breaking in on Nick's thoughts. "But it sure beats me why he'd bother. She probably wears iron pants and a girdle to bed." Merilee looked up at Nick. "But I don't suppose you'd know about that, would you, Nick? Or maybe you're aiming to find out. Is that why you're moving in with her? You a little curious, Nicky? Decided maybe you're going to change your luck?"

His face went still. "We've been friends for a long time," he said. "I hope we can keep on being friends, but don't interfere in my personal life, Merilee. Abby's my partner. She's a damn fine woman, and I like her. A lot. I'm moving out to the mine to make sure nothing happens to either her or the mine."

"You're going to be living with her."

"For as long as she's here," he said.

Two bright spots of color appeared in Merilee's cheeks. "You're making a mistake," she said quietly. "Abby Sedgewick isn't a love-'em-and-leave-'em type, Nicky. If she's playing, she's playing for keeps. If you don't watch your step, you'll wind up with a lasso around your neck."

"Nobody lassoes me," he said. "Nobody." He turned away from Merilee. "I'm going to see Jacinto now. Stick around if you want a ride home."

"I'll stick around," she said. "And I'll be right here waiting when Abby goes back to Ohio. Remember that, Nicky."

* * *

There was very little that Abby could tell Jake. She had awakened a little after two this morning. She'd heard what sounded like a scuffle, then a gunshot. She had seen the taillights of a car, but no, she didn't know the make or the model and she hadn't seen the license plate.

"Have you had any trouble out at the mine?" Jake asked. "Any problem with the men? Anything?"

"Everybody gets along," Abby said. "The men have all worked for both Nick and Uncle Jonah before."

"Have you heard any more from that outfit in Denver?"

"Nick and I had a meeting with Simon Taylor. I refused his offer. We've heard nothing since then. You don't think they had anything to do with it, do you?"

"I don't know, Abby, but I sure am going to check 'em out." Jake stood up, hat in his hand, hesitating before he said, "There's something going on between you and Nick, isn't there?"

And when Abby didn't answer, he said, "I'd sure appreciate it if you'd tell me the truth."

Abby liked Jake McClinton almost as much as any man she'd ever known. She didn't want to hurt him, but she didn't want to lie to him, either.

"Yes," she said. "There's something going on between us. I don't know what it is, Jake, and I don't know if it will last. But for now . . . yes."

"Are you in love with him?"

"Jake, I . . ." She took a shaky breath. "Yes," she said. "I'm in love with him."

"Lord." Jake shook his head, and his blue eyes were sad. "Then there's nothing I can do, at least right now, is there? But I want you to know I'm your friend, Abby, and that I'll be here and waiting when it's over." He took her hand. "And it will be over one of these days because Nick's not a marrying man, never has been, never will be. You ever want anybody to talk to, I'm here for you. No strings, no demands. You remember that."

Tears stung Abby's eyes. She couldn't speak; she could only nod.

"I'm going to be investigating whatever it is that's going on out at the mine. Meantime, don't go out alone. If you need to go into town, have Nick or one of the men go with you. And if you think of anything else you can tell me, call. If anything turns up on my end, I'll let you know."

"Thank you, Jake." She stood on her tiptoes and kissed him, a gentle kiss on his mouth. "I'll call you," she said.

"I wish..." He swallowed so hard his Adam's apple bobbed painfully. "I reckon you know what I wish," he murmured.

He turned away and collided with Nick. "Sorry," Jake mumbled over his shoulder. But he didn't stop, he kept on going.

"What was that all about?" Nick asked.

"Nothing. He...he asked me about last night, about the car and whether or not I'd seen anything. How's Jacinto? Did you speak to the doctor?"

"Yeah, I did. He thinks that with a little luck, Jacinto's going to make it."

"Thank God."

"I was able to talk to Jacinto for a couple of minutes. He barely got a look at the man who shot him. He heard something, but before he could do anything, the other man jumped him. He says he remembers seeing the gun and trying to grab it."

Nick hesitated, not sure he should tell her the rest, then decided that for her own safety, she had to know everything.

"There's something else," he said. "When Jacinto was down, he remembers the gunman standing over him saying, 'Next time, it will be them.'"

"Them?" Abby's eyes widened. "Us?"

"I'm afraid so. That's why I'm moving in with you."

She looked at Nick, her eyes questioning. "Is that the only reason?"

"What do you think?"

"I think it doesn't matter what your reasons are. I'm glad you're going to be with me."

And she did not add, for whatever time we have.

When Nick moved in that day, he explained to the men that because of what had happened, he had decided to stay in Jonah's house so that he could keep an eye on things. He said the same thing to the Crimmses and to Evie, ignoring Evie's crooked eyebrow and her murmured, "Hmm."

Though he had insisted on moving in with Abby and knew that he should, at the last minute, Nick hesitated because he had never lived with a woman before. He liked his privacy; he hated the idea of sharing a bathroom with a woman. If he didn't feel like shaving on a Sunday morning but chose, instead, to read the Sunday paper wearing old, grungy clothes with his feet propped up on a hassock, that's what he wanted to do. A weekend in Aspen was as much closeness as he'd ever wanted.

But it was different with Abby. For one thing, she was as neat and tidy as anyone he'd ever known. She didn't hang pantyhose on the curtain rod or leave wet towels strewed over the bathroom floor. On the other hand, if he left his boots in the living room at night or hung his pants over a chair instead of in the closet, she didn't complain.

During the day, they worked side by side in the mine office because she insisted on learning every aspect of the operation. She read all the books she could find about mining, studied charts and went through all of the records that had been kept when the mine had been in full operation.

"Three-twentieths of an ounce of gold for a ton of rock!" she'd said when Nick explained how the rock was milled. "That's like one-ninth of an ounce."

"That's right," Nick said. "But when you hit a vein, the profit is overwhelming. Right now, we're not showing enough gold to even pay the salaries of the men. It's pretty much the general opinion around here that the Lucky Lady's produced all the gold she's ever going to."

"But Jonah was convinced there was another vein, and because he was, you're willing to invest a year."

"That's right."

"If it hadn't been for the stipulation in the will that we reopen the mine, what would you have been doing?"

"I'd have been in Mexico."

"Will the job still be open when the year is up?"

"Probably not. But it doesn't matter. Jonah was my friend. I hope he was right about there being another vein of gold, but if he wasn't, if we don't find it, I'll never regret the year I spent trying." He touched her hair. "Especially now. Especially with you, Abby."

At night after dinner, she read while he worked at Jonah's desk, going over diagrams of the mine. Sometimes when the hour grew late, she went into the kitchen to prepare hot chocolate or coffee that she would put on the table in front of the fire.

"It's getting late, Nick," she'd say, and he would leave his work and sit on the sofa beside her.

And sometimes, he would take down her hair and undress her, and they would make love on the sofa or on the thick hearth rug. There in the half darkness, with only the glow from the firelight to see by, he would watch her eyes grow smoky with desire and know that she wanted him as much as he wanted her.

Because he couldn't find the words to tell her what she meant to him, he tried in every other way to show her that he cared. With gentle hands and hungry kisses, he brought her to the edge of ecstasy and sometimes, he held her there and made her wait because he loved her whispered entreaties, her frantic pleas of "Please, Nick. Now, Nick. Oh, darling, please."

And afterward, he held her and stroked and soothed her and cradled her close in his arms.

He did not want to think about tomorrow or of the tomorrows without her. It was enough now to make love with her, to sleep with her, to awake with her. And to look across the room and know that she was there.

In two weeks, Jacinto had recovered enough to go home from the hospital. The ex-sheriff's deputy whom Jake had recommended and who Nick had hired to take Jacinto's place, was a rawboned, taciturn man in his sixties. Looking tough enough to spit nails, he wore a long-barreled gun in a holster that was strapped around his waist, and he carried a double-barreled shotgun.

His name was Mordecai Ungerliter. Abby was willing to bet that nobody had ever made a joke about it and lived. He called her Girlie and he called Nick, Bossman. He worked six nights a week, from six in the evening to six in the morning.

"I don't work on Sundays because I'm a churchgoing man," he'd said when Nick hired him. "I don't drink hard liquor when I'm on duty, and I can shoot the head off'en a rattler more'n sixty feet away. Only kilt a man once, and that was because he was a low-down, rotten, no-good skunk and he had it coming. I'll watch over your house and guard your mine, and ain't nobody sneaking up on me, because I've got ears like a hound dawg."

"And a disposition like a bear with a thorn in his paw," Nick said later.

"I like him." Abby grinned. "He's a no-nonsense, Wyatt Earp, go-get-'em kind of a man."

"And he's got fourteen kids to prove it."

"Fourteen?" Abby started to laugh. But laughter or not, she felt safe with Mordecai Ungerliter outside and Nick in the house with her.

During the third week in December, the temperature fell to way below zero and a snowstorm left three-foot drifts. Nick and Abby rarely went out, preferring, instead, to spend their evenings and their weekends alone, but when Evie invited them for Christmas dinner, along with Jake, Blanche and Henry Crimms, and Merilee, they accepted.

"I couldn't *not* invite Merilee," Evie told Abby when she saw her in town at the grocery store. "It's kind of a tradition that the bunch of us always get together on Christmas Day. She irritates the stuffing out of me sometimes, but her folks were friends of mine, and ever since they died, I've tried to go on being a friend to her." She picked up a bunch of Christmas holly and put it in her shopping basket along with several sprigs of mistletoe.

"Poor Merilee's been as mean and as miserable as a skunk with a busted stinker ever since Nick moved in with you," she said.

"He thought it was the best thing to do. I mean, after Jacinto was shot . . . because he wanted to be right there at the mine. In case something happened, I mean."

"Uh-huh. You like pumpkin or mincemeat pie?"

"I like them both."

"Then I'll make both." Evie pushed the cart toward the produce section. "Isn't anybody's business that you and Nick are living together," she said. "Folks talked about Jonah and me at first, too, but after a while they forgot about it and acted like we were old marrieds. I guess in a way, that's what we were, after twenty years or so."

"Nick and I . . ." Abby tightened her hands around the handle of her own shopping cart. "It won't be that long for us. I'll go back to Toledo next summer. That will be the end of it."

"Will it?" Evie studied her. "I don't reckon it's ever over if a woman loves a man, Abby."

"It is if the man doesn't love the woman." She waited until her voice steadied. "This is the happiest I've ever been in my life, Evie. Nick is a wonderful, caring and sensitive man. But I knew when I went into it how he felt about a long-term relationship. I'm not going to try to pretend that it doesn't hurt, because it does. I love him, but when it's time to leave, I'll leave and I won't look back."

"I don't suppose you'd want me to talk to him."

"Talking won't do it, Evie. I'm gambling that maybe love will."

And if love wasn't enough? Abby felt her heart constrict with pain. Then I will leave, she thought. But I will never be sorry that Nick came into my life, however brief the time, for I will have known love.

Abby and Nick had Christmas Eve dinner alone. They toasted each other with a bottle of red wine and kisses, and when they finished dinner, they had their coffee in front of the fire.

"I have something for you," Nick said. He went into the bedroom and returned with a small package wrapped with Christmas paper and a big red bow.

Abby hadn't dared to hope that a Christmas miracle might happen and that he would give her a ring, but still, when she saw the oblong box, she felt a stab of disappointment.

But in spite of it, she held her face up for his kiss, and when she opened the box and saw the diamond-studded wristwatch, she said, "It's beautiful, Nick. Thank you, darling."

"You wear Jonah's old watch all the time and it's too big for you. I thought you needed a watch of your own."

"I have something for you, too." She went to the desk and came back with a gift-wrapped envelope.

"What's this?"

"Open it."

He took off the green-and-red paper and opened the envelope. Inside was a legal-looking document. "What is it?" he asked. "I don't understand."

"It's a deed to the house, Nick. And to my half of the mine. I had Henry draw it up last week."

"But I can't accept this."

"Both the mine and the house are more yours than mine. You were Uncle Jonah's son in every sense of the word, and you were here for him when he needed you."

"Abby, I can't—"

She silenced his words with a kiss. "I'd like to live here until I go back to Ohio," she said softly. "But the house is yours to do whatever you want with."

He had known, of course, that when the year was up, she would go back, but it bothered him that she could speak so casually about leaving.

"You might change your mind," he said. "Maybe you'll decide to stay in Cripple Creek."

"I don't think so, Nick."

He had little to say after that. He stared into the fire, so angry he couldn't even speak. Hadn't these past few weeks meant anything to her? Did she care so little about him that she could talk so easily of leaving? She'd deeded the house and her share of the mine to him in a final, good-bye-I'm-never-coming-back gesture. He didn't want the house and the mine. He wanted . . .

Abruptly, he stood. "I'm going out and have a look around," he said.

"All right, darling. But be careful."

Darling! He wanted to throttle her! Instead, he picked up his mackinaw and went out, slamming the door behind him.

He came back thirty minutes later, so cold his teeth were chattering.

Abby was in bed. She had on a lacy, pale pink gown that was cut low enough in the front to show the softly rounded contours of her breasts. Her hair was down and soft about her shoulders. The bedroom was warm and dimly lighted.

"Was everything all right?" she asked. "You look awfully cold."

"Yes, everything was all right," he growled. "And, yes, I am cold, cold as hell!"

"Would you like a cup of hot chocolate?"

"No, I would not like a cup of hot chocolate."

"Is something wrong, Nick?"

"No, nothing is wrong."

He took his clothes off and without bothering to fold them, tossed them over a chair.

The bed was warm and when he settled into it, she turned the light off and moved closer.

"Poor Nick," she said. "You're so cold, darling. Let me warm you."

She tightened her arms around him and turned so that his head rested against her breasts. He felt the brush of her lips against his hair. He had only to turn his head to kiss the small nipple that peaked so enticingly close.

But he didn't. He was still angry because she had spoken so casually of leaving him. How could she after what they had shared?

She shifted and her breast brushed his cheek. His body hardened and suddenly, everything that he was feeling, the need, the desire and the unreasoning anger all came together with a terrible force. With a muttered curse, he rolled her beneath him, grasped her hips and entered her.

She gave a little yelp of surprise. "Nick?" she said. "Wait, I..."

But he was past waiting. He drove into her and groaned aloud when her tight warmth closed about him. It was good. Damn, it was so good. His cadence quickened.

She moaned into his mouth, but he didn't stop. He drove her on, wild in his need to possess her, unrelenting when he heard her small whimpers of, "Nick, oh, Nick, please..."

She clung to him, helpless against his onslaught. An excitement unlike anything she'd ever known set her on fire. She lifted herself to him and pleaded for more. "Yes, Nick. More, Nick."

She heard his labored breath, his groans of pleasure. She felt the quickening of his body, the tautness of his muscles, and it began to build for her. Build and build until she cried aloud with the intensity of it.

He took her mouth and with a terrible paroxysm of force, his body shattered over hers.

"Too much," she whispered incoherently. "Too much, darling. Too..."

He tightened his arms around her. "I won't let you go," he murmured against the spill of her hair.

"What?" she asked. "What did you say?"

"Nothing." He kissed the side of her face. "Sleep now, Abby."

She curled her body close to his. "I love you, Nick," she said.

He kissed the top of her head and held her. But he did not answer.

## Chapter Fourteen

The snow began again when they were having breakfast the next morning.

Abby smiled across the table at Nick. "Merry Christmas, darling," she said.

"Merry Christmas, Abby." He got up, came around to her side of the table and kissed her.

In the clear, cool light of day, his anger of the night before seemed childish, and worse, cruel. He had taken her so forcefully, so abruptly that he was afraid he had hurt her.

He'd never done anything like that before. He didn't understand why he had with Abby. He wasn't sure he even understood his anger. Abby had every right to leave Colorado if she wanted to. That had been the idea from the very beginning, hadn't it? She had only come in the first place because of the stipulation in the will that said she had to if she wanted the money Jonah had left her.

Nick knew he had told her that he did not believe in love or in making a commitment. She had understood and accepted their arrangement, but last night, she had told him that she loved him, and while the words had warmed him, he wished she had not said them, because he could not say them back to her.

His anger had vanished, but in its place there was a terrible confusion about his feelings for Abby. He looked at her now, across the table from him, dressed in a navy blue wool robe, her face fresh and rosy from her shower. He didn't understand why she affected him the way she did, or why he had only to look at her to desire her. It bothered and bewildered, and yes, it angered him that he had so little control over his emotions where she was concerned.

When she got up to carry their dishes to the sink, he followed her and drew her into his arms. She seemed fragile, as delicate as a porcelain doll, and he cringed to think of how rough he had been last night.

He kissed her and said, "I'm sorry if I hurt you last night, Abby. I was too rough. I'm sorry."

Abby cupped his head between her hands, and looking up at him she said, "I'm not that fragile, Nick. I won't break easily. I know you would never hurt me, darling."

Never hurt her? He put his hand on the back of her head and held her against his shoulder so that she would not see the expression on his face. "I'll make it up to you tonight," he murmured against her hair.

She loved him so, and oh, how she wanted him to love her back. And perhaps because she wanted so badly to believe it, she told herself that it was only a matter of time before he told her that he did. And when he finally said the words, he wouldn't let her go. She had to believe that.

They stood that way for a moment longer, her arms around his waist, his lips against her hair. When he let her go, he said, "Tonight, Abby," and his voice was low and husky with an emotion he could not put into words.

Abby put on a pale blue wool dress. It was long sleeved and high necked, but it molded to her body like a second skin. She had on a pair of high-heeled, blue pumps, and she'd brushed her hair soft and loose about her shoulders. She'd even touched a pale coral lipstick to her lips.

"You're beautiful, Abby," Nick said. "Let's forget going to Evie's. Let's just stay home."

Home. Their home. Abby clung to him. She thought of next Christmas and of the Christmases to come without him. A shudder went through her, but she made herself smile and say, "We're late now, Nick. We have to go. We promised Evie."

The snow was coming down harder when they left, big, fat flakes that fell gently onto the already snow-encrusted ground.

"You drive," Abby said. "I don't know how to manage snow this deep."

The road leading to the highway was bad, and the highway itself was slick and wet, with four- and five-foot drifts banked on each side of the road. Nick drove carefully, but as careful as he was, the station wagon skidded sideways and he had to fight for control.

When at last they reached Evie's big two-story house in the section of Cripple Creek that was known as Millionaire's Hill, Abby said, "If the snow doesn't stop, it's going to be almost impossible to drive back tonight."

"If it gets any worse, we'll stay in town," Nick told her. "Don't worry."

He turned off the ignition, but when he didn't take the keys, Abby said, "You forgot the keys."

"Habit." And imitating Mordecai's manner of speech, he said, "This here ain't New York or To-ledo, Girlie. This here's Cripple Creek. Nobody ever worries about locking their cars here."

Abby kissed him. "Whatever you say, Bossman." Then she jumped out of the car.

Christmas lights had been strung on the outside of the house, and an evergreen-and-holly wreath festooned the door where Evie waited with a welcoming smile.

"I wanted snow for Christmas," she called out, "but this is ridiculous." She hugged Abby and kissed Nick. "We're all in the living room by the fire. Come in where it's warm."

There was a six-foot-tall Christmas tree in one corner of the room next to a baby-grand piano. Blanche was seated at the piano, and the others—the Crimmses, Jake and Merilee—were gathered around her.

Evie took Abby's and Nick's coats and said, "Go stand by the fire while I pour you a cup of mulled wine to take the chill out of your bones."

Blanche got up from the piano to hug Abby, and Henry shook hands with Nick. Then Merilee kissed him on the lips, and Jake took Abby's hand and said, "Merry Christmas," and kissed her cheek.

Evie brought the mulled wine, which spurred a round of toasts. Everyone chatted in front of the fireplace until Sybil May Harley, a tall, raw-boned woman who had worked for Evie for over thirty years, announced that dinner was ready. As they started into the alcove leading to the dining room, Blanche grabbed Henry's hand and pulled him under the mistletoe that hung above the door. "Merry Christmas, Ducky-Love," she said, and kissed him.

"Ducky-Love?" Evie hooted with laughter while the rest of them applauded.

Henry's face turned scarlet. "Anybody tells anybody she calls me Ducky-Love, I'll sue."

"Wouldn't think of it, D.L.," Jake said with a straight face.

That's the way it went through dinner. "Have some more sweet potatoes, Ducky-Love." "How about another piece of turkey, D.L.?"

Abby was having a good time in spite of the fact that Merilee had eased her way in next to Nick and didn't talk to anybody else but him.

Jake had pulled out a chair for Abby between Evie and Henry, and he'd taken the chair across the table from her. "Any trouble out at the mine?" he asked Nick.

"Not since Mordecai Ungerliter's been there," Nick said.

"Still carrying his double-gauge shotgun?" Henry laughed. "He's a tough old coot. Anybody try anything while he's on duty, he'll blow 'em to kingdom come."

"What kind of a deputy did he make?" Nick asked.

"The best Cripple Creek has ever had," Jake said. "Any time there was trouble, all Mordecai had to do was walk down the street and everybody scattered." He looked across the table at Abby. "That doesn't mean you don't have to be careful," he told her. "Whoever it was who shot Jacinto is still running around loose."

"You haven't turned up anything yet?" Nick asked.

Jake shook his head. "I'm willing to bet it's that bunch over in Denver, but I can't prove it. Unless something else happens, and I sure hope it doesn't, there's not much I can do. I still wish Abby'd move into town where I'd know she was safe."

"She's safe with me," Nick said.

"I'll bet she is," Merilee said, and laughed. It was an unpleasant sound and Evie shot her a look that silenced her.

After the pumpkin pie and the mince pie had been served, they took their coffee into the living room.

"Snow's getting worse," Blanche said. "I wanted a white Christmas but enough is enough."

Henry nodded. "If we don't leave soon, the roads will be impassable."

"You're all welcome to spend the night here." Evie's smile took them all in. "I've got plenty of room, and I'd love the company."

"We'll see what happens in an hour or so," Nick said. "Abby and I might take you up on that."

"In separate rooms?" Merilee murmured.

"Mind your manners," Evie said.

Blanche began to play the piano and when some of the others gathered round to sing Christmas carols, Abby joined them. There was an almost Currier-and-Ives feeling about this warm room, she thought—friends gathered around the piano; the room cosy and warm in the glow of the fireplace. Holly and mistletoe had been strung from the beamed ceiling. The air smelled of pine from the Christmas tree that was laden with lights, colored balls and silver tinsel. She smiled at Nick, who was standing next to her, and thought of the promise of later, when they were alone.

She gazed at the faces of the new friends she had made, at Henry, who looked lovingly at his wife, at Jake and at dear Evie. And at Merilee, with her gamin face and her too-tight red angora sweater. As Abby watched she saw Merilee smile across the piano at Nick, her lips forming a kiss.

And Abby wondered, when I am gone, will he be with Merilee?

Then Blanche, in a sweet contralto voice, began to sing *"Adeste Fideles,"* and Abby forgot Merilee. It was only when the song ended that she realized Merilee was no longer across the piano from her and that Nick was not beside her. But before she could wonder about it, Blanche began to play, "Silent Night."

Halfway through the carol, Abby started to sneeze, and Henry, in the middle of it, "all is calm, all is bright," said, "Bless you."

"I'll just get a hanky out of my purse," Abby whispered. "I'll be right back."

She hurried toward the downstairs bedroom where Evie had put their coats. Her purse was on a chair beside the door. She picked it up... then stopped, frozen.

Nick was next to the bed, his back to her. Merilee, on tiptoe, was pressed close to him, her arms around his neck.

How long did she stand there, her purse clutched to her chest, staring in disbelief? How long before the moan whispered from her throat?

Nick swung around. He stared at her, his face white, shocked. She saw the smear of lipstick on his mouth.

"Oops." Merilee giggled.

Nick thrust her away from him. "Listen..." he said.

But Abby wasn't listening. Before he could move, she turned and ran out of the room, through the dining room, into the living room, past the startled group at the piano.

Evie called out to her, but Abby didn't stop. She ran out of the house, down the steps. Her feet sank into the cold, wet snow, but she didn't feel it. She yanked the car door open, reached for the keys and started the engine. She had to get away from here. Away from Nick.

Tires skidding in the snow, she backed out of the driveway, then swung the wheel around, skidded again and raced down the hill toward the town.

Tears streamed down her face. She could barely see. "Oh, God," she said, over and over again. "Oh, God. Oh, God."

She was shattered, so torn with grief and shock that she did not see the big, gray car that had been parked and waiting at the bottom of the hill.

Nick ran into the living room.

"What's going on?" Evie cried. "What . . . ?"

Jake grabbed Nick's arm. "What did you do to her?" he shouted.

"Get out of my way."

"You get out of *my* way. I'm going after her."

"The hell you are!"

"The hell I'm not!" Jake tried to strong-arm Nick aside, and when he did, Nick raised his fist. Before he could strike out, Evie grabbed his arm.

"Hold on just a damn minute!" she roared.

"I'm going after her," Nick said.

"You haven't got a car." Jake started toward the door. Nick was right behind him.

"Take your coats," Evie yelled, but neither man paid any attention. They ran to Jake's car, got in and slammed the doors.

Jake backed out. "Where will she go? Back to Jonah's?"

"Yes."

Jake cursed. "She'll never make it, not on these roads." He shot a look at Nick. "What happened? What in the hell did you do to her?"

Nick sucked air into his lungs. "She saw me with Meri-lee. In the bedroom."

"You bastard!"

"It's not what you think. I went to the bathroom. When I came out, Merilee was standing there in the bedroom, waiting for me, dangling a piece of mistletoe. She said, 'Merry Christmas' and all of a sudden, she was giving me a tonsillectomy."

"Sure. Poor Nick, what else could you do but take it like a man?"

"It wasn't like that. She had her arms around my neck, and I thought, 'okay, a second or two and I'll break it up.' Then Abby was in the room and..." He ran a hand across his face. "Damn! If anything happens to her—"

"I'll kill you myself," Jake finished.

The road was bad; the snow was coming down so hard, they could barely see the road ahead of them. They made it through town and onto the highway, unable to see more than five feet in front of the car.

"Can't you go any faster?" Nick said in a fever of impatience.

"Not if I don't want to wreck us."

Nick's hands were balled into fists. He watched the side of the road, trying to see through the swirling snow. Abby wasn't used to driving through a blizzard like this. She wouldn't be able to see. What if she ran off the road? What if she had car trouble and tried to walk? People had frozen to death in storms like this. He had to find her, had to explain that it wasn't the way it seemed. He didn't care about Merilee; he didn't want Merilee.

"Take it easy," Jake said.

"If anything happens to her..."

"I know," Jake said. "I know."

\* \* \*

Abby turned her headlights on, but she still couldn't see the road because the windshield wipers couldn't handle the snow. She slowed the car, rolled the window down and tried to reach around and wipe the snow away. It didn't help.

She had to get back to the house, get a coat...she was so cold...pack her suitcase and leave. Just leave. Get away from Nick, from Cripple Creek. She didn't need the eight and a half million. She didn't want it. Let Nick have it. Let him have it all.

She saw the headlights behind her and because she thought it was Nick, she pressed her foot down on the gas. The car swerved, but she righted it and held it steady.

The headlights grew closer. One was too bright, the other beamed off to the left. She tightened her hands on the steering wheel. The car behind her pulled up and around her.

It won't do you any good, Nick, she thought. I won't stop. I won't—

The car slammed into hers. Abby gasped. What was Nick trying to do? What...? She swung her head around. The other car was only inches from hers. She could barely see through the slanting snow, but the window on the empty passenger side was rolled down. Nick wasn't driving. She'd never seen the man before. Why...?

He hit her car again. It skidded, and Abby thought for a moment that she'd lost control. But she pulled out of the skid, hit the gas and shot ahead of the other car. A gray car. She had to remember that.

He pulled up alongside of her again and she saw his face...white, like his hair and eyebrows. He held his arm out. He was holding something, pointing it at her. Oh, my God...

She held one hand up to try to shield her face, and instinctively fell to her right as the explosion ripped through the car. She felt a jolt. The car went off the road, skidding, sliding, out of control. The car hit something and began to roll. Abby screamed. The car hit something else and jolted to a stop. Suddenly, she was flying out into the snow.

Into oblivion.

Nick had never known this kind of pure panic before. What if something happened to Abby? What if she had an accident? He cursed himself, Merilee and the snow. And though he had told himself he did not believe in prayer, he found himself whispering, "Please, God. Please, God, don't let anything happen to her."

The snow slackened off. They could see the road now, but there was nothing, no car, no taillights.

Suddenly Jake's hands tightened on the steering wheel. "I think I see something." He slowed the car. "Look! Pairs of parallel tire tracks. What in the hell ... ?"

"Stop!" Nick cried. He saw the skid marks ahead, skid marks that ran off the side of the road. He opened the door and jumped out before the car rolled to a stop. He raced down the slope, breath coming fast, heart pounding hard against his ribs. "Please," he prayed. "Please ..."

He saw the station wagon on its side against the trunk of a tree. He screamed her name, "Abby!" and staggered like a drunk man through the snowdrifts.

"Lord," he murmured. "Oh, Lord, please ..."

He fell, got up and fought his way to the overturned wagon.

Behind him he heard Jake shout his name, but he didn't stop. He reached the car. The door on the driver's side was open; the wagon was empty. He whirled around, frantic in his need to find her.

Jake was beside him. "Is she all right?" he said. "What happened? What...?"

Nick raced toward the front of the car. He saw a patch of blue, and a great cry tore from his throat. He ran toward her and fell onto his knees beside her.

She was facedown in the snow. He rolled her over, crying, "Abby! Abby!"

She was unconscious; her face was as white as the snow. He saw the blood. "She's been hurt," he cried. "We've got to get her to the hospital."

"Wait." Jake knelt beside him. He felt her neck and her shoulders. He saw the bullet wound that Nick in his panic hadn't seen. "She's been shot!" he said.

"Shot?" Nick stared at the blood slowly oozing from her arm. Somebody had shot Abby. Somebody had...

He picked her up. Her body was cold. He started running toward the car. Jake ran ahead of him to open the back door. They put Abby inside, and Nick got in with her. Jake handed him a blanket from the trunk and Nick wrapped it around Abby.

"Hurry," he said to Jake. "For God's sake hurry."

## Chapter Fifteen

A voice called out to her, but Abby was too paralyzed with cold to speak or to move. Was death this cold? Was this what it felt like to die?

"Can't you go any faster?"

"I'm going as fast as I can. How is she? Is she responding?"

"No." The word sounded choked, strangled.

"I'll call ahead to the hospital. They'll be waiting for us."

"Hurry..."

A time of nothingness.

Then bright lights above her. Strange faces surrounding her.

"Put a pressure pack on," a man said. "We'll worry about the wound later. Right now, we have to take care of the hypothermia. Fast!"

"Abby? Abby, can you hear me?" She felt a kiss on her cold lips.

"You'll have to leave now."

"I'm staying."

A mumble of voices. Sounds. Her skin prickled, hurt. Everything hurt. "Please," she whispered. Then darkness and silence closed in around her.

Nick sat beside Abby's bed all that night. Evie brought him coffee that he didn't drink, but she didn't try to talk or to tell him that everything would be all right.

Every half hour, a nurse came to check on Abby. "The bullet didn't hit the bone," she said. "The wound was clean, her shoulder will heal. She's lost a lot of blood and she's weak, but she's going to be all right."

The next morning, a doctor came in. He listened to her chest while a nurse took her temperature. "She has pneumonia," he said.

Abby dreamed about her mother. In her dream, her mother was well and happy, her father was handsome and kind.

Uncle Jonah's gold earring sparkled in the bright lights of the carnival. The Ferris wheel went around and around. The music played, dum de-de dum, over and over again. She tasted cotton candy, and Nick kissed the pink sweetness off her lips. She started to smile, but then, it wasn't her that he was kissing, it was Merilee. Merilee with shiny eyes and red, red lips. Lipstick marks on his mouth, all over his face.

A nurse in a white uniform put a needle in her arm. It hurt, and she said, "Don't do that!"

"It's all right, Abby." Evie patted her other arm. "Everything's all right, dear."

She slept again, and all the while, the carnival music went around and around in her head.

Jake and Blanche came to visit. They stood near the door. Blanche cried, and Jake's face looked white and grim.

"Merilee's outside. She wants to see you," he told Nick.

"I don't want to see her," Nick answered. So Evie went out.

"How is she?" Merilee asked. She started to cry. "It was only a joke. Nick didn't kiss me, Evie, I kissed him." She covered her face with her hands. "He probably hates me now. Tell him I'm sorry, Evie. Please."

"I will," Evie said.

"If there's anything I can do . . ."

"When Abby's better, you can tell her the way it was."

"I will. I promise I will." Merilee swiped at her eyes with her fingertips. "I—I don't suppose Nick wants to talk to me."

"Not now, Merilee. Maybe later. You and Nick have been friends for a long time. He'll remember that when this is over."

When this is over, Evie thought. Then she went back into the room to keep her silent vigil beside Nick.

Later that night, when the hospital corridors were silent except for the rustle of starched uniforms and the quiet pad of rubber-soled shoes on the tiled floors, Evie went to the all-night coffee shop next door to the hospital to buy sandwiches.

When she returned, she pushed open the door to Abby's room. And stopped.

Nick was on his knees, his face against the white coverlet. He was holding Abby's hand. "Please," he said, "if you can hear me, hear my prayer. I'm not sure I know how to say the right words. But don't let her die. Give me another chance to show her how much I care. Please. Oh, please.''

Evie went back into the corridor. She placed the bag with the food on the floor and leaned her face against the wall. "Help him," she whispered. "God, help him."

Morning came and Nick told Evie to go home and get some rest.

But she wouldn't leave, not until she knew that Abby was out of danger.

Doctors and nurses came and went, their faces solemn, worried.

Abby mumbled as she drifted in and out of consciousness. She talked of Uncle Jonah, of a carnival and pink cotton candy. And once she said, "Nick. I want Nick."

"I'm here, Abby," he said. "I'm here, sweetheart."

"Don't leave me."

"I won't, Abby. I'll never leave you. I love you, Abby. Can you hear me? Can you understand? I love you, sweetheart."

But her eyes were closed. She didn't hear.

In the late afternoon, her temperature began to go down, and finally, Nick was able to convince Evie to go home and rest for a while.

"What about you?" she asked.

There were dark patches of fatigue under his eyes. His face was ravaged with worry. "I'm fine," he said. "I don't want to leave. I want to be here when she opens her eyes."

All that night he sat beside her, and when his eyes grew heavy with sleep, he rested his head against her hip because he had to be close to her, touching her.

In the first faint light of morning, he felt her hand against his hair. "Nick?" she whispered. "Is that you, Nick?"

He raised his face and looked at her. Her eyes were open. The hand against his was cool.

"Why are you crying, Nick?"

He shook his head, unable for a moment to speak. "How do you feel?" he asked when he could.

"Tired. My shoulder hurts."

"It will be better soon."

"But why am I...?" Her eyes widened. "Somebody shot me!"

"I know, Abby, but don't think about it now."

"All right, Nick." She held on to his hand and closed her eyes. "I think I'll sleep for a while," she murmured.

He kissed her forehead. "I'll be here when you awaken, Abby. I won't leave you."

She slept then, and when she awoke, Jake was sitting beside Nick.

"How are you, honey?" he asked, and kissed her. "Do you think you can answer a couple of questions?"

"Sure." Her voice sounded wobbly weak.

"Did you see the man who shot you?"

She hesitated. "Yes... but only for a moment. The window on the passenger side was rolled down when he... When he pointed the gun at me." She closed her eyes, trying hard to concentrate. "I had the impression of whiteness. I mean, his face was white, and his hair. It wasn't like gray, it was white, snow white. So were his eyebrows."

"Good, Abby. That's good. Do you remember the car at all?"

"It was gray. I don't know what kind, only that it was old and that one of the headlights kind of went off to the side."

Jake patted her hand and said, "That helps a lot."

Nick walked out of the room with him. "Do you think there's a chance of catching the guy?" he asked.

"Maybe. I've heard of somebody, a hired thug, who fits Abby's description. I'll see what I can find out." He looked at Nick. "You look like hell," he said.

"I'm okay, now that Abby is."

Jake put his hand on Nick's shoulder. "I hope everything works out the way you want it to," he said. "But I have to be honest with you, Nick. If it doesn't, if you're fool enough to let her go, I'm going to do my best to win her."

Nick's jaw hardened. "You do and you'll have a fight on your hands."

"Yeah?" Jake shook his head. "You're the one who doesn't believe in making a commitment. Why should it make any difference to you?"

Before Nick could answer, Jake turned and walked quickly down the corridor.

Ten days later, Nick brought Abby home from the hospital. She was still weak, but the doctors had assured him that she was going to be all right.

He carried her into the bedroom, helped her undress and put her to bed. But that night when he started getting ready for bed, she said, "I'm awfully tired, Nick. The doctor said I needed a lot of rest. I—I think it would be better if I slept alone. I hope you don't mind."

"No, of course not."

But he did mind. Terribly. All the time she had been in the hospital, all those nights he had sat at her bedside, watching her, praying for her, he had thought of how it would be when they were home again. He wanted, he needed, to hold her and feel her warmth next to him so that he would know that she was safe and well and his again.

But she didn't want him with her, and he knew that it wasn't because she thought she would sleep better alone. It was because of Merilee. Because Abby couldn't forget or forgive.

"I'll leave our bedroom doors open," he said. "If you need anything, just call out."

She forced a smile. "I will."

At the doorway, he hesitated. "It's good to have you home, Abby."

"It's good to be home," she said.

He lay alone in Jonah's bed and thought about the word *home* and what it really meant. Four walls and a roof over your head? Furniture? Pictures on the wall? A closet full of clothes? And he knew that those were not the things that made a home.

This house had been a home for Jonah because Evie had shared it with him. For a few weeks, it had been a home for Nick because Abby had been here. And as he lay there, staring at the ceiling, he vowed that somehow, she would be with him again. He would do anything he had to, to show her that he cared.

The room she slept in was only a few steps down the hall, but so faraway. His body ached with the need to be with her. But he couldn't, not as long as she held him off. She was the one who had made the decision that they would be together once before. Now he had to wait to see if, once again, she would come to him.

He would wait for as long as it took.

Jake came to the house three days later. Abby had gotten up and dressed that morning, and she and Nick were having breakfast when he arrived.

"I think we've got the man who shot you, Abby," Jake said.

She stared at him. "You found him? But how?"

"From the description you gave me. I remembered hearing about an albino who was a professional hit man. I don't know who hired him, but I've got a pretty good hunch that bunch in Denver are responsible."

"Simon Taylor," Nick said as he poured Jake a cup of coffee.

Jake nodded. "We can't prove it unless we can make Blanquito—that's Whitey in Spanish—talk. But first, Abby has to identify him."

"She's not up to that yet," Nick said.

"Of course, I am." She turned to Jake. "Is he here in Cripple Creek?"

"No, Abby, he's in Colorado Springs. We could drive over right now if you don't mind. Might do you good to get out of the house."

"Yes, I think it will." She finished her coffee and stood up. "I'll just get my coat," she said.

"This might be too hard on her. She's still not strong." Nick frowned. "Couldn't it wait for a day or two?"

"I suppose it could, Nick, but I want to nail this guy and the Denver group before they do anything else to you or Abby or to the mine. Unless we've got an ID, we can't keep holding Whitey Mason." He shoved his chair away from the table. "What about the mine? How's it going?"

"Joe Hart was in charge while I was at the hospital with Abby. The men are working double shifts, but we're not producing. We've already worked three of the tunnels without coming up with anything. Beats the hell out of me why anybody'd want to buy the mine, because I honestly don't believe there's any gold left. I think Jonah dug out everything there was to dig years ago."

He looked up when Abby came into the room. "You sure you want to do this?" he asked.

"I'm sure." She smiled at Jake. "Ready," she said.

Jake took her arm when they went down the stairs to his car. On the bottom step, he turned back. "I don't know how long this will take. We'll probably have lunch in the Springs."

Nick nodded. "Drive carefully," he said.

He stood in the doorway and watched them drive away.

The air was cold and crisp but there wasn't any snow. It felt good to be out of the house, and Abby found herself humming along with the radio.

"You look good," Jake told her. "Maybe a little too thin, but good."

"Thin is stylish," Abby said with a smile.

"Not for you. You have a style all your own, a kind of natural beauty that knocks me out every time I look at you."

"Jake..."

He shook his head. "No, I'm going to say it, and then we won't talk about it again. I'm crazy about you, Abby. I told you before that I'm here for you, and I am. I don't know how things are now between you and Nick, whether or not anything has changed. But if it has..." He took a deep breath. "Maybe he's not a marrying man, Abby, but I am. I can't think of anything better in this world than being married to you. I want you to remember that. If you ever change your mind, I'll be here waiting for you."

She covered one of his big, competent hands with one of hers. "I'll remember," she said.

The only time Abby had ever seen a lineup had been on television. Now she was frightened, but determined.

"I'm going to bring out a group of men," the sergeant in charge told her. "They won't be able to see you. Look at each one of them carefully and tell me if you recognize any of them. You ready?"

Abby nodded. "Ready," she said.

The sergeant spoke into a microphone. "Bring 'em out."

Six men walked into the small room, separated from where Abby, Jake and the sergeant were by a thick plate of glass. "Line up," the sergeant ordered. "Face forward."

Abby looked at them, one by one. Her gaze stopped. Her throat went dry. "That's him," she whispered as she indicated the third man.

"You sure?"

"Yes."

"Turn sideways," the sergeant told the men.

Abby started to shake.

Jake reached for her hand. "You're absolutely sure?"

"Absolutely."

"Take 'em out," the sergeant said. And when the men had filed out, he said, "That's it, McClinton. We've got him now."

Jake put his arm around Abby, and when they were outside, he took her arm and led her to his car. "Do you like Italian food?"

"Yes, I..." She took a deep breath of the cool, clean air. "I love it."

"Good. I know a place that serves the biggest antipasto and the best pasta in town."

A small glass of red wine steadied her nerves and settled the queasiness in her stomach. The antipasto was as big as Jake had said it was, and the lasagna was wonderful.

"Are you feeling better?" he asked when the waiter cleared away their dishes.

"I'm fine, Jake. Too full, but fine." Abby took a sip of the strong, hot coffee. "What will happen now?"

"They'll question him, and maybe they'll offer him a bargain if he tells who hired him. I don't think whoever was behind the shooting will try anything else, but I want you and Nick to be careful." He smiled across the table at her. "All right?"

She smiled back. "All right, Jake," she said.

Nick was on the porch waiting for them when they drove in. Hands on his hips, legs spread, jaw clenched, he said, "Where in the hell have you been?"

"We stopped for lunch," Jake answered. "Then I drove Abby around the Garden of the Gods."

"It's her first time out of the house," Nick snapped. "It was bad enough, going in to the Springs to identify that creep. You should have brought her right home afterward."

"I'm perfectly all right," Abby said.

It took every bit of his willpower not to order her into the house, lock the door and keep her there. Instead, he made himself say, "Were you able to identify the guy?"

She nodded. "Yes, it was him."

Nick looked over her shoulder at Jake. "Now what?"

"Like I told Abby, they'll try to get him to tell who hired him."

"And if he doesn't?"

Jake shook his head. "I don't know. Maybe you'd better think about hiring another guard. Just in case."

Just in case? Nick thought when he and Abby were alone. Were they still in danger? And if they were, why? If there wasn't any gold, why were they, whoever *they* were, so determined to get the mine?

That night when Abby was safely tucked into bed, Nick sat at Jonah's desk and began going through all of the records of the past years. He studied the notations that Jonah had carefully recorded, hoping to find a clue to what Taylor and his men were after. There were mentions of minerals that had some small value, but certainly not enough to warrant attempted murder or the amount of money Taylor's people were willing to pay for the mine.

By four in the morning, Nick's eyes were bleary and his head ached, but he still hadn't the slightest idea what Taylor was after. He stood and rubbed the back of his neck. It was late, he had to get some sleep. Tomorrow, he'd go over the records they kept in the office. Maybe he'd find something there.

## Chapter Sixteen

A week later, while Nick and Abby were having breakfast, Sam Crocket knocked on the back door. His face was bright red with excitement, and he couldn't stand still.

"Never saw the like," he said, jigging on first one foot then the other and slapping his woolen stocking cap against his leg. "Goes back into the ground as fer as you can see. Derndest dang thing I ever seen."

"Slow down," Nick said. "I haven't the slightest idea what you're talking about."

"I'm talking about silver, boss! By dang, we found silver!"

"Silver?" Nick stared at him, dumbfounded. "You found silver?"

"Bet your Aunt Nellie's britches. Prettiest sight I ever seen. Old Jonah must be whoop-de-doing like billy-blue-blazes up there in heaven."

"What's going on?" Abby asked, coming toward the door. "What's all the commotion?"

"Sam says they've found silver!" Nick picked her up and whirled her around the kitchen. "We've got a silver mine!"

"Silver? What in the world are you talking about?"

"Danged if we didn't discover silver, Miz Abby," Sam told her. "Abel's the one that seen it, him and Joe. Said it was the prettiest thing they'd ever seen. A whole vein of it right there just waitin' to be dug out."

Nick grabbed a leather jacket off the hook in the kitchen. "I've got to go see it," he said to Abby. "You coming?"

"Of course, I'm coming!"

Together, with Sam skip-hopping in front of them because he was too excited to walk, they hurried to the mine.

The men were gathered at the entrance, grinning and passing around a jug of whiskey. "Beats anything I've ever seen," Joe Hart said. "Abel and I were working Pad Number Four. All of a sudden, he started hollering, 'Silver! By jingo, I found silver!'" He handed Nick a chunk of rock. "See for yourself."

Nick took it out into the sun. He turned it around in his hand and when he got a good look at it, he sucked in his breath. It was silver, all right, pure and perfect. He held his hand out for Abby to see. "It's the real thing," he told her.

"Do you think there's more? That there really is a vein?"

"More'n a vein," Abel said. "Lessen I miss my guess, it's something that could go on forever, just like that Valenciana Mine in Mexico. The Spanish started digging silver out of it back in 1765 and it's still going strong."

"I want to see it," Nick said. "Show me where it is."

"I'll take you down." Joe started into the shaft, Nick, Abby and the other men behind him.

"I'd like to see it, too," Abby said.

"In a couple of days," Nick told her. "I don't want you down in the dampness yet, not after what you've been through."

She frowned at him, but thinking better of it said, "You're probably right. But no more than a couple of days. Okay?"

"Okay." He grinned at her. "How does it feel to be a rich lady?"

"Danged good," she said, grinning back.

He went down into the mine with Joe, down to Pad Number Four, and followed him into the tunnel.

"Right over here." Joe indicated a section of the wall. "It's streaked with silver, Nick. All we've got to do is take it out."

"I'll be damned." Nick shook his head in disbelief.

"I wonder if Jonah knew about it," Joe said.

"If he had, he would have told me." Nick shone his light on the wall. "This is what they're after," he said almost to himself. "It's why Jacinto was attacked and Abby was shot. We've got to be careful, Joe. There's no telling what they'll try next."

"I've already alerted the men, Nick, and it wouldn't hurt to have a daytime guard."

"I've already hired somebody to work with Mordecai. He'll start next Monday." He walked farther into the tunnel. "What kind of production do you think we'll have?"

"Hard to tell. I'd say we could easily bring up about three hundred, three hundred and eighty tons of ore every day. That ought to bring in over eighty grams of silver per ton."

Nick whistled. "That much?"

"I think so." Joe grinned. "We've got something to celebrate, Nick. How about treating the boys to an evening at Zeke's."

"You're on!" Nick said, and he slapped his raised hand against Joe's in a gesture of triumph.

The word spread fast that silver had been discovered at the Lucky Lady Mine, and half of Cripple Creek made it into Zeke's that night. This wasn't only good luck for Nick, it was good news for everybody in Cripple Creek. The discovery of silver in the Lucky Lady meant that maybe there was silver in the other mines, as well.

Abby, along with Evie, Blanche and Henry, took a table in the far corner of the room away from some of the noise.

"Lord, I wish Jonah could be here tonight," Evie said. "Wouldn't he be busting his buttons? He worked like a dog the last five years of his life trying to find more gold, and all the time, there was silver. Doesn't that just beat all?" She reached across the table and squeezed Abby's hand. "I'm glad for you and Nick. The two of you are going to be sitting right on top of the world once you start bringing the silver out."

But I'll be sitting there alone, Abby thought sadly. Nick could do whatever he wanted with her half of the mine. She was glad they'd found the silver, glad for Nick and for the men who had worked so hard in the terrible darkness underground. For as long as she was here, she would work with them, doing whatever she could to help. And when her year was up... But she didn't want to think about that. Not tonight.

Jake came over. "Great news, Abby," he said. "You must be walking on air."

"I am," she said with a smile.

"Up to dancing on air?"

"Sure, Jake. As long as it's a slow number. I'm not as young as I was a month ago."

"None of us are." He took her hand and led her to the minuscule dance floor.

"What news from Colorado Springs?" she asked when he put his arms around her."

"A lot of legal stuff going on. It'll be five or six months before Mason's brought to trial." He looked down at her. "You know you'll have to testify, don't you?"

Abby nodded. "I'm not looking forward to it, but I will, of course."

"Atta girl." He tightened his arms around her. "Just tell me when you're tired and you want to sit down."

"I'm fine, Jake. It's been a long time since I've danced. I came here the first night I was in Cripple Creek, but I haven't been back since."

"The boilermakers scared you away." He laughed. "You were so damn cute that night, Abby. So proper and ladylike, and so pixilated. You—"

"Mind if I dance with my girl?" Nick tapped Jake, not too lightly, on his shoulder.

"I mind, all right." Jake let her go, and to Abby, he said, "I'll be back."

Nick put his arm around her. "Don't know what I'm going to do with him," he muttered. "Can't leave you 'lone for a minute."

Abby looked up at him. "You planning to get drunk tonight?"

"Already am. Everybody in town's buying me a drink. Can't refuse 'em." He stared owlishly down at her. "You mind?"

"Not too much. Just as long as you let me drive home."

"Will do." He planted a moist kiss on her brow. A lock of his hair hung over his forehead and she brushed it back, feeling oddly protective. She'd seen his vulnerability once before, when they were in the mine together. She saw it again now, in his tousled hair and his lopsided smile.

And, strangely, it seemed to her that she could see the child Nick had been, vulnerable as only a child can be, a little boy whose mother had run away and left him with an angry and abusive father.

She understood the defenses he had built up to protect himself from ever being hurt that way again. She knew how difficult it must be for him to believe in love, and the thought that he would go through life afraid of loving or ever being loved made her want to weep.

As for the incident with Merilee, she knew now that was all that it had been, an incident. She had believed Nick when he'd said it hadn't meant anything. She knew Merilee, and, yes, she believed that Merilee probably *had* had a stranglehold on Nick.

But Merilee wasn't the reason she had not wanted to resume her relationship with Nick. She had pulled back to give herself time to regroup, to think of where they were going and where it would end. And when it did, she wanted to be the one to leave him, before he left her.

Reflectively, Abby tightened her arms around him. I love you, she thought. Oh, Nick, Nick, I love you so.

He nuzzled her ear. "You're my baby," he whispered. "My Abby-girl. Won't drink much more tonight. 'Kay?"

"Okay."

"You feeling all right, sweetheart?"

"I'm fine, Nick."

"Good. That's good. I gotta get back with the boys. Is that okay?"

"Sure, Nick."

He led her, with her arm around his waist to support him, back to her table. With slow, deliberate movements, he pulled out Abby's chair. "She's my woman," he told the others, and toasted her with the rest of the Scotch in Evie's glass.

"And you, my friend—" he hiccuped and poked a finger against Jake's chest "—my best, best friend, you stay 'way from her or I'll whup you good."

"You couldn't do it when we were kids, you probably couldn't now."

"That's right," Nick said solemnly. "Absolutely right." He shook a warning finger. "Remember that." Then, with his arm clamped around a well-wisher's shoulder, he went off toward the bar.

"Whew!" Evie said. "I've never seen him like that before."

"Well, I guess he's got something to celebrate," Blanche commented with a laugh.

"Lord, yes." Henry took a sip of his beer. "You'll get the money that Jonah left you at the end of the year, Abby, that's sure and certain, whatever happens. But this discovery of silver is going to make you an extremely rich woman."

"I know," she said, but she did not tell him that she had deeded her part of the mine to Nick.

The hour grew late. Finally, Zeke himself announced that it was closing time, but it took another half hour before everybody straggled out the door.

Jake helped Nick to the car. "You want me to come with you?" he asked.

Abby shook her head. "I can get him home, all right. No problem."

Nick put his head on her shoulder. "No problem," he murmured.

He sang, in a dreadfully off-key voice, all about Minnie the Mermaid on the way home. When Abby pulled up in front of the house, she tapped the horn. Jasper began to bark and in a couple of minutes, Mordecai came around the corner of the house.

"We could use your help," Abby said.

He came over to the car, looked at Nick and shook his head. "Don't hold with drinkin'," he muttered. But he got Nick out of the car and into the house. "Where you want him?"

"In the back bedroom." Abby led the way into Jonah's old room, grateful that the clothes Nick had worn earlier were over a chair so it would be obvious to Mordecai that this was where Nick slept.

Mordecai pulled Nick's boots off. "If you'll excuse me, Girlie, I'll undress him now," he said.

Abby backed out of the room.

When Mordecai came out, he said, "He won't be bothering nobody tonight. Iffen he does, just whack him over the head with a piece of kindlin'. That'll cool him down. Anything else I can do for you?"

Barely restraining a smile, Abby said, that no, she didn't need anything else, and thanked Mordecai for his help.

When he left, she locked the door and went in to check on Nick. He was asleep, curled up on his side, his head buried in the pillow, as peaceful as a child.

She smoothed the hair back from his forehead. "Good night, darling," she whispered. And she kissed his lips.

"Love you," he murmured.

But she had already turned out the light and tiptoed out of the room.

Nick had never in his life had such a headache. Drums throbbed behind his eyelids. Trumpets and tambourines pounded against his skull. He struggled to a sitting position and groaned aloud. Holding his head in his hands he said, "Lord. Oh, Lord."

"Feeling a little under the weather this morning?" Abby asked from the doorway.

"I'm a dying man."

She came in with a cup of coffee and handed it to him. "Maybe this will help," she said.

"Only death will help." He took a gulp of coffee and closed his eyes. He drank half of it before he spoke again. "How did I get in here?" he asked.

"Mordecai put you to bed. He said if you gave me any trouble I was to whack you over the head with a piece of kindling."

Nick laughed, then said, "Oh, Lord," again and held his head.

"Do you think you're up to eating breakfast?"

He started to shake his head, groaned, then said, "Not for a while. But I'd sure like another cup of coffee." He reached for her hand. "I'm sorry I got drunk last night, Abby. Are you mad at me?"

"No. I understand. It's not every day a man finds a fortune in silver."

"A man and a woman," he said. "Both of us, Abby."

She shook her head. "The mine belongs to you."

"It belongs to the two of us. Before we went out last night, I tore up the papers you gave me on Christmas Eve."

"Nick, I—"

He rested a finger against her lips. "The two of us," he said.

Later, after Nick was able to eat breakfast, they went down to the mine together. The men, all looking just the way Nick felt, were gathered around the stove in the office, drinking coffee.

"I signed the pledge last night," Moe said. "I'll never touch another drop of liquor as long as I live."

"Neither will I," Abel chimed in. "Least ways, not till next time."

"I didn't see any point in working all day today," Joe said. "Everybody's pretty much under the weather after last night. If it's all right with you, we'll knock off in a couple of hours and start bright and early Monday morning. You can take Abby down sometime this weekend and let her see the vein for herself."

Sam stood up and poured her a cup of coffee. "I reckon we all acted up pretty bad last night," he said. "I'm sorry as can be, but it sure was one hell . . . excuse me, one heck of a party. I'm sorry Jonah missed it."

"Maybe he didn't," Abby said. "Maybe, somewhere, he knew and was celebrating right along with you."

"That's a pretty thought, Miz Abby." Abel took a red kerchief out of his pocket and blew his nose. "A right pretty thought."

They talked more about Jonah, about the good times, the good days when they'd brought gold up out of the earth.

After a while, Abby went back to the house. She took a pot roast out of the freezer, defrosted it and put it in the oven with potatoes and carrots and onions. When it was done, she made brown gravy and biscuits, and went down to the mine office to invite all of the men to dinner.

They sat around the table in the warm kitchen, napkins tucked up under their chins, a little quiet at first, but when they began to eat they forgot their shyness. Once again, the talk began about the old days and the way things had been then.

Nick smiled at Abby across the table. She hadn't had to do this, but he was glad that she had, proud that she had wanted to.

When the men had cleaned up every bit of the roast and had mopped up the gravy with the last of the biscuits, Abby put two apple pies on the table, along with a pot of coffee.

''My, oh, my,'' Sam said. ''This here was the finest dinner I've had in a long time, Miz Abby. I purely thank you.''

''*Sí,*'' Paco said. ''*Todo,* everything, was delicious, Señorita Abby. *Muchas gracias.*''

''*De nada,* Paco.''

''Come Monday, we're all going to be working hard, Miz Abby,'' Abel said. ''We're going to bring more silver outta that mine than anybody's ever seen before. You just wait'n see, ma'am.''

''I want to go into the mine, Nick,'' Abby said on Saturday morning.

He lowered his copy of the local newspaper he had been reading. ''Let's wait until Monday when the men are here.''

''I don't want to wait. I want to go today.'' She got up from the chair by the fire and stood in front of him. ''I'm so anxious to see it, Nick. Please.''

He hesitated. It really wasn't a good idea to go down when no one was on the surface. But he supposed it would be all right. The men would be so anxious to start work on Monday, they'd be impatient about showing Abby around. It would only take fifteen or twenty minutes. He'd show her the vein of silver and they'd come right back up.

''All right,'' he said. ''But let's wait until it's warmer.''

She fixed a light lunch for them at one o'clock, and after they had eaten, she asked, ''Now?''

Nick grinned across the table at her. ''Now,'' he said.

There had been a light snow during the night and the ground was covered with a thin, hard crust of it. Jasper went with them, barking as he raced ahead. But as always, he stopped at the entrance of the mine.

So did Nick. He knew how badly Abby wanted to see the silver, but he hesitated about taking her down when no one else was around. The extra security man he'd hired wouldn't start until Monday. Mordecai wouldn't arrive until after dark.

"Maybe we ought to wait until Monday," he said.

"Oh, come on, Nick. I'm dying to see the vein." Abby started toward the office. "We won't stay down long. I just want to have a look."

"Fifteen minutes and we're up," he said.

"Okay, okay." She picked up her hard hat and strapped the battery belt around her waist. "It's cold in here," she said.

"It'll be colder underground. You're just now getting over pneumonia, Abby. I don't think—"

"I'll be all right," she insisted. "We'll just go down for a little while, and when we come back up, we'll have a cup of hot chocolate and sit in front of the fire."

"Together?" he said, challenging her.

She looked at him, then away. And though her wounds, emotional as well as physical, had healed, she still was cautious, still not sure she wanted to open herself up to being hurt again.

"I don't know, Nick," she said. "I need more time. I hope you understand."

His mouth tightened. "Sure," he said. "Forget that I said anything." And he turned away so that she wouldn't see the hurt and the longing in his eyes.

At the entrance to the mine, when he saw that she had Jonah's watch on, he said, "Better take the watch off. I told you before that it's liable to catch on something."

She nodded, and slipping it off her wrist, she placed the watch on a rock at the entrance.

They went into the mine and at the shaft, Nick opened the door of the cage. He helped her in and they slowly began the descent.

This was one of the things she didn't like, this descent into what seemed to her like the very center of the earth.

"How far down are we going?" she asked, her voice sounding strange and ghostly in the dark and narrow shaft.

"Almost to the bottom. About a thousand feet down."

Abby tightened her hands on the iron bar and closed her eyes. She wanted to see the silver, but she really hated going down underground this way.

Nick stopped the cage. "Here we are," he said. "Give me your hand."

She didn't need any urging. She grasped his hand and followed him into the tunnel.

"It's a way back. Hang on."

"I'm hanging."

When they were almost at the end of the tunnel, he said, "Right about here." He flashed his light in front of him. "This is where it starts, Abby."

He chipped off a piece of ore with his penknife and handed it to her. Tracing the streak of silver with his finger he said, "See how it flows through the rock?" He shone his light on the wall of rock. "It . . ." He hesitated.

"What is it?"

"I heard something."

She stepped closer to him. "What?"

"I'm not sure. I . . . It's the cage! It's going up!" He grabbed her arm. "Come on!" he urged. "Hurry!"

"Is it one of the men? Joe? Do you think he came to check the mine?"

"That's probably it." Nick didn't want to tell her that he didn't think it was Joe or any of the other men, that he had a feeling, that he'd had a feeling ever since they'd talked about coming down this morning, that they shouldn't do it. He should have followed his instincts, he shouldn't have let her talk him into it.

They ran back to the shaft. The cage wasn't there. Nic
pushed the button that would bring it back down. Noth
ing happened. There was no whir of the cable to indicat
that it was moving.

There was only silence. He pushed the button again an
again.

"Maybe it's stuck." Abby tried to keep the fear out o
her voice. "Push it again, Nick."

He did. Nothing happened. They were alone in th
darkness, almost a thousand feet underground.

It was like that other time. With Steve.

His mouth went dry, his throat clogged with fear. H
had to get out of here, had to...

"What are we going to do?" Abby whispered.

Nick looked at her. He took a deep breath. It steadie
him. The other men wouldn't be here until Monda
morning. He and Abby couldn't wait that long. "We'r
going to climb up," he said.

"Climb?" She swallowed hard. "Climb?"

"There's a ladder, Abby. Remember I told you about it
We'll climb up the ladder."

It was dangerous. Terribly dangerous. If they fell... No
he wouldn't think about that.

It would take hours. He wasn't sure Abby was stron
enough to make it. He put his arms around her. "It's
long, tough climb," he said. "But we can do it, Abby. To
gether, we can do it."

She clung to him, fighting to stay calm, trying with ever
ounce of her will to subdue the sheer terror that made he
want to scream like some wild and frightened creature. Sh
tried to slow her breathing, and she made herself step awa
from him.

"Where..." Her teeth were chattering so badly, she
could barely get the words out. "Where is the ladder?" she
finally managed to say.

"Over this way." Nick led her to the other side of the shaft. It started four feet from the ground and he had to boost her up. "You go first," he told her. He did not add that if she were ahead of him, he'd have a chance to catch her if her foot slipped.

The ladder was narrow, no more than a foot and a half wide. The metal rungs were thin and round.

Abby started up. The only light came from the lamp on her hat and the lamp below on Nick's hat. What if the lights went out? They hadn't checked the batteries. What if . . . ?

She tried not to think about what ifs. She had to concentrate on taking one step up at a time. One step.

It was freezing cold, but she could feel the sweat running down from her armpits, gathering on her upper lip. It was hard to breathe. The iron rungs hurt her feet. She tried not to think about what would happen if she slipped and fell. She tightened her hands on the ladder.

"Easy does it," Nick said from below. "We'll reach another tunnel in a little while. We'll rest then."

His earlier panic had disappeared, but in its place was a growing apprehension about who had taken the cage up and why? Mason was in jail, but the men who had hired him were still free. Was it one of them? What were they trying to do? Drive him and Abby out with terror tactics?

It took them almost an hour to reach the next tunnel. With his hand on her bottom, Nick eased Abby up from the ladder. She slumped against the ground, rubbing her hands together to try to relieve the ache.

"What happened, Nick?" she asked. "Somebody had to take the cage up. Why would anyone do that? I don't understand."

"Neither do I," he said grimly.

"Does everybody know there's a ladder? I mean, do all mines have them?"

"No, as a matter of fact, it's fairly unusual. But it was something Jonah insisted on because he wanted to make sure there was a way out in case something like this happened."

"Then whoever took the cage up might not have known about it. They wanted to trap us down here. It's Saturday. We'd have been down here all weekend. We—" Her voice started to shake. She covered her mouth with her hand as though to still the hysteria she felt rising in her throat.

Nick put his arms around her. "We're going to be all right, Abby," he said. "It's a long climb, but we can make it."

She looked at him. His face was streaked with dust. His hair under the hard hat was disheveled. She remembered that he had once been trapped in a mine for almost three days. She touched his hand as though to reassure him. "This is hard on you, too," she said. "I've only been thinking of myself. I should have remembered that this must be terrible for you."

Nick shook his head. "It was for a minute or two, but I'm all right now." *Because I want to take care of you,* he almost said. *Because you're the most important thing in my life, and no matter how hard it is, no matter how long it's going to take, I'm going to get you out of here.*

When they started out again, he helped her onto the ladder. "Remember," he said, "one step up at a time. I'm right behind you. I won't let you fall."

Abby went steadily upward. The air was stale; her throat was so choked with dust, she found breathing difficult. Her hands hurt and the rungs cut into her feet so painfully, there were times when she didn't think she could take another step up. But she did.

Another hour went by. Two. Three. They rested whenever they reached a tunnel, too exhausted to speak, only reaching out for each other's hand.

Nick began to worry about their lights. He had only glanced at the time gauges when they'd strapped their belts on because he'd known there would be three or four hours of life left in the batteries. But three or four hours had already gone by. What if the batteries died? What if they were left in darkness?

When they reached the next tunnel and stepped off the ladder, Nick said, "Maybe we'd better snap off the lights."

"Our lights?" Abby gulped, but she made herself reach behind her for the switch. Nick reached for her hand and holding it tightly in his, he turned his light off, too.

Abby had never known this kind of darkness. It was tomb black, so heavy and dark, she could almost feel it pressing in on her.

Nick leaned back against the wall and drew her into his arms. "Sleep if you can," he said.

She closed her eyes and tried to pretend that night had come and that she was safe in bed with Nick next to her. "Hold me," she said without opening her eyes. "Hold me, Nick."

He tightened his arms around her. "I'm here, Abby. We're going to make it, sweetheart. Together, we're going to make it."

"Together," she said.

In a little while, they started out. They were halfway up to the next tunnel when Abby's light went off.

She froze, clutching the iron sides of the ladder so tightly, she felt her muscles pop. "Oh, my God," she cried. "Nick! My light! I can't see! I can't—"

"Just take it easy," he said quickly. "I'm going to try to come around and over you."

"You can't! You'll fall!"

"No, I won't. Listen to me, Abby. I want you to move your hands and feet closer together, toward the center of the ladder."

"I can't." She began to weep. "I can't, Nick."

"Yes, you can." His voice was firm. "Do what I tell you, Abby. Now!"

She moved her hands a notch or two, then her feet.

"I'm going to step up over you," he said. "Hang on."

She pressed her forehead against the iron rung. His feet grazed her fingers but she was too frozen with fear to move them. She felt his body against hers, then he was over her, above her. She opened her eyes and saw his light.

He looked down into her frightened face. "We're going to start climbing again," he said in the same firm voice, and prayed that she would be able to.

She did, step by painful step.

Finally, after a long and terrible time, they reached the last tunnel before the surface. Nick looked at his watch. It was almost midnight; they'd been in the mine for over ten hours. He was exhausted, and if he was exhausted, he could only imagine how near the end of her strength Abby was.

"We're almost there," he told her. "We've got less than two hundred feet left to climb."

She could barely hold her head up, and her hands were so sore, she didn't think she could close her fingers. But she'd do what she had to do. With Nick. For Nick. She'd—

"The cage is coming down!" He stood and pulled her to her feet. Was it one of their men? Had one of them come back to check on something? But what if it was somebody else, somebody who wanted him and Abby out of the way?

The cage grew closer. Should he turn off his light. Should he . . . ?

Before he could do anything, the cage was level with them.

"Bossman!" Mordecai called out. "Girlie? You down here?"

"Here! Yes, we're here!" Nick cried.

The cage jerked to a stop.

"What the hell are the two of you doing down here this time of night?" Mordecai got out of the cage and hurried toward them. "Why'd you send the cage up? I saw old Jonah's watch at the entrance and thought you might be down here. What in the sam hill's going on?"

He shone a light on Abby and saw the tears coursing down her dirt-smudged face.

"Now don't do that," he said plaintively. "If there's one thing a man can't stand, it's a woman's tears. Plumb tears us apart."

Before Nick could help her, Mordecai picked Abby up in his arms. "Old Mordecai's here, Girlie," he said. "Going to take you out of this fearful place, up to where there's light and air. You're going to be just fine."

Nick followed them into the cage and pushed the switch that would take them up to the top. The cable began to whir. They were safe. They had made it.

## Chapter Seventeen

Nick eased her against him in the warm, soapy water. "That's it, Abby," he murmured, "lean back against me, honey. Relax."

She lay in the water and felt his arms around her. After the nightmare and the terror of the mine, it was pure heaven to be warm and safe again.

He bathed her shoulders and her back, and made soapy circles around her breasts with his fingertips. Through the groggy haze of her tiredness, Abby felt a warm stirring. She leaned her head back against his shoulder, too tired to respond, but awake enough to find pleasure in his touch.

When they came out of the tub, he dried her as gently as he would a child, while she simply stood there. So tired, she could barely lift her head. He took her to their bed and came in beside her. There was no question of passion tonight, only of closeness and of warmth and the feeling of safety they gave to each other.

As she drifted to sleep, Abby's last thought was that she and Nick had come through the darkness together and that they were safe in each other's arms.

When she awoke in the morning, she heard voices, so she dressed quickly, and when she went into the kitchen, she found Nick, Jake and Joe at the table, drinking coffee.

"How do you feel?" Nick asked, and getting up, he led her to the table.

"Tired." She smiled a greeting to the other two men and accepted the cup of coffee that Nick poured for her when she sat down.

"That was some experience you and Nick had yesterday," Joe said. "I want to tell you, Abby, there aren't many men who could have climbed up that ladder the way you did. The thought of being down in a mine scares most people to death. I've been doing it for a long time and I'm used to it, but I don't know how I'd react to being trapped down there with no way out except for that skinny little ladder. That would scare me to death."

"It scared me to death, too," Abby said. She reached for Nick's hand. "Nick kept me going. He gave me the strength to go on."

Nick smiled at her. "We kept each other going."

Jake tightened his hand around his steaming mug of coffee. "We caught the man who did it," he said.

Abby stared at him. "How did you find him?"

"Mordecai remembered seeing a black pickup parked down the road when he came to work last night. He called me after he got the two of you out, and I came on up here. We saw the tracks where the fellow had been parked, and we saw them coming down toward the mine. I didn't hold out much hope of finding the pickup, even though Mordecai had given me a pretty good description of it. But we took a chance. I drove back in to Cripple Creek to check the hotels and motels, and Mordecai went on over to Victor. About six this morning, I got a call from him that he'd found the pickup and had corralled the man who owned it."

Jake took a drink of his coffee. "I hightailed it over to Victor. Went into the motel with my gun drawn." He chuckled. "But I didn't need it. Old Mordecai had just about worn the guy out. First time I ever had a suspect begging to be taken to jail."

"He talked?" Nick asked.

"Not at first, but when I threatened to leave him alone with Mordecai, I couldn't shut him up. He told me all about Simon Taylor, and he implicated anybody and everybody connected to that bunch in Denver. We've got it all on tape, Nick. There's not a way in the world any of them will get away with what they've done."

"And it was the silver they were after," Nick said.

Jake took a drink of his coffee. "They knew all about it, and they wanted it, any way they could get it. The guy we caught said they hadn't meant to shoot Jacinto. That had been an accident. They were only poking around when Jacinto saw them and made the mistake of trying to grab the gun."

"What about Abby? Don't tell me that was an accident, too," Joe said.

"Mason was just supposed to run her off the road to scare her. When he couldn't do that, he tried to kill her. The guy we caught said Taylor hadn't wanted to hire him but he'd been overruled by the others. The way it stands now, every one of those good old boys will be tried for attempted murder."

"And trapping us down in the mine yesterday was just another scare tactic?" Nick asked.

"That's right." Jake looked at Abby. "It's over now," he said. "You can rest easy."

"And start digging all that silver out of the mine." Joe pushed his chair back and stood. "I'll get the crew going, tomorrow, Nick. You take it easy. Everything's under control."

Joe and Jake went out together. When they were alone, Nick put his arms around Abby. "You're tired," he said. "Why don't you go back to bed for a little while?"

"Why don't you come with me?"

For a moment, Nick didn't speak. He looked into her eyes and knew that she was his again, so infinitely dear, he never wanted to let her go.

He picked her up in his arms and cradled her head against his shoulder. He carried her to their bed and when he laid her down, she raised her arms to welcome him.

They came together with gentleness and with love.

He touched her breasts with his hands and with his lips, with exquisite tenderness. He feathered kisses up and down her skin, his touch so light, it was as though she had been brushed by butterfly's wings. And when at last their bodies joined and met, they took each other to a wondrous place that was quite unlike anything they had ever known before.

And yet, in that final moment when she cried his name and said, "I love you, Nick. Oh, darling, I love you," he could not say the words that would forever make her his.

Merilee came to the house the next morning while Abby was doing the breakfast dishes. She knocked, and when Abby opened the door, Merilee said, "Hi, uh . . . it's me. Can I come in?"

Abby hesitated for just a fraction of a second, wondering why in the world Merilee had come to call. But she said, "Of course," and opened the door.

Merilee thrust a bag of donuts at her. "I meant to come before," she said. "I did when you were in the hospital, but I—I didn't go in. To your room I mean. I just didn't have the guts after what I'd done. It was my fault, you having the accident and getting shot.''

"You didn't shoot me." Abby motioned Merilee to a chair. "But maybe there were a couple of times when you wanted to."

The shadow of a smile crossed Merilee's face. "Maybe." She accepted a cup of coffee, and after she had stirred and stirred and stirred the dark liquid, she finally looked at Abby. "I've been jealous of you," she said. "I always thought that someday, maybe Nick and I would...you know."

"I know."

"Even though I knew deep down he never really felt that way about me. I mean we've never..." Color rose in her cheeks. "Nick's never really been serious about anybody before, but I knew right away that there was something between the two of you. I could tell by the way you looked at each other. I was jealous and I was angry because Nick had never looked at me the way he looked at you."

Merilee reached for a chocolate-covered donut and after she had dunked it in her coffee, she said, "On Christmas, over at Evie's, I followed Nick when he went to the john, and when he came out, I grabbed him and just hung on. That's when you saw us."

Merilee looked down at her coffee. "I'm sorry—sorry that you got hurt and that I've acted so awful every time we've been together. And I'm sorry I put the burr under your horse's blanket."

Abruptly, she shoved her chair back. "I know you don't like me, so I'll get out of here. I just came to tell you how it was so you wouldn't go on being mad at Nick."

"Sit down!" Abby said in her best no-nonsense voice.

Merilee looked startled, but she sat back down.

"I would like to like you because Nick likes you," Abby said. "The two of you have been friends for a long time, and you mean a lot to him." She held her hand out. "What do you say? Shall we bury the hatchet?"

Merilee grinned and held out her hand. "But not in each other's skulls, okay?"

"Okay," Abby said. And they shook hands.

They drank more coffee and ate most of the donuts. After they had chatted for a while about Abby and Nick being trapped in the mine and the discovery of silver, Merilee said, "So what's happening? With you and Nick, I mean? Has he said anything? Like anything serious? Do you think he's ready to settle down and maybe get married?"

Abby didn't want to discuss Nick with Merilee, but because the other woman had made an offer of friendship, Abby didn't want to be abrupt. So she shook her head and said, "No, he hasn't said anything about marriage. I doubt he ever will."

Elbows on the table, resting her chin in her hand, Merilee said, "Don't take this wrong, okay? But maybe if you...well if you fixed yourself up a little bit, it would make a difference. I don't want to hurt your feelings, Abby, but Nick has always liked his women a little flashy. Maybe if you did something with your hair and wore some makeup. If you dressed a little bit zippier and wore your dresses shorter, it would make a big difference. You know what I mean?"

"I think so. But Nick has never said—"

"He wouldn't. He'd never want to hurt your feelings like that." She leaned across the table. "Why don't you give it a try, Abby? We could go into Colorado Springs, and I could help you pick out some things. I know a really classy beauty shop there. They can do makeup, too. How about it?"

"I—I don't know, Merilee. I don't think—"

"C'mon, Abby. Give it a try. What can you lose?"

Abby hesitated. Maybe it would make a difference in the way Nick looked at her. Maybe if he could see her all dressed up and glamorous, like the other women he had known, he'd take a second look and realize he loved her. It might be worth a try.

"Well?" Merilee asked.

Abby took a deep breath. "I'll do it," she said.

"Tomorrow?"

"Okay, tomorrow," Abby agreed. And she hoped to heaven she wouldn't live to regret it.

They had lunch first, and after lunch, they shopped. Merilee talked Abby into buying a black crepe dress a size smaller than she usually wore. The neckline plunged, and the skirt came four inches above her knee.

At Merilee's urging, Abby also bought a silky red dress, equally plunging and short, and a pair of black pumps with four-inch heels.

The beauty salon came next.

Mr. Roberto, a man in his mid-forties, with orange-tinted curls, tight, white pants and a black silk muscle shirt, slapped his hands to his cheeks when he saw Abby's hair. "A twist!" he squeaked. "My God, a French twist! That went out with Joan Fontaine and the Duchess of Windsor, dear lady. Oh, my. My, my, my, we must, we absolutely must do *something* with you."

Abby wanted to run, but it was too late. A shocking pink cover-up had been fastened around her neck, and Mr. Roberto had picked up his scissors. With a barely contained cry of glee, he attacked.

Abby closed her eyes and kept them closed.

Mr. Roberto hummed while he worked. Every once in a while, Merilee said, "Oh, it's going to be precious. Just precious."

And finally, Mr. Roberto said, "Open, open. See what a surprise I've got for you."

It was a surprise, all right.

Eyes wide with shock, Abby put her hand on the back of her head. She'd been shorn. Wisps of hair no more than an inch and a half long stuck out all over her head.

"I...I..." She tried to speak, but the words stuck in her throat. For the first time in her life, she was speechless.

"Wait till I put a little life in it," Mr. Roberto said.

"I don't think—"

"It's going to be wonderful, Abby," Merilee said. "You can trust Mr. Roberto. He does all the models and the TV anchorwomen. Believe me, you're going to be beautiful."

Abby had little to say on the trip back to Cripple Creek. Her new purchases were in the back of her recently re-paired station wagon. Every now and then, she glanced at herself in the rearview mirror and shuddered.

"Don't worry," Merilee said. "You look sensational. Nick is going to have the surprise of his life." She turned on the seat and faced Abby. "Will he be there when you get home?"

"No." Abby stared down at her new, red acrylic finger-nails. "He and Jake drove over to Denver to the district attorney's office there. He won't be back until after seven."

"That's perfect! You can get all dressed up and have a candlelight dinner waiting for him. I wish I could be there to see his face when he sees you, Abby. He's going to be so pleased. Just wait and see."

Abby put a bottle of white wine in the refrigerator to chill, made a hearts-of-palm-and-artichoke salad, stuffed two Cornish hens with sherried wild rice, and baked a loaf of cheese bread.

The table was set in front of the fireplace with a pale blue linen cloth and matching napkins. White candles waited to be lighted.

At six, she went in to bathe and dress. When she passed the mirror in the bathroom, she started in surprise. "Who...?" she asked aloud, then realized the "who" was she with short, wispy, blond hair. And makeup. A *lot* of makeup.

"Don't wash your face when you bathe," Merilee had warned her. "You're perfect just the way you are."

Abby stared at her face in the mirror. Eyes outlined with a dark brown pencil and touched with turquoise and gray stared owlishly back at her. She blinked her mascaraed lashes and touched her blushed cheeks. With a sigh, she lowered herself carefully into the tepid bath water, tepid because Merilee had warned her not to have the water too hot. "You don't want to spoil your hair," Merilee had said.

As far as Abby was concerned, there was nothing else that could possibly happen to her hair.

She got out of the tub and dabbed on some of the new expensive perfume she'd bought. When she tried to put the new black bra on, she almost couldn't get it fastened because her fingernails felt as though they were three inches long. It was the same with the sheer, black stockings with the seam at the back that Merilee had insisted went with the dress.

Abby put the dress on and groaned. It showed the rise of her breasts and came halfway up her thighs. She tried to tug it down, but when she did, it showed even more of her breasts, so she let it alone. She stepped into the shoes with the four-inch heels and teetered.

This had all better be worth it, she thought when she looked at herself in the mirror. She was doing this for Nick; she hoped he'd appreciate it.

Abby returned to the living room, dimmed the lights and put a CD of Ravel's *Bolero* on to play. Just as she took two crystal wineglasses out of the cupboard, she heard the crunch of tires in the driveway.

"Please," she whispered.

"Abby?" Nick called from the front door. "Where are you, sweetheart?"

"Here." The word came out in a squeak to rival Mr. Roberto's. "I'm coming."

She took a deep breath, ran her hands down the side of the new black dress and teetered into the living room.

"I'm glad to be home," he said. "It's been one hell of a day and I'm—" His words stopped. His mouth fell open and he stared at her.

"Hi, darling," she murmured in what she hoped was a softly seductive voice. "I—"

"What in the name of..." His voice rose to a roar. "What in the hell have you done to yourself?"

"I—" She moistened her ruby red lips. "I thought I needed a change," she managed to say. "I—"

"You look like hell!"

Abby's chin began to wobble. She blinked hard and tried, unsuccessfully, to keep the tears back. The mascara began to run.

"What's happened to your hair? It's yellow! You look awful!"

So mad she wanted to kill, Abby teetered and tottered until she was nose to nose with him. "I *know* I look awful," she cried. "But I did it for you."

"For me?"

"Yes, dammit, because I wanted to be pretty for you."

"You are pretty." He glowered at her. "Or you were, th
way you were. I *liked* the way you looked. I love you.
don't want you to change. I—"

"You love me?" she said.

"Of course, I love you," he shouted.

"Oh."

"You ought to know that I do."

Abby sniffled.

"But I never really said it, did I?"

She shook her head.

"It's hard for me to say the words, Abby. I know
should have said them. I wanted to."

"Say them again."

"I love you."

"Once more."

He put his arms around her. "I love you, Miss Abigai
Sedgewick. Now and forever, even with your yellow hair."

"It'll grow back," she said. "And I can dye it brown
again."

"Tomorrow. Maybe tonight it would be fun to go to bed
with a blonde."

She socked him on the shoulder.

He laughed and hugged her, then his face sobered. "
want to spend the rest of my life with you," he said. "
want to be married to you."

Abby let out the breath she didn't even know she'd been
holding. "I love you so much, Nick," she whispered. "
wanted so much for you to love me back, but I though
you never would."

"I fell in love with you that first night at Zeke's. I knew
then, Abby, but I was afraid."

"Of love." She understood.

And it was all right. She would make it up to him for al
of the bad childhood years, for all of the pain he had eve

suffered. It was love that he needed, and it was love she would give. With open arms and an open heart.

Forever.

\* \* \* \* \*

## *Silhouette Special Edition*

### salutes

# MOMENTS OF GLORY

# from Lindsay McKenna

In a country torn with conflict, in a time of bitter passions, these brave men and women wage a war against all odds . . . and a timeless battle for honor, for fleeting moments of glory, for the promise of enduring love.

**February: RIDE THE TIGER (#721)** Survivor Dany Villard is wise to the love-'em-and-leave-'em ways of war, but wounded hero Gib Ramsey swears she's captured his heart . . . forever.

**March: ONE MAN'S WAR (#727)** The war raging inside brash and bold Captain Pete Mallory threatens to destroy him, until Tess Ramsey's tender love guides him toward peace.

**April: OFF LIMITS (#733)** Soft-spoken Marine Jim McKenzie saved Alexandra Vance's life in Vietnam; now he needs her love to save his honor. . . .

SEMG-1

# *Silhouette Special Edition*

### is pleased to present

# A GOOD MAN WALKS IN
## by Ginna Gray

The story of one strong woman's comeback
and the man who was there for her, Travis McCall,
the renegade cousin to those Blaine siblings,
from Ginna Gray's bestselling trio

### FOOLS RUSH IN (#416)
### WHERE ANGELS FEAR (#468)
### ONCE IN A LIFETIME (#661)

Rebecca Quinn sought shelter at the hideaway on Rincon
Island. Finding Travis McCall—the object of all her childhood
crushes—holed up in the same house threatened to ruin the
respite she so desperately needed. Until their first kiss...
Then Travis set out to prove to his lovely Rebecca that man
can be good and love, sublime.

You'll want to be there when Rebecca's disillusionment turns
to joy.

### A GOOD MAN WALKS IN #722

Available at your favorite retail outlet this February.